# CHARMING
# THE VICAR

**Visit us at www.boldstrokesbooks.com**

## By the Author

A Royal Romance

Heart of the Pack

Courting the Countess

Royal Rebel

Dapper

Unexpected

Charming the Vicar

# CHARMING
# THE VICAR

*by*
# Jenny Frame

2018

This Trade Paperback Original Is Published By
Bold Strokes Books, Inc.
P.O. Box 249
Valley Falls, NY 12185


First Edition: January 2018

---

**CREDITS**
EDITOR: RUTH STERNGLANTZ
PRODUCTION DESIGN: STACIA SEAMAN
COVER DESIGN BY SHERI (GRAPHICARTIST2020@HOTMAIL.COM)

# Acknowledgments

Big thanks to Radclyffe and all the BSB staff. I'm grateful for your tireless hard work and how much you all help to make our writing community a wonderfully supportive environment.

Thank you to my editor, Ruth. Your help, encouragement, and patience are greatly appreciated. I couldn't have wished for a better or kinder editor.

This year has been one of the most difficult years my family and I have had to face, but through it all, love and support have seen us through. Love is the most powerful thing in the world. It brings people together through adversity, and gives us hope for the future. There is nothing more important than love and family. So thank you to my family, for everything they do.

My darlin' Lou, I'm the luckiest girl in the world. The day I met you was the biggest gift the universe could have given me. I'll always love you, and I'll always be on your side.

To my Barney Boy. You keep me company as I write each day, and with your presence I know that I'm never alone. You're crazy, but we love you.

For Lou,
I'm always on your side…

# PROLOGUE

Even though Finnian Kane, master magician and illusionist, was hanging by her feet from a burning rope one hundred and eighty feet above huge spikes on the London Arena floor, she was centred and happy. The atmosphere in the auditorium was tense to say the least, but the show had gone like clockwork, and this illusion was the finale, the one the audience left talking about every night.

Finnian's show had a steampunk circus style, so the audience was circled around the middle of the arena floor, which Finnian made her stage. As Finn struggled with her straitjacket, she kept her eye on the fire burning its way through the rope above her feet, burning its way down to the threads. She then looked below her at the floor covered with four-foot high razor-sharp spikes. A large piece of meat was impaled on them, a piece of meat one of her stagehands had thrown down from the platform, before the illusion started, to prove to the audience that the spikes were real.

Everything was going to plan, and Finn had her audience in the palm of her hand. The trick was to delay her escape from the straightjacket until the rope was nearly on its last thread, to heighten the suspense. Finn fed off the audience's trepidation, fear, worry, wonder, and amazement. Here onstage she was accepted and loved for being different, not chastised for it, and that was why she loved it so much. There was risk, but the risk made the payoff even more exciting. If she had her environment and the people around her in her control, then it worked. Finn always kept ten steps ahead—if she didn't, she'd get hurt, both physically and mentally.

The rope was down to its last few threads, and the audience was starting to squeal with fear for her. She released herself from the straitjacket and unclasped her feet just in time for the rope to break.

Everyone in the crowd screamed, and she landed miraculously, on two feet, perched on spikes beside the impaled meat. There was silence for a few seconds, and then Finn looked up, smiled, and gave a nod of the head, and the audience roared.

The stage went black, and when the lights came up again, Finn was on the ground a few feet away from the spiked floor. Finn's dancers appeared and the music played while the crowd cheered. Finn took her ringmaster's jacket and steampunk top hat, with a playing card and feather tucked in the band, and put them on.

She walked around all sides of the audience taking their applause. The cheering crowd filled her with the high of performance. There was nothing like it, nothing like the pleasure of people loving her, wanting more of her.

Finn took off her top hat and gave one last low bow, revealing her trademark hair. It was brown, shaved in short at the back and sides, but on top she had a sweep of platinum blond, which she styled in many elaborate different ways, depending on her mood. Tonight it was gelled up into a longer version of a fauxhawk.

"Thank you for coming, everyone!"

She ran backstage while the noise was still at its loudest. "Great show, Finn," her PA Christian said. He took her top hat and handed her a bottle of water and a white towel.

Finn was physically tired and her muscles burned, but she felt energy coursing through her veins. She took a long drink of water and said, "Thanks. Is my guest here?"

Christian nodded. "In your dressing room waiting."

"Thanks. Get the car ready to take us to the restaurant in an hour."

Finn walked down the corridors leading from the arena stage to the dressing rooms. The corridors were busy with her dancers and stage crew, who all congratulated her on a great show.

Normally after the show she experienced a gradual comedown after the high of performance, a downer which Finn tried to fill with sex and clubbing. But tonight the most special woman in the world was here, and she couldn't wait to see her.

At the corner of the corridor, next to her dressing room, one of her main dancers, Layla, waited for her, and Finn sighed internally.

Finn didn't know when it happened, but gradually the appeal of sex with her dancers or groupies who followed her entourage to a club afterwards had lost its appeal. She didn't understand why, because she loved sex, loved women, but there was something missing now. *Maybe there's something wrong with me?* Maybe she was losing her sex drive?

Layla had been with the show for a long time and knew that Finn usually wanted no-strings fun, and that had suited her completely. There was never going to be any other woman in her heart apart from the one sitting in her dressing room just now.

"Fantastic show, Finn," Layla said, slipping her palms under Finn's jacket.

"Thanks."

Layla trailed her fingernails down Finn's cheek. It should have made her feel something. The touch was meant to be seductive, and it was anything but.

"There's a new girl in the troupe that wants to meet you. These new girls always fall for you, don't they? They don't realize what a cold-hearted bastard you are." Layla laughed.

That assessment of her character stung Finn somewhere deep inside her. But that was part of her illusion. Only one woman knew who she really was. "You know me only too well, Layla."

"Why don't we head to the club and then see if she's interested in coming back to the hotel with us?" Layla said.

Finn couldn't think of anything worse. Threesomes or more, which used to be so exciting to her, now were just boring—but she had to keep up the mysterious, in control, untouchable, Finnian Kane illusion. So she took hold of Layla's waist and backed her against the wall.

"That sounds like fun, but I can't tonight. My baby sister is at the show tonight. I'm taking her out for dinner."

Everyone knew Finn's sister. Charity was the most important woman in the world to her, and when she came to visit, all her plans changed.

Layla brought her lips close to Finn's. "Oh, well. There's always tomorrow. You know I'm always here, ready to have any kind of fun you want."

"Yeah, I know you are," Finn said with a sigh. *And the rest of the women I meet.*

Layla squinted quizzically. "Is there something wrong?"

"No, nothing," Finn said, anxious to get away and to see her sister.

Layla reached up and tried to stroke Finn's long fringe, but she caught Layla's wrist to stop her.

"I better go. Carrie will be waiting."

She disentangled herself from Layla's grasp and walked towards her dressing room.

❖

Finn stepped into her dressing room and found Carrie waiting for her on the couch. "Come here, baby sister."

Charity jumped up and flew into Finn's arms. "Finn! The show was totally amazing."

Finn squeezed her sister tightly and spun her around in her arms. Five years younger than Finn at age twenty-two, Charity Maxwell was the apple of her eye, and the only permanent woman in her life.

As she hugged her she felt the always petite Charity was slimmer. She pulled back and said, "Have you lost weight?"

Charity was unusually silent for a few seconds, and then just brushed it off. "I don't know, probably. I hardly get time to eat, the café and shop are so busy." She ran her hand through Finn's hair, and softly grasped her blond fringe. "When are you going to get this thing chopped off?"

Finn laughed. It was a running joke. Carrie pretended to hate her hair, but secretly Finn knew she liked it.

"It's my thing. It makes me"—Finn swirled her hands in an elaborate fashion—"mysterious. Come and sit down."

She took Charity's hand and pulled her over to the couch. When they sat Finn realized her sister looked tense. She knew her sister inside out—she had been solely responsible for her since age sixteen. Charity was the driving force behind Finn's career. She had always promised her sister she would be a success and look after her the way their father never could.

Magic and illusion had been her life from an early age, and when she and Charity found themselves on their own, Finn worked two jobs and did some street magic and performed in clubs in London to make ends meet. She'd launched her own YouTube channel, and with her distinctive steampunk image to build a following, she soon was being noticed by media. Add hard work and perseverance, and she was finally able to give Charity the security her sister wanted. Finn had purchased a piece of prime London property and made Charity's dream come true of owning a vegetarian café and New Age shop.

Finn was a staunch atheist, but her sister had found her own personal solace in the New Age world.

"They repeated your exposé on spiritualists and psychics last night on TV."

"They did?" Finn smiled. "I didn't even know it was coming on again."

Not only a mentalist and magician, Finnian Kane was a crusader against the frauds and fraudsters of the religious and spiritualist worlds—faith healers, psychics, anyone who took people's money and promised them something that was not humanly possible. For the benefit of the TV audience, she would show how the fraudsters made the alleged supernatural happen with nothing more than tricks and illusion.

Charity leaned on Finn's shoulder. "You know your shows always bring in big TV audiences. Thank God my customers don't know you're my sister." She joked, "It would be bad for business."

"Don't worry, you know I'll never do a show on crystal healing and angels. That's your thing and I respect that. Help me take off my make-up and we can go out for dinner."

Charity suddenly looked uncomfortable and serious. "I need to talk to you first."

"What is it? You haven't got a new boyfriend I have to threaten with bodily harm, have you?" Finn joked, but she had a sinking feeling.

"No, no boyfriend for you to frighten as per usual. Let's just talk for a while."

"Something's wrong, isn't it?" Finn said seriously.

Charity simply nodded, and her eyes filled up with tears.

# CHAPTER ONE

The function room of an upscale London gay and lesbian bar was an unusual venue for a Church of England strategy meeting, but although attended by vicars from all over the country, and one bishop, this meeting was highly unofficial.

Bridget Claremont, vicar to the parish of Axedale, sat at the head of the table, chairing the monthly meeting of the Christian LGBT group, Love and Hope.

Bridget smiled as she watched her colleagues—Kate, a vicar from Manchester, and Jerry, who ministered a parish in Leeds—argue over the tone of their next campaign.

Kate banged her hand against the table and said, "We need to, if you'll forgive the pun, stop pussyfooting around this issue and trying to get change with gentle persuasion. We need to act now."

Bridget didn't blame Kate for her advocacy of more direct action. She had a beautiful spouse, who was her civil partner, and wanted to be married in the fullest sense of the word.

Jerry interjected, "But we don't want to frighten the Church hierarchy off. We know a lot of them are dinosaurs, and some of them are so far in the closet they are in Narnia. If we don't tread carefully, we could set our campaign back years."

Bridge decided to step in, since they were coming to the end of the meeting. "I think I could sum up the feeling of the meeting by saying this: We are all frustrated by the inconsistency over the sexual freedom of gay clergy. As I know from experience, being gay in the Church means your freedom is based on the whims of your bishop. If you have a sympathetic bishop, you can be more relaxed in your personal relationships, but if you don't, you can feel an alien in your own church.

Before we work on the campaign for the marriage proposal at the next synod, we need to first have the Church recognize that they should not be looking into our private lives, or our bedrooms. Do the bishops ask our straight colleagues if they remain celibate before marriage? I think not. We must have equal rights with them. At our next meeting, we can look in detail at that question."

Kate raised a hand to be granted one last chance to speak.

"Yes, Kate?"

"I just wanted to add that if we do not achieve our goals by the synod meeting next year, I will be prepared to marry and force the Church into action."

Bridget could see the anger and frustration in her eyes. If the Church reprimanded her, she could see Kate dragging the Church through the courts. Hopefully it wouldn't come to that.

"Thank you, Kate. I think we all understand your frustration. We'll end there, and get some tea and coffee, shall we?"

Everyone agreed and started to stand. As the meeting broke up, Bishop Claremont, who had been sitting to the side, made her way over to Bridget with a big smile on her face.

"There's my little Bridge. Give your old aunty a hug."

Bridge embraced her favourite aunt tightly. "You're far from old, Aunt Gertie. You have more energy than most of us here put together."

Gertrude Claremont had dedicated herself to the Church and its many causes from an early age and, after a long campaign, became one of the country's first female Church of England priests, then the first woman bishop, and was Bridget's inspiration to join the Church.

"Oh, I don't know about that," Gertie said.

She kissed Bridget's cheek and they walked arm in arm over to the side table, where tea biscuits and cakes had been provided for the meeting.

After they each took a sip of tea, Bridget said, "Thank you for coming to the meeting. The support of a bishop is really important to our cause."

"It's my pleasure. Gay rights are very important to me, and should be to the Church if we wish to stay relevant in a modern world. You can always count on me."

Bridget was lucky to have such a supportive family. The Claremonts were from a long line of trailblazers, rebels, and libertarians. Whether it was her mother, her father when he was alive, her brother, or her aunt, she could always count on their unstinting support.

Aunt Gertie took a bite of cake and asked, "How is Harry? Married life still suiting the once-committed bachelor?"

Bridget chuckled softly. "Amazingly, yes. I've never seen Harry happier in all her life than she is with Annie and Riley. It's their anniversary today and we're having a bit of a celebration at the church hall tonight for them."

"Wonderful. I'm always happy to see young people happy and in love. It must be your turn next, eh?"

"Oh, I don't know about that."

Bridget kept a forced smile on her face but inside she felt a sadness that had been creeping up on her slowly since Harry had gotten married. Love was something she craved, but in a small village like Axedale it was hard to meet someone, let alone deal with all the problems her position as vicar would bring to any relationship.

"And your parish? Is Axedale still enjoying their modern woman vicar, in biker jacket and heels?" Gertie joked.

That was something Bridget could answer honestly and enthusiastically. "My parishioners are wonderful. I couldn't have been luckier to have the pastoral care of such wonderful people. The village is going from strength to strength, now that Harry and Annie have rebuilt the estate to what it once was. There's plenty of work for the locals and the tourists are flooding in. Mrs. Peters the postmistress says she's never done as much trade in years. It's wonderful to see."

Gertie cleared her throat and asked, "And your new bishop?"

Bridget placed her tea down on the table and sighed, facing the difficult question. "Bishop Thomas Sprat. He certainly is a huge change since old Henry Lovejoy hung up his cloak—"

"And his heels!" Gertie interjected.

Bridget chuckled. "Quite so. Going from the world's most gay-friendly bishop to the most antigay one I've ever met has not been easy. I got into a lot of hot water for giving Harry and Annie a blessing in church."

Gertie shook her head. "Yes, I heard about that, but don't take it personally. Sprat has been gunning for me for years too. He led the campaign against women bishops, if you remember."

"Indeed I do. If you're not a white middle to upper class male, he has a problem," Bridget said.

Gertie took Bridget's hand and squeezed. "Don't let him distract you from your good work in Axedale. Carry on as you are, and remember—you're a Claremont. We are not shrinking violets and we don't run from the good fight."

"I won't, Aunt Gertie."

"Excellent. Would you like to have dinner before you return to the country?" Gertie asked.

Bridget looked at her watch and scowled. "I'm sorry, Aunty, I'm going to have to get back to Axedale pretty sharpish. I promised to help set up for Harry and Annie's surprise party."

"Next time then," Gertie said.

They exchanged kisses, and Bridget said goodbye to the other group members and headed out into the London streets in search of a taxi.

Bridget felt a sense of melancholy descend upon her as she walked down the street. Her aunt had verbalized something she had secretly been turning over in her mind. She was thirty-six years old and had no one to share her life with, and no prospect of such.

Being single hadn't always bothered her. Before she took holy orders, her social life and her sex life had been more than healthy, but that part of herself had been locked down inside once she dedicated her life to the Church. She was so consumed with her vocation and looking after her parishioners that it didn't seem that worrisome.

That all changed when Harry met Annie. Daily, she saw the joy and the happiness that love and the comfort of a partner brought to the once grumpy, career driven countess, and it made her heart ache for the same.

Bridge stuffed her hands in her leather jacket's pockets and sent up a silent prayer to God.

*God, if I am meant to walk through life alone, help my heart make peace with that, but if there is anyone out there for me, please guide them to me.*

Her prayer was interrupted as she walked past a newspaper seller.

"Evening news! Famous mentalist and magician Finnian Kane does own disappearing act after sister's death. Evening news!"

Bridget stopped and looked at the front page of the newspaper on display. It showed a picture of the famous magician in her steampunk gothic-inspired ringmaster's outfit, complete with top hat and cane.

She had never seen one of her shows but did know that Finnian caused upset in the religious community for her evangelical atheism, debunking faith healers, psychics, and the like.

Bridget quickly hailed a taxi, and as she got in a bus passed displaying a full-length picture and advert for Finnian Kane's stage show, *Mysterium*.

*I pray you find peace*, Bridget said from her heart and then got into the taxicab quickly.

"St. Pancras train station, driver."

Harry and Annie held hands as they walked down to the village from Axedale Hall. Riley ran ahead, crossing the river and the bridge that led to the centre of the village.

Annie heard Harry sigh and said, "What's wrong, sweetheart?"

"Remind me why we changed our anniversary plans. Riley was delighted to be having a sleepover with her friend Sophie, and we—" Harry stopped, pulled Annie close, and whispered in her wife's ear, "And we were going to play master and slave in the Roman pool room. But instead the church council calls an emergency meeting about street lighting."

Annie laughed and gave her a swat on the behind. "Behave, your ladyship. If it's important to the village then it's worth changing our plans. Besides"—Annie sneaked her fingers under Harry's shirt and scratched her nails along her stomach, just the way Harry liked—"we're leaving in the morning for a month in Rome, and I'm sure when your mother meets us there, she'll be delighted to babysit Riley."

Harry groaned as Annie continued to touch her. "Darling, you know what that does to me."

"I do, just reminding you that I'm worth waiting for. Imagine— you, me, Rome, alone in the villa we've rented. What could be a better place to play master and slave, hmm?"

Annie painted quite the picture in her mind, and it was worth waiting for. "I'd wait forever for you."

They shared a sweet kiss before Riley shouted at them to hurry up. Once they started walking again, Harry said, "Why did you insist we dress so formally for a council meeting anyway, although I'm not complaining about you in that dress?"

Annie giggled, held up her hand, and gazed at the anniversary present Harry gave her. "I couldn't wear my beautiful eternity ring for the first time in jeans and a jumper, Harry, and I have a feeling we might want to be dressed a little nicer tonight."

"How do you know?" Harry said with confusion.

"Just a feeling."

When they got to the church gates Riley said, "Wait here a minute. I need to go in first."

"Why?" Harry asked.

Riley hesitated, as she seemed to search for an excuse in her head, but Annie saved her. "It's okay, sweetie. On you go."

Harry really had no clue as to what was happening. "Annie? What is this? You know I don't like surprises. Do you know anything?"

"Relax, sweetheart. I don't know anything for sure, but I have an idea the village might be up to something."

Riley came out with a huge smile on her face, and said, "You can come in now."

Annie pulled Harry by the hand.

"I don't like this."

When they walked through the doors of the church hall, what looked to be every one of the villagers jumped out from behind the tables, and shouted, "Surprise!"

Harry instinctively tensed up. She did not like to be taken by surprise and not be in control of things, but then she looked down at Annie's smiling, happy face, and all her tension left her.

❖

The church hall was filled with music, laughter, and the sound of happy children running around. Bridget sat on the edge of one of the tables, with her glass of wine in hand, watching Harry and Annie dance closely on the dance floor. She sighed, but smiled at the sight. It was wonderful to see her best friend so happy, but that little niggling part of her wondered if she could ever find the same.

Harry and Annie looked like they were unaware that they were not alone. They were lost in each other, and the way they touched, Bridge half expected to see sparks of electricity fly from their fingers. She looked to the side and saw Quade, Harry's assistant estate manager, talking with one of the other farmers.

"Quade?" Bridget pointed to the dance floor.

When Quade looked to where she was pointing, Bridge said, "I think we better cut in before they make Mrs. McCrae blush."

Quade laughed and followed her over to their friends. Bridge tapped Harry on the shoulder, "May we cut in?"

Before Harry could start to complain, Quade had danced off with Annie.

"Bridge, did you really have to? I was enjoying dancing with my wife, and now she's been stolen by a rugged farmer," Harry said with mock anger.

Bridge smacked her on the shoulder. "Oh, shush and dance with me. You'll have Annie for a whole month. I want to see you before you go."

"Very well." Harry slipped her arm around her waist, and they started to dance.

"So, have you had a fabulous anniversary, your ladyship?" Bridge asked.

Harry twirled her around and said, "It's been wonderful, Bridge. We both really appreciate everything you've all done, and how much the whole village has taken Annie and Riley to their hearts."

"It's our pleasure, and we all wanted to thank you for everything you've done for the village. There's work for everyone, the tourists are bringing much needed income to the shops and tea rooms—"

"All because Annie whipped me into shape and changed me," Harry finished for her.

"No," Bridge replied. "All because you allowed love into your heart, and let go of your hurt. This Harry has always been inside you."

"I'm very lucky. I just wish I could see you happy too, Bridge. You deserve it."

Bridge tensed, and then laughed it off. "Please. Who wants a celibate vicar?"

The song finished and Harry gave her palm a kiss. "Perhaps it's time to move on, Bridge?"

Bridge saw images of a nightclub, heard the thumping of music, and then someone call her name across the club...

"Bridge. Bridge?" Harry shook her from her thoughts.

"Sorry, I was miles away." Bridge forced a smile.

Harry leaned in and kissed her cheek. "I know, but it's been a long time."

"Don't worry about me. Worry about a rugged butch stealing your fair lady." Bridget pointed over to Quade hugging Annie.

"I think I see a rent increase in Quade's future," Harry joked.

❖

Bridge kicked off her heels, sat down putting her feet up on the chair in front of her, and yawned. It had been a busy, tiring day. After Harry and Annie headed home, the other partygoers started to disperse, well fed, watered, and happy. Bridge and Quade stayed behind to clear up.

She watched Quade busily sweeping up the hall floor and said, "Quade? Please take a pew and chillax for a minute. You're making me feel more tired than I ought to be."

Quade laughed and placed her brush against the wall. "Chillax? You're so down with the kids, Vicar. It's no wonder the village young people love you."

"Oh, shush. Bring me a glass of wine on your way, and something for yourself. I think we deserve it."

Quade went to the drinks table and poured out a glass of wine, then drew a pint from the barrel of home-brew beer that she had brought to the party.

Bridge accepted the glass from Quade and took a large glug. "Oh, I needed that." Quade sat, and Bridge said with a smile, "Your Axedale Ale went down well with the locals. You'll soon have to be selling by the barrel—I know Mr. Finch at the pub has said so."

Home-brew real ale was somewhat of a hobby of Quade's and was starting to become very popular with the Axedale locals.

"I don't know about that, but everyone seems to enjoy it."

Bridge chuckled to herself. That was Quade, modest and self-deprecating. The more she got to know Quade the more she liked her. They had always been friends, since Bridge came to the village, but they had gotten closer since Quade started managing the estate and often joined Harry, Annie, and her for a weekly meal.

It was just typical, thought Bridge. The one other lesbian in their village, and the only chemistry they had was as friends.

"It was a great party, wasn't it?" Quade said. "Everyone seemed to enjoy it."

Bridge took a sip of her wine and smiled. "I loved the look on Harry's face when she walked in. She doesn't like surprises. They make her feel out of control, and there was a split second of the old grumpy Harry ready to come out, but Annie squeezed her hand and smiled, and Harry immediately relaxed and beamed back at her with happiness. It's amazing what love has done for her. They have an intense chemistry. When you watch them gazing at each other, you're surprised they don't tear each other's clothes off right there and then. It must be wonderful to have that feeling with someone you love."

Bridge was no stranger to sex. She had always been a very sexual creature, which might have been God's sense of irony given her current occupation, but when God called her to his service she felt she had to choose, and her love for God won.

Her position meant she had to toe the party line, follow Church rules, and remain celibate, until such a time as she and her LGBT colleagues received marriage equality within the Church. Some queer vicars, she knew, flouted that rule in the privacy of their bedrooms, but they took the chance of losing their position. Bridge was not willing to lose this life she had built for herself. It meant everything to her.

Quade looked down and swirled her beer around her glass. "Yeah, it's an amazing thing, love. Harry's lucky to have Annie just walk into her life. Have you ever been in love, Bridge?"

Bridge took another large gulp of wine. "No, I wasn't lucky enough to have somebody love me, but I did a lot of looking, if you know what I mean."

Quade gave an exaggerated sigh. "It's a bad day when your vicar has more experience with women than you do."

"Oh, come now, Quade. A strapping butch like yourself must have ladies banging your door down."

"Not even a knock. I've lived in this village practically all my life, and in that time, there have only been three other lesbians here—Harry, Annie, and you, Vicar. Harry and me? Just...no. Annie was perfect but she had eyes for someone else and—"

"There's me. Clearly not compatible, although you are extremely handsome," Bridge said with a wink.

"You have way more experience than me, Vicar. Tell me, why aren't we compatible?" Quade said with a mischievous question in her voice.

Bridge smiled as she thought back to her pre-church days when celibacy was not part of her make-up and the things she got up to would have frightened the life out of poor Quade. "Our energies are too similar, let's just say."

"Oh? How?"

She leaned forward into Quade's personal space and said in a very seductive voice, "Well, you might like my short skirts, stockings, and heels, but you wouldn't like those heels walking up and down your back."

Quade's eyes went wide with shock, and then she started to laugh. "You're right. I like my women a bit softer than that, Vicar."

Underneath their jovial conversation, Bridge felt a melancholy creeping up on her. "I wish I could meet someone to love me, Quade. I wouldn't like to think that I'll grow old alone, and I have to have faith that God has a plan for us both and will guide the right people to us at the right time."

Quade held up her pint and said, "From your lips to God's ears. Let's make a pact. If neither of us is married by the time we're forty-five, we get hitched. What do you say?"

Bridge smiled. "Is that a proposal, Sam McQuade?"

"Of sorts."

Bridge got up and walked around to the back of Quade's chair. She leaned over and whispered in her ear, "Can I bring my whip?"

Quade jumped and turned to look at her friend with horror, "Christ, no. I just proposed to a vicar who has her own whip? I think we need to check with your bishop that you really are a vicar."

Bridge picked up a rubbish bag and snorted. "He would tell you I'm the devil incarnate. Let's get this place cleaned and locked up."

Quade shook her head in amusement and grabbed her broom. "Is it wrong to say I hope you and your whip find that person to love before the task falls on me?"

Bridge's designer heels clicked on the floor and echoed around the room as she walked over to Quade. She gave her a peck on the cheek and said, "You're a good friend, Quade."

# CHAPTER TWO

On Sunday morning, Bridge shook hands with her parishioners as they filed out of church. It had been strange without Harry, Annie, and Riley in the front pew. They were such an integral part of the community now, and the church and the village seemed empty when they were gone. Normally Bridge and Mrs. Castle, and sometimes Quade, would go to Axedale for lunch after church for one of Annie's famous roast dinners, but today would be a much longer, lonelier day.

"Lovely sermon, Vicar," Mr. Finch from the pub said. "But here's hoping no mere mortals can turn water into wine, or I might go out of business," he joked.

"Fear not, Mr. Finch—" Bridget's witty retort was interrupted by the roar of a motorcycle engine. The sound was out of place in the quiet village.

Everyone looked around and gazed at the bike which slowed down just across the road from the church. It pulled up next to Mr. Butterstone, who had just left the church, and then he started directing the rider with some animated hand gestures. Although she couldn't see the rider's face, Bridge admired their leather jacket, biker boots, and jeans. She had always had a thing for leather and motorbikes, and wasn't an expert, but it looked like the bike was a classic Harley-Davidson.

The rider then nodded and zoomed off towards the other end of the village, and Mr. Butterstone hurried back over to the church. In this insular village, newcomers were big news and those still at the front of the church gathered around to hear his report.

"Mason's cottage is rented at last," Mr. Butterstone said excitedly.

"Who was it?" Mrs. Peters said. "Did they give a name?"

Mr. Butterstone shook his head. "No, don't even know if it was a bloke or woman I was talking to. They weren't very chatty."

"I'm sure they will soon warm up," Bridge said. "I'll call in on them later and give a welcome to the village."

Bridge was always happy to be welcoming to anyone, but someone with good taste in leather and motorbikes was even more welcome.

❖

"That's everything, mate."

Finn put down a box marked *delicate* on the coffee table of her new cottage and walked over to see the movers out the cottage door.

"Thanks Bob. I—"

She was cut off midsentence by her mobile, which had been ringing incessantly since she arrived.

"Looks like someone is desperate to get hold of you," Bob said.

As if her management, PR company, and show entourage calling wasn't bad enough, somehow the press had gotten hold of her number and had been calling constantly since this morning, and it was driving her mad.

Finn had kept her destination secret, even from her management company, so determined was she to have her privacy.

She looked at Bob and realized he and his crew knew exactly where she was and when she arrived. They'd known who she was as soon as they'd arrived at her London apartment this morning to start the job. Her look was distinctive and unmistakable. Since Finn and her show—and her two-tone hair—were plastered all over billboards and buses in London, it didn't take her movers long to suss her out. If she wanted to keep her anonymity, she would have to buy their silence.

She took out her wallet and pulled out a wad of notes. Unlike most people who normally carried cards and a few coins, Finn always carried paper money in her wallet. It was a quirk that had developed as she'd started to earn good money. She knew what it was like to be poor. When she had to take the sole responsibility for herself and her sister at age seventeen, sometimes all the money they would have left to feed themselves for the whole week would be five or ten pounds. The pressure and anxiety of trying to make that last would never leave Finn. So when she started to make money, it made her feel safe to know her wallet was full.

Bob eyed her wallet greedily. She took out some notes and started to count them.

"Listen, Bob, I'm down here for an indefinite break, and I don't want anyone to find me."

She let him see the notes at the back of her wad of money were hundreds.

"Would you and your guys like to help me with that?"

Bob nodded enthusiastically. "Yeah, no problem. We can do that."

Finn took out a hundred pound note for every one of the movers, and a little extra for Bob, and held it out to him.

"You have no idea where I moved to, do you?"

"Haven't the foggiest, mate."

She handed the cash to him and he just about snatched it from her hand.

The door shut and Finn was finally alone. She walked over to the box on the coffee table and opened it up. On top of the box was a large framed photo of Finn and Carrie, taken on the first night of her first arena tour three years ago.

Finn sat down on the couch and let her fingers caress the glass, hoping to connect with her. She felt the tears start to well up in her eyes, as they had done so many times before. She hurt unbelievably and didn't feel like the pain would ever end. That's why she'd come here, to this little village no one had ever heard of, to hide from the world and work out where she went from here.

In the space of a few months, her whole life had been broken, and she didn't have the first idea of what to do to make things better, or if she should even try.

*This was my fault.*

Finn put the picture on the table and scrubbed her face in frustration. She was so tired of these emotions, so tired of feeling empty.

Her head snapped up when she heard the screech of the garden gate, and then the unmistakable sound of high heels on the path.

Great, a bloody local. Just what she needed.

Finn's heart sank when the person knocked on the door. The last thing she wanted was a nosy welcoming committee. She ignored the knock, and luckily the living room curtains were shut, so the visitor would have no idea she was in.

The insistent knocker at the door then began to speak. "Hello? Hello? Is there anyone in there?"

"Clearly not. Bugger off," Finn said in a whisper.

But they didn't give up. "My name's Bridget and I'm the vicar here."

"Perfect, fucking perfect. A bloody vicar." Finn started to pace.

"I know you're in there." The vicar certainly wasn't giving up easily. "I saw the movers just leave."

"Fuck me, why can't people just leave me alone?" Finn said with anger.

In the end, Finn thought it would be easier to open the door and get rid of the no doubt frumpy, old, do-gooding vicar directly. She pulled open the door and said, "What is it? I've no time—"

Her words died in her throat when she saw who was standing there. Instead of a frumpy grey-haired crone, there was a stunningly good-looking woman in a tight miniskirt, heels, and a biker jacket.

The woman gave her an open smile, and Finn's eyes dropped to her legs, in *that* skirt, in *those* heels. She had always been a leg woman.

"Good afternoon. My name's Bridget, and I'm vicar here. I just thought I'd pop over to welcome you to the village, check if you were settling in okay, and…"

Finn never heard the rest of the sentence. Her eyes travelled up the vicar's body and soon were captivated by her lips, and the deep, dark lipstick she wore.

She quickly pulled herself together in time to hear Bridget say, "Is there?"

Finn was lost in the conversation, and her annoyance had returned. "What?"

"I wondered, is there anything you need?"

"I don't need anything from anyone, and I certainly don't need ministering to," Finn replied sharply.

Bridget's brow furrowed as if she was assessing Finn and how to handle her. "Well, if that's the case, I'm delighted." Bridget reached into the pocket of her biker jacket and pulled out a church leaflet. She held it up for Finn to take. Finn did, and as her fingers touched Bridget's highly polished manicured nails, a jolt of static electricity made them both jump.

Bridget chuckled and said, "As a woman of God, I'd say that was a sign. We'd be happy to see you in church on Sunday, if you would like to join us."

Finn looked down at the leaflet and saw it contained all the times and information for church services. "I'm gay and an atheist. You wouldn't want me."

Instead of provoking surprise or anger, which was Finn's intention, Bridget gave her a wink and a quick reply. "So am I—gay, that is—and we can work on the atheist bit."

*She's gay?* Axedale had a gay female vicar in heels and a biker jacket? Had she walked into the twilight zone?

Finn was lost for words. Being well schooled in human response, cold reading, and suggestion usually allowed her to steer most conversations wherever she wanted them to go, but in this moment, with this strange woman in front of her, her mind was blank.

Feeling a little bit panicked, she tore up the leaflet, threw it at the vicar's feet, and slammed the door.

Bridge felt a lingering annoyance all day. She couldn't remember anyone being as openly rude to her as their village newcomer had been today.

"Bloody obnoxious fool," Bridge said under her breath as she walked into the village pub, The Witch's Tavern.

She was greeted warmly by the villagers as she entered, and she soon spotted Quade at one of the tables by the open fire in the corner.

Quade waved her over. "Evening, Vicar. I got your usual."

Bridge sat and just about downed her usual drink of Campari and soda. Quade looked surprised. "Bad afternoon, Vicar?"

"I paid our new resident a call." Bridget swirled what was left of her drink around her glass.

"And? Man, woman, or beast?" Quade joked.

"Woman—and a beast, by my reckoning."

"Uh-oh. It takes a lot to rile you up, Bridge. What happened?"

Bridge sighed and placed her glass down on the table. "I took over the church leaflet and my best smile, and she slammed the door in my face."

Quade raised an eyebrow. "She must be brave to slam a door in a vicar's face."

"It seemed to be the vicar part that was most egregious to her. The worst thing was she's one of us."

"One of us?" Quade asked.

"As gay as the day is long." Bridget sipped her drink. "But with the worst attitude, and very rude."

Quade leaned closer and smiled. "Sounds intriguing. Another lesbian in the village. Your type?"

Bridge snorted. "Hardly."

"Mine?" Quade said hopefully.

Bridge shook her head. "I doubt it. She's boyishly butch with the strangest haircut."

"Looks like our impending marriage is safe then," Quade joked.

"Exactly. I was sure I knew her face from somewhere though." Bridge stood. "I'll get some more drinks." The newspaper Mr. Finch was looking at behind the bar caught Bridge's eye. Now she was seeing the newcomer everywhere.

"Bridge? What's wrong?"

She went over to the bar and asked to see the tabloid, confirming her suspicion. *It's her.*

Bridge turned and showed Quade the picture, gesturing. "This is her. The famous magician who's gone AWOL."

"Finnian Kane?" Quade said.

The low chatter in the pub stopped suddenly. Obviously, they all knew the celebrity better than she did.

Bridge nodded. "That's her."

Suddenly Bridge felt a sense of guilt welling up inside. From what she had picked up from the news media, Finnian Kane had gone to ground after her younger sister died of an aggressive cancer.

She was grieving.

## CHAPTER THREE

The next day, Bridge was walking back from visiting one of her parishioners when she noticed a motorcycle parked outside the post office. There was only one person in the village who owned a motorcycle, and that was the enigmatic Finnian Kane. Bridge stopped for a second and admired the bike from afar. *You do have very good taste, Ms. Kane.*

Although she had never ridden herself, Bridge always had a liking for motorcycles—the leather and everything that went with it—which, she believed, would account for the ripple of excitement running through her body at the moment.

The one thing that didn't seem to fit the Harley was the artist's easel strapped to the back of the bike. She would never have guessed Finnian Kane to be the arty type. Bridge resumed her walk and saw Kane exit the post office with a gaggle of schoolchildren behind her. At the head of the bunch was Riley's best friend Sophie, saying, "Please show us a trick, Finn! Please, please?"

Bridge smiled at the exuberance. It was a big thing for a small village like this to have a celebrity living here, no less a famous magician.

Her smile soon wavered when she heard Finn snap, "No, I don't practice magic any more, okay?"

Bridge was only a few feet away now, and Finnian looked up and met her eyes. There was so much pain, anger, and confusion in those eyes that her heart ached.

"Good morning," Bridge said.

Finnian held her gaze for a few more moments, and said, "Is it?" She pulled on her helmet and mounted her bike. The children looked entirely crestfallen, but just then Finnian flipped up her visor and rummaged in her pocket and handed some money to Sophie. "Buy some sweets for you and your friends."

With that she drove off and the children hurried back into the post office.

*So, you're not as bad as you want to make out.* Bridge walked into the post office and up to Mrs. Peters at the counter.

"Good morning, Vicar. You'll never guess who we had in here."

She watched as Mr. Peters tried to serve the excited children at the sweetie counter.

"Finnian Kane?"

"Yes, she's nothing like she is on TV though. Mr. Peters and I always enjoy watching her shows. She's bright, happy, charismatic, but here she was moody, and a little lost."

"A lost sheep," Bridge said.

That was exactly what she thought when she'd looked into Finnian's hurt and emotional eyes.

"Although," Mrs. Peters added, "she is as good-looking in real life as she is on the TV."

"Yes, indeed." Bridge thought back to meeting her at the cottage and outside the shop. There was no doubting she was a delightfully good-looking butch, but very different than her friend Quade. Quade was what she would call old-school butch, rugged, handsome, and traditional, whereas Finn was what she would describe as boyish in her looks and charm.

*I wonder how old she is. She looks younger than me.*

Bridge realized she had become lost in her thoughts when Mrs. Peters said, "Wouldn't you say so, Vicar?"

"Sorry, Mrs. Peters. Say again?"

"Ms. Kane is very intense. She walks around as if she is carrying the weight of the world on her shoulders."

"I think you are right."

As rude as Finn had been to her the twice she had met her, Bridge did feel as though she should persist in trying to help her. After all, wasn't it every vicar's job to lead the lost sheep back to their flock?

❖

"Fuck! You can't do anything right." Finn pulled her headphones from her ears and threw them on the ground beside her easel.

Finn couldn't stare at the four walls of her cottage any longer and had to get out. One of the reasons she had rented the cottage was the summer house in the garden. The previous tenant had been a potter and it was fully set up and ready to be a painting studio, but today she needed some space and fresh air in her lungs. She had grabbed her easel and set off on her bike to find the perfect spot.

She'd stopped when she saw a car park and signs for the beginning of a forest trail, and eventually made her way up to the top of a small hill. It had a bench that looked out over a valley, and a ruined castle in the distance. Perfect for painting.

Finn had been there since the morning but had been making frustratingly slow progress. Painting was something she had always enjoyed but hadn't had the chance to do in a long, long time. The last few years of her life had been twenty-four-seven performances and travelling to venues all over the world. She had been so busy, she hadn't stopped to appreciate what she had, and now her happiness was gone. The colour of life had deserted her, and she couldn't see how she could live on in this bleak world.

Finn looked down at her paint-covered hands and saw them tremble. It was no wonder she couldn't paint the way she wanted—she couldn't even control herself.

*Finn, I'm scared. What if you were right? What if there's nothing?*

The voice that haunted her thoughts threatened to bring tears to her eyes. She pulled off her baseball cap and scrubbed her face vigorously. Just then Finn heard the telltale sounds of footsteps on the gravel path leading to the lookout area.

She had been lucky that all day there had only been a couple of dog walkers passing her spot. Finn quickly smoothed back her hair and replaced her baseball cap, back to front.

As she had done with the others who had passed by, she kept her eyes low and hoped they would walk on without incident. But instead of a pair of trousered legs and a dog come upon her, she saw a pair of knee-high broad-heeled lady's biker boots that nearly made her swallow her tongue.

Finn's eyes travelled up the boots that had various buckles and zips all the way to the top and ended at the knees of the sexiest pair of legs she had seen.

"Good evening, Ms. Kane."

That upper-class voice she would recognize anywhere. The vicar.

Her brief arousal was extinguished by the image of the dog collar around Bridget's neck.

Finn was lost for words, and Bridget said, "Are you going to reply to me or my boots?"

She looked up and gave her a hard stare. "It's Finn, and I don't intend to talk at all."

"Such nonsense," Bridget said. "Budge up."

Before Finn had time to protest, Bridget plonked herself down on the bench beside her, and leaned in to her. "Budge up, unless you want me to sit on your knee."

Bridget was in such close proximity that Finn could smell her perfume, and her body reacted in a way it hadn't in a long time.

Whatever perfume Bridget wore, it made Finn think of sex, and that was wrong on so many levels. She was grieving, and the woman in question was a bloody vicar. Finn scooted up the bench like a frightened rabbit, something she had never felt like around a woman before.

Finn tried to feign nonchalance, and leaned back against the seat. "Didn't think you would be much of a walker, Vicar."

"Well that's good then, because I don't like to fit people's expectations." Bridget gave Finn a smile and a wink. It was always thrilling to surprise people. No one quite believed she was a vicar, anywhere she went or any *who* she met. "I like to walk here just before dinner and find some peace, sort out my thoughts, and make my sermon plan for Sunday."

"Just before dinner? What time is it?" Finn quickly looked at her watch. "Five thirty? I completely lost track of the time."

"Have you been up here since this morning?"

Finn nodded. "Got lost in my painting."

Bridge narrowed her eyes. Finn must have missed meals. "Have you not eaten anything all day?"

Finn scowled like a moody teenager. "Does it matter?"

She resisted the urge to bite back, and sat back against the bench. Bridget wondered again how old Finn was. She did seem to be much younger than her, but that could be simply the effect of Finn's boyish looks and appearance, today made even more apparent by her ripped jeans, checked hooded shirt, and baseball cap worn back to front.

There was silence for a few seconds before Bridge said, "It is beautiful up here, isn't it. I like to think of this as God's back garden."

Finn laughed cynically. "Or simply a beautiful landscape created by billions of years of natural evolution."

Bridge mentally rubbed her hands together. *Oh, don't even go down this road, Finn. I'll have you for breakfast.*

But maybe if played correctly she could get Finn to open up and have a conversation, and the human contact she was clearly crying out for.

"There you go making assumptions again. You think I don't believe in evolution?"

Finn started to put away her paints and wipe her brushes. "No, I wouldn't think a vicar would."

"I'm not only a vicar, I'm a scholar as well. I was well educated not only in Bible texts, but in Greek, Latin, Egyptian, and esoteric doctrines. I know there are truths and myths in all ancient documents."

Finn put down her brushes and turned to face her. Bridge could see a spark in her eyes that hadn't been there before. Had she hit on something to make her lost sheep engage with the world?

"Do you believe God made the world in seven days?" Finn said quickly.

"No," Bridge fired back.

Finn scooted closer to her on the bench. "Do you believe in Adam and Eve?"

"Or Adam and Steve?" Bridge corrected her.

"Exactly. Adam, Eve, Steve, whoever?"

This was becoming jolly good fun, Bridge thought. "No, I don't. I believe that back in the mists of time we made those allegories and myths to try to make sense of concepts we didn't understand, but I do believe God made everything happen, and the message is always the same. God is love, and love is all that matters."

"Oh, please. Do you know how many men and women of God I've heard say that while they line their pockets with money? Faith healers, so-called miracle workers that turned out to be two-bit magicians and cold readers, and not very good ones at that."

She hadn't seen much of Finn's work, but Bridge knew that Finn was a controversial figure within the Christian and spiritualist communities, making it her life's mission to debunk the darker sides of those religions.

"That's not the faith or the God I represent, Finn. I don't promise miracles, or healing. I talk to people about being the best they can be.

Loving your neighbour, helping those worse off than yourself, being kind, and loving one another. That is the God I've given my life to."

"The God of love who takes away the only love you've ever known? No, thanks."

As Finn threw her painting things into her bag, Bridge thought how different she was to the confident, charismatic performer she had seen on YouTube clips she had looked up last night. Now she was angry, bitter, and perhaps on a path of self-destruction, if the bottle of vodka peeking out of her bag was anything to go by.

Bridget said the first words of comfort that came to her mind, *"The righteous perish, and no one takes it to heart. Merciful men are taken away, and no one considers that the righteous is taken away to be spared from the evil."*

Quick as a flash, Finn finished the quote for her. *"He enters into peace. They rest in their beds, each one who walks in his uprightness.* Isaiah 57:1–2. Don't quote scripture at me and hope I'll find comfort in it. There is no comfort," Finn said coldly and calmly.

Bridge was taken aback by Finn's biblical knowledge. "You're not what you seem to be, Finn."

"That's because I'm not. I'm an illusion. Everyone presents an illusion of themselves to others—very few people see us as we really are. Look at you, for example."

Bridget was surprised the conversation had rounded on her. "What about me?"

"You are an illusion of your own making. You're not the vicar people expect."

"You've only known me for five minutes. You know nothing about me. I am everything I seem, a vicar who…likes fashion. Maybe a bit different, but nothing wrong with that."

Finn put her canvas in her bag and folded up her easel. "That's where you're wrong. You see, I am excellent at reading people. I've trained myself over my life to look beyond the illusion and read a person's psyche. That's why I'm so good at what I do, at cold reading."

She swung her bag onto her shoulder and lifted her easel. "I think you are hiding behind that dog collar, and all the other mumbo jumbo you preach. You're hiding a part of yourself, a part that will never quite let you go."

"How dare you—" Before Bridget could continue her rant, Finn walked off, leaving Bridget fuming.

❖

After dinner Bridge walked up to Axedale to check on the house and the horses. She walked into the stable and the horses whinnied and neighed when they saw her holding the bag of goodies her housekeeper had sent for them.

"At least someone's pleased to see me," Bridge said.

She took out her bag of carrots and gave one to each horse before stopping at Willow's stall. Willow was Riley's beloved horse and she had left strict instructions to bring her an evening snack. She took out an apple and rubbed Willow's nose as she fed her the fruity treat.

Bridge smiled as the horse gobbled up the apple and whinnied for more. She reached into the bag and got her a carrot, which Willow gratefully received.

"If only all the members of my parish were as easy to help."

She just couldn't shake the conversation she'd had with Finn earlier. Even though the woman was obviously going through a lot of grief, her attitude irked her. Bridge had always had a natural need to help people, but now that she was a vicar, the need was also a duty. It wasn't nice to have her attempts to make a connection thrown in her face.

She also felt a sense of guilt that she felt angry at Finn's petulance and distrust. "Bloody arrogant—"

"Penny for them?" a voice behind her said.

Bridge nearly jumped out of her heels. She turned around and saw Quade standing there. "Dear God, Quade. You nearly gave me a heart attack."

Quade came closer and patted Willow. "Evening, Vicar. Sorry about that. Who's driven you to swear on this lovely evening?"

"Oh, just a lost sheep I'm having trouble trying to welcome to the flock."

Quade leaned on the stall door. "You mean our new resident celebrity?"

Bridge nodded, and Quade replied, "Maybe she thinks you're a wolf, Vicar."

"What? Why would she think that? There's nothing scary about me."

Quade raised an eyebrow and said, "Oh, I could list a few things."

Bridge gave her a soft hit to the arm. "Behave, Quade. I'm not scary. I'm just a vicar with fabulous heels."

Quade laughed. "No, seriously. You just said it yourself. You're a vicar. Isn't she known for being an evangelical atheist?"

"Yes. So?"

"Well, sometimes the thing you hate the most is what scares you the most. You, Vicar, represent the Church. Maybe that's what it is?"

Bridge thought about her last conversation with Finn. She'd implied that Bridge was hiding behind her dog collar. Maybe Finn did resent what the dog collar represented.

She grabbed Quade and gave her a kiss on the cheek. "That's brilliant! You're not just a handsome face."

Quade rolled her eyes. "Yeah, so handsome the women are beating down my door. Listen, maybe I should try first, maybe take a keg of Axedale Ale? Surely no one can refuse that."

Bridge rubbed her hands together with satisfaction. She loved finding a new positive angle to try to relate people to each other and to God. She had helped Harry, with the huge help of Annie, so there must be hope for Finnian Kane.

She shouldn't care since Finn was so rude to her, but the pain she had seen in Finn's eyes the two times they had met was not something she could easily ignore. Bridge's calling was to help others, and in her parish, the buck stopped with her.

"Yes, you go first. She might relate to you better. Then I'll come up with something and try again."

# CHAPTER FOUR

Finn was trying to work on the landscape she had started the day before. She hadn't had time to paint in a long time, but it was a natural talent.

After long months on tour, she used to paint to de-stress in her home studio for hours at a time, knowing that her sister Carrie, with whom she shared her home, was taking care of all the domestic issues. Making sure there was enough food in the fridge, making sure she ate, bringing her endless cups of tea, and keeping all but the most urgent phone calls away from her. They were a team, they looked after each other, but now Finn was alone.

Finn picked up her bottle of water for a drink and looked at her picture despairingly. Rustiness was to be expected after so long away from her art, but this was more than that. Somehow working on her canvas felt impossible, like climbing a mountain. Every single little stroke of the brush was a huge effort. There was something missing from inside her, and she didn't know how to fix it.

She looked over at her sister's plants, sitting on the summer house windowsill, and the guilt began to gnaw at her guts.

Finn threw down the water bottle and pulled off her paint-splattered checked shirt, scattering the playing cards she always kept in her pocket all over the floor, and leaving her in a sleeveless T-shirt.

She felt constrained, suffocated, and just wanted the pain to be over. Finn reached for the small bottle of vodka she'd propped on the workbench and glugged down a few mouthfuls of the burning liquid.

Looking at the canvas in front of her just made her more aware of how hopeless she was. Finn's anger spilled over. She slammed down her bottle on the bench, smashed her knee through the canvas, threw it against the wall, and pushed over the easel. Her paints and brushes were pushed off the workbench, and then her frenzy and anger dissipated, leaving her with intense and overwhelming sadness.

Tears welled over and she slid down the summer house wall, to sit amongst the frenzy and mess of her emotional breakdown. "I can't do this, Carrie, not without you."

The sight of her playing cards strewn all over the floor made her feel even more out of control. Her deck of cards never left her person—they were both her security blanket and part of her identity. She'd had them since she was a child. They were a part of her rebellion, an integral part of her personality.

Finn frantically began to collect them back into a pile, and then sat back against the wall, shuffling them while they brought her calm.

She gazed over at her broken landscape and let out a breath. It seemed she just couldn't paint pictures like that any more. Her creativity had deserted her. All she had inside were these dark, raw emotions.

On impulse she got up, picked out a fresh canvas, and started to paint broad red and black strokes.

❖

After working out her frustrations in paint, Finn was cleaning her brushes and equipment in the garden, and she heard someone at the back garden gate.

"Knock, knock?"

She looked up and saw a woman holding a cask of some sort. "Can I help?"

"The name's Sam McQuade. I thought to bring you a cask of Axedale Ale to welcome you to the village. I make it myself."

You didn't need gaydar to guess that Sam McQuade was gay—she certainly out-butched Finn. She got up and walked over to the gate. "Thanks. I appreciate it, Ms. McQuade."

"Call me Quade, mate. Everyone does." Quade handed the small cask over the gate to her.

It was strange, but she didn't feel on the defensive with Quade, like she did with the do-gooding vicar. Perhaps because she was a kindred spirit. "Would you like to come in?"

"I won't, but thanks. I'm expected up at Axedale Hall. I'm assistant estate manager there."

"That must keep you busy. I noticed the tourists going in the gates in droves when I passed yesterday."

"Yeah, it's been redeveloped by the present countess. Keeps us all busy. Anyway, I thought since I was passing, I'd bring you the ale as a welcoming present."

"I'm sure I'll enjoy it."

"I hope you settle in quickly. It is a lovely little village, even if I say so myself. The locals are all friendly. Come to the pub and we can have a pint together sometime. There's a pub quiz every Saturday, which is always a good laugh."

"Sounds great," Finn lied. She couldn't think of anything worse than mixing with a pub full of people at the moment.

"I usually team up with the vicar. I think you've met her?"

Finn thought about the easy way she was talking to Quade, and felt a little guilty at the rude way she had spoken to the vicar.

"Yes, I've met her."

Quade smiled. "Bridge really is a character, and we are so lucky to have her. She works tirelessly to help everyone in the village. Always puts others before herself. And it's nice to have a vicar who is gay."

"Yes, it must be."

Quade held out her hand and Finn shook it. "I better get going. I hope I'll see you in the pub so we can have a chat."

❖

Bridge took Quade's advice, and the next day after dealing with church business, got changed into something less intimidating. She replaced her dog collar with a fine V-necked cashmere jumper. She stood in her bedroom and looked at her image in her full-length mirror. Her uniform of heels and leather jacket was only slightly changed by the cashmere jumper, but she was so rarely in civilian clothes these days, she did look strange to her eyes. She felt vulnerable, like a knight without his shield, and was reminded of the time before she entered the Church.

Something Finn had said to her floated across her mind. *I think you're hiding behind that dog collar.*

Was she? Bridge's gaze went across the room to the large built-in wardrobes. In there lay some memories she didn't want to think about.

She shook the thoughts away quickly, and hurried downstairs to the vicarage kitchen. Mrs. Long, her housekeeper, had a basket of food on the table for her.

"Is this everything, Mrs. Long?"

Mrs. Long smiled proudly. She dried her hands on the kitchen towel and made her way over to the basket, and picked a few items.

"Indeed, Vicar. There's some bread fresh from my oven, Mrs. Ashworth's jam and marmalade, some tomatoes from Mr. Pratt's greenhouse, Miss Nuttal's scones, and finally Mr. Butterworth's damson gin. Perfect to welcome Ms. Kane to the village. I only wish we had some of Lady Annie's Death by Chocolate cake."

"Don't we all," Bridge said. "I'm going to have withdrawal symptoms by the time they return from Italy."

It secretly tickled Bridge, and she knew Harry felt the same, that the villagers had taken to call her wife Lady Annie out of respect. Legally Harry was unable to share her title with her wife, although everyone hoped that outdated law would relax in the future, but despite this Annie was Axedale's lady of the manor in the true spirit of the word, and deserved their respect.

She had done so much for the village, least of which melting the heart of their countess, and that had changed everything in the village for the better.

Bridge lifted the basket and said, "I don't know how long I'll be. Ms. Kane may not even let me through the front door, but if anyone needs me, just call my mobile, and if I'm not back for evening prayers, then our resident magician has probably made me disappear into the ether."

Mrs. Long chuckled. "Will do, Vicar."

She set off to Mason's cottage, hoping to herd the lost sheep of the parish into the welcoming flock. Bridge chuckled, remembering Quade describing her as a wolf. Surely, she wasn't that frightening a woman?

Bridge walked up to the cottage gate and noticed the front door open, and some wood, broken shelving, and broken and smashed painted canvases—abandoned halfway through by the looks of it—lying up against the fence.

When she had met Finn on her evening walk, she'd noticed she was painting a beautiful landscape, but these abandoned artworks were abstract, and dark angry colours only.

"Oh, dear. One is feeling rather angry, my little lost sheep."

Bridge knocked on the open front door, and no one responded. "Hello? Is anyone at home? It's Bridget."

There was no reply so she moved further into the living room. Immediately something caught her eye on the hatstand in the corner. It was the top hat she had seen Finn wearing in the YouTube clips she had watched. She placed her basket of goods on the floor and picked it off the stand, fascinated by all the unusual adornments it had.

The broad band around the hat held a feather, two playing cards, two little silver cogs, and a brass clock face with no hands. Above the band was a brass keyhole, complete with key.

"How very steampunk."

"Funny, I don't remember inviting you in, Vicar," a voice behind her said.

Bridget jumped and clasped her hand to her chest, and turned around quickly. It was Finn.

"Dear God! You gave me such a fright."

Finn folded her arms and gave her an accusing look. "Well, you must forgive me for giving you a fright after you walked into my house uninvited."

It appeared that Finn was hostile and defensive with her already. Yet Quade said she had been normal and polite. *What am I doing wrong?*

It annoyed Bridge that she got that reaction. She was used to warmth and friendliness from people she met. Usually her position bought her some immediate goodwill, but it seemed to be just the opposite with Finnian Kane.

"I'm sorry. I did knock, but I got no answer." Bridge settled the top hat back on its resting place.

"And so you just walked in?"

Bridge couldn't help but take in Finn's ruffled appearance. She was wearing a white sleeveless T-shirt and jeans, both spattered with paint, with a painting rag hanging out of her pocket. Her feet were bare.

That infuriating long fringe held in a topknot at the back of her head emphasized the short, shaved in sides and back of her head. She imagined running her fingernails down that soft short hair, and her heart sped up. Finn was very attractive, in a boyish way. Delicious.

Bridge shook off the feeling quickly. What was she thinking? Finn wasn't her type. It wasn't that she didn't find butch women attractive, but just that normally their energies didn't mix. She was too much of a femme top for most butches.

"I'm sorry from my presumption, but it's just habit. In Axedale we don't lock doors and are in and out of each other's homes."

She noticed again Finn's gaze travelling up and down her legs, as she had when they'd met on her walk. Maybe Finn was a leg woman, and maybe she did notice her, even though she seemed determined to be rude.

Finn closed her eyes for a second and returned to her cool impassive gaze. "So now that you're here, what do you want?"

Bridge picked up her basket and walked over to the coffee table. "I brought you this. It's some things the people of the village have put together to welcome you here. There's bread, scones, jam, and Mr. Butterworth's damson gin. I'll warn you though, it's very potent."

Finn walked the few steps to her and looked in the basket. She nodded and said, "That was kind. Thank them for me."

Bridge was more than a little annoyed. Thank *them*? Why was it that everyone else got a better reception than she did?

"Have I done something to offend you?"

Finn took another step into her personal space. "Do you push your way into the lives of everyone you meet, Vicar?"

They stood toe to toe. Finn had a few inches of height on her but her heels cancelled out the difference.

"Or is it just that you want to get your hooks into the famous lesbian who's moved into your village?"

Bridge laughed sarcastically and moved to within inches of Finn's lips and whispered, "I wouldn't worry, Magician. You are not my type."

Finn appeared to be taken aback by that answer, then bit back, "Where's the dog collar today, Vicar?"

Bridge cleared her throat and stuffed her hands into the pockets of her biker jacket. "I simply felt like dressing in civvies today."

"Bollocks." Finn laughed. "You think I have a problem with religion and what your dog collar represents, so you came over without it, hoping I would be more amenable to your ministering."

Bridge spluttered, "I—"

"Don't try and psychologize me. I'm the master of psychology and the human mind. Why can't you just leave me alone and direct your do-gooding to someone else?"

Finn clearly had an arrogant streak a mile wide, but instead of angering Bridge, Finn's outburst made her chuckle thinking how much fun it would be to wipe that uppity sneer right off her face—preferably with Finn on her knees. A ripple of excitement spread throughout her body at the thought.

Those feelings had been lying in cold storage for a long, long time, and now she felt them, standing in front of this cocky butch.

As that part of herself started to waken, she stood a little straighter and said confidently, "You're the master, are you?"

"Haven't you seen my shows on TV?"

"Only snippets. Conjuring isn't my thing." Bridget was amused by the look of annoyance on Finn's face.

"I am not a *conjurer*. I'm a mentalist and master of illusion."

"Oh, how marvellous. Can you pull a rabbit out of a hat?"

"Sit down at the table, Vicar, and I'll show you just how good I am."

❖

*Conjurer? Bloody woman*, thought Finn as they sat down at the dining room table. This vicar, who knew nothing about her or her skills, was laughing at her.

She took her pack of cards from her jeans pocket and began to shuffle them in her trademark elaborate fashion.

"Are you going to show me a card trick?"

"No. I don't practice magic any more." Finn placed her cards on the side of the table.

"Why?" Bridge asked. "I understand from the newspapers you've been grieving for your sister but—"

"Don't. I told you not to minister to me. My private life is no one's business but my own. Now let me show you just how good I am, Vicar."

Bridge sat back and crossed her legs nonchalantly. "Off you go then. Impress me, Magician."

Finn's simmering annoyance ramped up a couple of notches. "Oh, I will. Now I need something of yours to pick up the vibrations. A watch perhaps?"

She watched with amusement as Bridge went to take off her watch and found her wrist bare.

"What? I was sure I put it on this morning."

Finn reached into her pocket and pulled out Bridge's watch. "Looking for this?"

"Wait—how did you get that?"

"I told you I'm the master," Finn said with extreme confidence.

She looked at the watch face: Cartier. That was part of the puzzle she had to work out about Bridget Claremont. Everything Bridget wore was designer, and a vicar's salary didn't normally stretch to those types of items. Added to that her upper-class accent and admitted good education—Bridget clearly came from a family of some substance. This was all information she could use in her cold reading.

Bridge tapped her fingernails on the tabletop and Finn couldn't help but gaze at the bright red nails. She could certainly imagine Bridge using them as claws on someone's back, and that thought made her shiver.

Bridget slapped her hand down sharply on the tabletop, breaking Finn's focus. "I'm up here, not down there, you know."

Finn immediately looked up. *Get a grip.*

"Vibrations?" Bridget said. "I thought you didn't believe in the supernatural? I thought you were some atheist crusader?"

Finn set the watch between them. "I'm going to show you just how good I am, and why you shouldn't even attempt any psychology tricks with me. Put your palm on the watch."

Bridget sighed but then did as she was asked. Finn rubbed her palms together vigorously and closed her eyes for a few seconds. She then placed her palm on top of Bridge's.

Finn felt a spark, then felt warmth spreading up her arm. She heard Bridge gasp. She obviously felt it too.

Why did this happen every time they touched? She opened her eyes slowly and found Bridge's soft gaze like a caress.

"Show me you're the master then," Bridge said with a hint of challenge in her voice.

"I can see an old box of photographs at home." She felt Bridge tense immediately, and knew she was getting a hit. "Yes, it's becoming clearer, an old box of photographs, in a wardrobe or cupboard. Does that mean anything to you?"

Bridget nodded briefly and cleared her throat nervously. Finn knew she was on the right track, and now she just had to follow the scent.

"The box of photographs has been in the wardrobe for a long time, and you've been meaning to sort through them, and scan them onto your computer. Does that make sense?"

Again, Bridge nodded, the tension in her hand rising.

"Now there's a woman in those photographs, and she's coming through to me now."

Bridge looked up at her sharply. Her breathing increased and the tension deepened by the second. Finn had a hit.

"This woman—" Finn brought her free hand to her forehead and rubbed it tensely. It was all part of the showmanship.

"What about her?" Bridge said out of nowhere.

"She's very faint, but she's trying to give me her name…It starts with an *E*. Is there someone who's passed on with the initial *E*?"

"Ellen," Bridge blurted out.

Finn could feel Bridge's hand tremble underneath her own. This Ellen clearly meant a lot to her. All the visual cues were telling Finn she was getting hits with every word. Even though Bridge should have known this was all tricks and showmanship, Finn was sucking her in, as she always did. People were predictable, no matter where they came from in life or what they did for a living. They were all susceptible to illusion.

"Yes, Ellen. That's right. She's telling me that you feel a great sadness at her passing, that you had unfinished business?"

"Yes." Bridge's voice cracked with emotion, and Finn was sure she could see the start of tears well up in her eyes.

She had taken this too far. Finn didn't like the vicar's persistence, but she would never want to hurt someone who'd recently lost a loved one, especially since she knew what that felt like. Finn assumed Ellen would be an aged great-aunt or something. She had to make this better.

Finn looked into Bridge's eyes with sincerity and said, "She said you shouldn't feel bad about her passing—"

Bridge snatched her hand away and stood up quickly, hurrying out the front door.

Finn immediately tried to run after her. "Vicar, wait!" But she was gone.

"Fuck! What were you playing at?" Finn slammed her hand against the front door in anger.

❖

Bridge hurried home, barely raising her head to anyone who tried to engage with her. She felt the world closing in on her, and all she wanted was to get home to her bedroom.

She walked through the door and ran up the stairs. She heard a voice behind her shout, "How did you get on with Ms. Kane, Vicar?"

She opened her bedroom door and called back, "I'll fill you in later, Mrs. Long. If anyone calls, I'm not available."

Bridge shut and locked her bedroom door, took off her biker jacket, and threw it on the bed. She held her hands over her face and couldn't stop the tears she had been holding in.

Her brain couldn't process what had just happened. How could Finn know about Ellen?

Bridge got a tissue and dried her eyes. Her gaze was drawn to the wardrobe in the corner. It was calling to her, as it always did, but was she strong enough to look?

*I must do this.*

She walked across to the wardrobe and rested her hand on the knob. Her heart started to beat rapidly. "Come on, Bridge. You can do this."

Bridge quickly opened the door and there on the top shelf was a box labelled *photographs*, just as Finn had predicted. It had sat in here since she'd moved to Axedale, and she had never once opened it. This wasn't just a box of photographs—it was a box of memories. Memories that she tried hard not to think about too much, memories that represented a different life.

*Maybe today should be the day.*

She took the box down, blew a cloud of dust off the top, and carried it over to her bed. Bridge sat beside the box and inhaled a long breath before taking the lid off. Pictures of all different sizes were piled in the box. One on top caught her eye, and she smiled as she picked it up.

It showed Bridge in her early twenties, dressed in a skimpy leather outfit with thigh-high lace-up heeled boots, a coiled whip rolled up in her right hand. She turned it over and written on the back was *Red's Christmas party. 2002.*

The next photo she picked up had her and Harry posing in it. Bridge wore a similar outfit, and Harry had on leather trousers, biker boots, and a black sleeveless T-shirt. They were both laughing with drinks in their hands.

Harry hadn't often gone to Red's with her, but occasionally she liked to join Bridge at her favourite club.

She remembered that night like it was yesterday, even though she hadn't thought about that time in her life much recently. Because of the person who was missing from the picture.

The one who had taken the picture. Her friend, and first love, her unrequited love, Ellen.

Bridge put that picture down and picked up another that brought new tears. Ellen. The woman who had changed the course of her life.

The woman in the picture was wearing a black catsuit, her beautiful red hair pulled back into a ponytail. Bridge was with her in the picture, and unbeknownst to Ellen, looking at her adoringly.

Bridge traced her painted fingernail over the picture of Ellen, hoping to feel connected. Even after all this time, the pain was still real, and she was hard to think about. Why this had to come up now, when she was supposed to be helping someone else with their grief, she had no idea.

As the pain was threatening to spill over, she looked over to the thing that had saved her from pain before, her dog collar. It was hanging with her black shirt from a hanger on the door. It represented her faith, the thing that kept her sane.

She shut the box and got up quickly to grab the collar and shirt. Once she was dressed, she looked at herself in the mirror, and felt so much calmer and stronger. The dog collar was Bridge's armour, against pain and the world. Was Finn right? Did she hide behind it?

Quickly shaking away those thoughts, she put the box of photos back in the wardrobe.

"I'll always keep you in my prayers and my thoughts, Ellen."

One day she would sort out the old photos, but today was not the day.

❖

Finn had spent the day wallowing in guilt. What she had meant as some sort of arrogant brush-off for the vicar had upset Bridge. She sat on the couch in her living room, shuffling the cards that helped her calm, and looking at the picture of her sister on the coffee table. Next to the picture was a glass and an open bottle of vodka.

"You would be so ashamed of me, Carrie. I hurt someone, just because I could."

She was agitated and didn't know what to do with herself. What she should be doing was going to the vicarage, and apologizing to Bridget, but she did not have the guts to face her.

Finn downed her drink, grabbed her coat, and went out of the cottage, determined to have a long walk to clear her mind.

She walked into the heart of the village and stood on the bridge that crossed the river which flowed through the village. Finn leaned over the side and gazed at the trickling water.

It was so calm and so unlike her troubled mind. Finn had done cold readings as part of her act, and to debunk psychics before, but never just to show off and play a cruel joke on someone. What she had done to Bridget made her no better than the charlatans she had debunked over the years or, more worryingly, her father.

When Finn's sister Carrie had died, she had promised herself she wouldn't perform magic ever again, and she had so easily and arrogantly slipped back into it as if nothing had happened.

*What a joke.* It turned out she was the charlatan.

"All right, mate?" a voice said behind her.

She turned around and found Quade standing there. "Oh, hi."

"Taking the evening air, eh? It's a pretty village, isn't it?"

"Yes, it is. Picture perfect."

"I was hoping I'd bump into you. I wanted to let you know that Bridge and I spread the word around the village. If any nosy newspaper blokes turn up, we won't say you're here. As far as we're concerned, you just passed through."

Finn was more than a little taken aback. She had been obnoxious and bad tempered, pushing everyone away since she arrived, and yet they wanted to help protect her.

Yet another reason to feel bad. Finn pushed her hands in her pockets and looked down at her shoes.

"That's really kind of you all. I really don't deserve it."

Quade put a friendly hand on her shoulder. "You're in Axedale now, and we all look after each other."

Finn took a couple of seconds to imagine what it would feel like to belong somewhere like here. She didn't have a home and had been a nomad for most of her life. Since her sister died, she'd been adrift physically, spiritually, and mentally.

"Thank you. You don't know how much I need my privacy right now."

"I get it," Quade said. "I was just on my way to the pub. Fancy a pint?"

"Oh no, thanks. I'm not really good company at the moment," Finn said.

"Come on, mate. It doesn't matter if you don't want to talk. It'll just get you out from your four walls at home."

Going to the pub was the last thing she wanted to do, but how could she deny Quade when she had just been so kind to her?

"Maybe just a quick one then."

Quade gave her the biggest smile. "Great, let's go."

It was a short walk to The Witch's Tavern from the bridge. When they walked into the pub, everyone went quiet for a second, then returned to their chatter.

"You get us a seat, mate, and I'll get the first round in."

Finn nodded, looked around, and saw a table free at the back of the room, the furthest away from the other patrons. She took a seat and gazed around. It was a classic small village pub. Warm, inviting, and she was sure full of good cheer. The problem was she didn't want to feel good cheer. In fact, after today, she had slipped even deeper into despair than before.

*Just one pint to be polite, and then I'll go.*

The walls of the pub were filled with old photographs of the village and estate, trophies, and posters. One poster advertised the village winter show, and another was a sign-up sheet for something called Witch's Night.

The pub was named The Witch's Tavern, and the village had a Witch's Night? The village must have some connection to witches or the occult.

Quade put a pint down in front of her and a big bowl of nuts. "There you go, get that down your neck, mate."

"Thanks."

Quade lifted her pint and said, "Cheers." She took a sip and asked, "So, how are you settling in at Mason's cottage?"

"It's nice. Like nothing I'm used to." Finn took a large gulp of lager.

"You're from the big city?"

Finn nodded. "Mostly, although in recent years it's mainly been the hotel rooms of cities I've lived in."

Quade took a drink and a handful of nuts from the bowl. "You must have seen a lot of amazing places on your world tours."

"I was never in any one place long enough to see them. I'd be packed on the plane ready to perform in the next place almost as soon as the curtain came down on my last show."

"Wow, going from that to a slow, quiet village like Axedale must be a big shock to the system."

"It was what I needed to do." Finn didn't want the conversation to veer into why she was here, so she asked Quade, "What do you do here, Quade?"

"Well, I run my farm, and I'm also assistant estate manager at Axedale Hall. Have you seen Axedale yet?"

"I just passed by the gates. It looked beautiful from what I could see."

Quade smiled proudly. "It is. The village is so proud of the estate. It's undergone a lot of refurb work since the countess inherited."

Finn had heard that Axedale had an interesting owner. "What's this countess like?"

"Harry? She's a good friend. She and the village had some rough times when she first inherited the title. There was a lot of bad blood between Harry and her late father, but then she fell in love with her housekeeper, Annie, and she helped Harry fall in love with the village and the estate."

Finn smiled. "Sounds like a fairy tale."

"Yeah, a bit of a beauty and the beast love story, but Annie tamed the beast."

Finn couldn't help but laugh at that description, and then the guilt she had momentarily forgotten churned inside her.

*I have to get out of here.*

Quade continued, "It really was. Bridge praises Annie's name because she even got Harry to come to church."

"The vicar?" Finn doubted Quade would be so friendly towards her if she knew what Finn had done that afternoon.

"Yeah, Bridge is Harry's best friend. They went to school together, but they chose very different paths in life. Bridge is so happy Harry found love."

Just then, the pub door opened and Bridge walked in. Their eyes met, and Bridge walked straight back out. Finn didn't have the strength to follow her.

"That's not like the vicar," Quade said.

Finn sighed. "It's my fault. I upset her today."

"Bridge is a very forgiving person. Just go and talk to her."

"I don't think it'll be quite that easy. I'm not ready to be around people, Quade. I hurt them. I'm sorry. I'll get you another pint and head home."

# CHAPTER FIVE

B ridget set off from the vicarage to start her day at the church. Bridge liked to start her day early. Her morning walk was peaceful, a time to contemplate and pray. She felt so tired this morning. Last night she could barely sleep with thoughts of the past, and when she did doze off she dreamt of the past.

If only Harry had been here to talk to. She would have understood—she was the only link to her past. Bridge knew the only way to find peace and solace was in her work, and in God, and so she hurried down to the church. As she walked through the high iron gate to St. Mary's church, she heard the comforting sound of Mr. Butterstone on the church organ. Now that he was retired, he always came early to get a head start on practicing the next week's hymns and church music.

Bridget walked through the graveyard at the front of the church and made her way to the back door, which led to her office. Her secretary Janice Street, a middle-aged woman who had dedicated her life to the Church, was waiting for her.

"Good morning, Vicar. How are you today?"

Bridge hung up her biker jacket on the coat stand and sat at her desk. "Very well, Jan," she lied. "Any messages for me?"

Jan brought over her writing pad. "Ten phone messages, and a lot of emails have come through to you."

Bridget was always drowning in messages. Administration was a huge part of the modern vicar's role, giving her less time to do what she really wanted to do, minister to her flock.

"Oh, and this is the post for today." Jan handed over a large pile of letters, the top one of which was from the bishop.

Bridget couldn't deal with Bishop Thomas Sprat this early in the morning, so she put his letter to the back of the pile.

"Could I get some coffee, Jan. I'm having trouble getting going this morning," Bridge said.

"Of course, Vicar. I won't be a jiffy."

Jan headed to the church hall kitchen, and Bridge sat back in her seat and closed her eyes. She'd started drifting to the sounds of the organ music gently filtering through to the office, when she heard a shuffling. Her eyes sprang open and she saw a note had been slipped under the door.

She got up quickly and picked up the note. *I would like to talk to you about yesterday. Meet me at the bench on your walk tonight, and I will explain.*

Bridge's anger and annoyance had dissipated somewhat from yesterday, but it still hurt that Finn would use her grief to make a point. When Bridge was in the moment, it was easy to believe Finn's performance was real, but as reality settled in, she realized it must have been some sort of trick. How Finn got that information, she would never know, but at the very least maybe this could be a catalyst for Finn opening up to the village. It was Bridge's calling to forgive and she would always give people a second chance.

That evening, after her day's work, Bridge set off for her walk, and as she reached the brow of the hill, she saw Finn waiting for her on the bench.

"Evening," Bridge said as she sat down next to Finn.

She could feel Finn move a few inches away from her on the seat, already trying to keep her distance, even though she was here to apologize. Finn was definitely hard work, and had no intentions of giving up the chip on her shoulder anytime soon.

"Hi," Finn said, meeting her eyes only briefly before returning her gaze to the view. "Thank you for coming. I want to make things right... about yesterday. Although I was annoyed with you, I shouldn't have used my skills and techniques to fool you and upset you."

Throughout the whole explanation, Finn never looked at her once, and that, coupled with the half-hearted apology, made Bridge's vow to forgive Finn start to weaken by the second. *Her skills?* Finnian Kane's arrogance showed no sign of dissipating.

"Well, I think I can honestly say I've never had such an apology in my life. So basically, you're not sorry because I deserved it?"

Finn whipped around to look at her, surprise and anger in her eyes.

"What? I go to all the trouble of inviting you here to make things right, even though you walked into my house like a trespasser, and you won't accept my apology?"

In that one sentence she realized why Finn had invited her up here. Everything was on her terms. She could have quite easily knocked on her church office door and spoken to her there, or come to the vicarage, but she didn't.

"You think it's that easy? You think you can give me your directions to come and have your apology bestowed on me? That might work on your entourage who follow you around, hoping you'll bless them with your attention." Bridge leaned in closely to Finn's shocked and angry looking face and breathed, "Well, that doesn't wash with me, Magician. You can take your conjuring tricks and stick them where the sun doesn't shine."

Bridge immediately got up and started to walk away. She smiled to herself when within a few seconds she heard Finn's footsteps catching up with her.

"Hey, don't walk away from me, Vicar."

She kept up her pace and didn't look back. She could feel Finn by her side, but still she didn't look.

"Bridget, stop. I'm talking to you," Finn said with frustration in her voice.

"But I'm not talking to you. You need to learn some manners, Magician."

"Excuse me? I need to learn some manners? Ever since I got to this village, you haven't left me alone."

Still Bridget didn't look at her but just smiled. She was starting to enjoy the hint of desperation in Finn's voice because she wouldn't give her the attention she was used to getting.

"Look at me," Finn demanded.

Bridge put her hands in her pockets and kept her gaze forward. "You don't deserve my attention. You may be grieving at the moment, but you're behaving like a spoiled brat, and I don't give my attention to spoiled brats. Yesterday you thought I didn't wear my dog collar because I was trying to psych you out. I wasn't. Plainly and simply I wasn't wearing it so as not to frighten you, because that's what you are frightened of—me, and what I represent. Come back when you can apologize properly."

She heard Finn almost growl with anger and frustration. Then the footsteps stopped and Finn shouted, "Don't hold your breath, Vicar."

❖

Finn attacked her canvas with her paintbrush like she never had before. Big bold colours were splashed across the surface as she tried to quell the frustration and anger she was feeling. She couldn't sit still since she got back from her time trying to talk to the vicar. She had so much energy and anger, and she just couldn't get the things the vicar said out of her mind.

"Frightened? I'm not bloody frightened by a vicar in short skirts and heels, and I most fucking definitely don't want her attention."

Her heart thudded as the conversation played over and over in her mind. Bridget had totally disregarded everything she said, and wouldn't even look at her. To top it off, every time Finn thought of Bridge calling her *Magician*, as if she was nobody, and not worth her time or energy, it made her feel…she couldn't quite work out what, but it made her want to snap her paintbrush in half.

"Fuck this."

Painting just wasn't cutting it. She cleaned up her brushes and headed out for a run. It was dark and quiet in the village, but Finn enjoyed the peaceful, calm atmosphere. Just what she needed for this feeling, like she had ants crawling under her skin.

Her run took her down towards the church. As she got closer she could hear the strains of organ music and singing. Finn looked at her watch and realized it must be an evening prayer service or something.

Being an atheist, it had been a long time since she had been inside a church, but she had been brought up in the Charismatic Christian community until she and her sister finally broke away when she was sixteen, so she was well versed in hymns and church practice.

Finn slowed to a stop when she got to the gates and took a drink from her water bottle. The singing stopped, and she was sure she could hear Bridget's voice.

Although she was taking a break from the exertions of running and cooling down, her heart started to speed up. She tried to picture the vicar in her pulpit, smiling and bestowing her attention on her willing congregation, and she had the urge to see her in the flesh.

*Don't be an idiot.* She hadn't been in a church since she was seventeen, and she wasn't about to start now. Finn took another drink of water and started to walk away.

Finn took a few steps and had the insatiable urge to look back. She couldn't stop herself, and as soon as she turned her feet started walking back to the church and through the gates. Inside the entrance door to the church, she saw a stone bench.

Maybe she could go that far, just to hear what Bridge was sanctimoniously preaching.

She took a chance and walked up to the threshold. Even walking through the front door was a huge psychological barrier for her, but as she had gotten closer, the louder she could hear Bridge. The louder she could hear her, the more she wanted to hear.

She looked down at the threshold nervously. "What are you frightened of? There's no God ready to strike you down."

But that was the problem. Since her sister died, she just wasn't sure any more. Everything that had once made clear, total sense, including her career, was now in flux.

Finn looked at the wristband she wore that had belonged to her sister. *If I've got Carrie, I'll be fine.*

She took the step over the threshold, and remained in one piece. She took a seat on the stone bench and listened to Bridge's words float through from the church. It didn't feel like enough. She was being pulled to the door. Finn knew she was acting irrationally, but somehow, she couldn't stop herself. She got up and inched to the door, before peeking around the stone door frame.

There was nothing to see but another archway and another set of big oak doors. Finn imagined that those doors opened onto the centre aisle of the church. Maybe she could open them, just a crack, and then she might be able to see her nemesis in action.

Finn plucked up her courage and moved to the next set of doors. They had huge iron hoops for door handles and she rested her hand on one. Her palm became sweaty, and her breathing quickened.

*Why am I doing this?*

Again, the urge to see Bridge just once pushed her forward, and she pulled the door open a few creaky inches. Luckily the congregation was singing so they wouldn't be disturbed. Feeling brave she opened the door a few more inches and saw her—Bridget Claremont in her full robes and regalia. She looked different, even more at peace with herself. Her countenance was warm and open, but despite her vestments, she wore her bright red lipstick. Finn wondered if she still wore her killer heels under her robes. The thought excited her for some bizarre reason.

The singing stopped and the congregation was seated. Bridge started to speak. "We are gathered here this evening to remember the greatest tragedy in Axedale's history. The death of one hundred and ten good family men in the mining disaster of 1922. It was a tragedy that left children without fathers, wives without husbands, and family and friends without good men who made this village the thriving community it was. Each successive generation has vowed to remember them on this night every year, so that their memories will never fade."

Finn was held captivated. Bridge's speaking and preaching style was gentle, reverent, and sincere. She immediately thought of her father, Gideon Maxwell, Evangelical pastor and faith healer. His preaching style was the opposite of Bridget's. It was brash and flash, and lacked sincerity, and of course his whole faith was based on a lie.

Bridget continued. *"Jesus said unto her, I am the resurrection, and the life: he that believeth in me, though he were dead, yet shall he live—"*

At that moment, Bridget looked up from her notes and appeared distracted for a few seconds as she scanned the congregation, seemingly looking for someone, and then her gaze fell on Finn. She had been rumbled. Finn held her breath and held Bridge's gaze for a second more, and then turned and didn't look back. As she ran home, she realized something was different since she had met Bridge on the hill by the bench this afternoon. She hadn't thought about her grief and her pain once, and she hadn't had one drink.

## CHAPTER SIX

A week had gone by since Bridge had seen Finn lurking at the back of her church, and she'd had neither sight nor sound of her since, and neither had Quade. It had been a big surprise to see the world-renowned atheist peeking in to their service. The Finn whose eyes she locked onto that night was very different to the arrogant, demanding brat she'd met in the afternoon.

It was early evening and Bridge was walking from the vicarage to the church hall for their weekly parish council meeting. She chuckled to herself remembering how much she enjoyed pricking Finn's arrogant façade, and how Finn had followed her, trying to demand her attention.

Why Finn had sneaked into the church she had no idea. With her arrogance left at the door, Finn looked like a lost little boy, and Bridge had to physically stop herself from giving in and paying another visit to Finn's cottage to check in on her.

*Maybe I should—*

Her thoughts were interrupted by Mr. and Mrs. Peters and Quade making their way to the meeting.

"Evening, Vicar," Mr. Peters said.

"Good evening, all," Bridge replied.

Finn offered Bridge her arm, and she happily took it. "Chivalrous as always, Quade."

Quade laughed. "I try my best."

Mrs. Peters rubbed her hands together. "Let's get inside, shall we? It's getting a bit chilly."

In the church hall they were greeted by Mr. Finch the pub landlord, Mrs. McCrae, Lady Harry's social secretary, Mr. Butterstone who took the minutes of each meeting, and deputy church warden Mr. Winchester.

They all greeted each other, and Bridge took off her jacket and placed it over the chairperson's seat. Normally that was Lady Harry's seat, as she chaired the meetings, but as she was away, Bridge was taking the chair in her stead.

They exchanged small talk for a few minutes before Bridge brought the chatter to an end and brought the meeting to order.

"Let's get started, shall we, and then we can share a drink at the pub sooner, eh?"

"Carry on, Vicar," Mr. Peters said.

Bridge looked down at her parish council agenda and said, "First, as you know, the countess sends her apologies for not being able to make the meeting tonight, but she and the family are in Italy at the moment. In fact, I received an email from Lady Harry only this morning and she asked me to show you these pictures."

Bridge took out her mobile and showed the committee the first picture of Harry and Riley, up to their waists in mud in an archaeological trench, both wearing baseball caps back to front and both smiling broadly.

This received a collective *Aww* from the committee members, all apart from Mr. Winchester, who sighed audibly. He had been close to Harry's father and his nose was put out of joint when Harry joined the parish committee.

"They are like two peas in a pod, that pair," Mrs. Peters said.

Then she showed the second picture of Annie being held lovingly in Harry's arms, in front of the Colosseum in Rome.

"They look so happy," Mrs. McCrae remarked.

"Could we get on with church business please, Vicar?" Mr. Winchester said. He had never been happy with a female vicar to start with, but a gay vicar was even worse.

Bridget gave him her most polite smile and said, "Of course, Mr. Winchester."

She put away her phone and went back to her agenda. "The first two items on the agenda are Witch's Night in a few weeks' time, and then the start of rehearsals for the winter show."

Both were big events on the village calendar. Witch's Night was a quaint old village festival that dated back to the early eighteenth century, and the village show helped raise funds for worthy village projects. Everyone put their all into it every year. She knew Riley was very sorry she was going to miss it this year.

"So…Mr. Peters, do you have all the fireworks purchased for Witch's?" Bridge said.

"Yes, indeed. I got them at the wholesaler's last week." He smiled broadly. "Got bigger and better ones this year. Quade and her estate staff are going to set them up on the day."

"Yep," Quade said and then gave her a wink. "It's all under control, Vicar."

"I'm sure," Bridge said with amusement. "Now, Mr. Finch, you've organized the outdoors drinks licence as usual?"

"Yes, Vicar. My boy has got together tables and equipment so we can offer drinks along the parade route and river. Quade has given us a few barrels of Axedale Ale for the night too, which will go down very well."

"Sounds excellent. We're all in good order then. I understand Lady Annie's housekeeper, Beverly, has also made similar arrangements for the food. Item two, the village winter show. Any thoughts on the theme this year?"

Bridge looked up and saw all the council members looking at each other nervously.

"Is there a problem?"

Mrs. Peters was the first to speak. "No, no problem. We just were talking between ourselves and wondered—"

"Wondered what?" Bridge asked.

"We thought since we have such a great celebrity and showman in the village, could we try and get her interested in helping us with the show, maybe directing?"

Bridget laughed. "Good luck to whoever you send to ask that. Finnian Kane is too busy scowling and feeling sorry for herself to get involved with the village in any way."

Again, the council members looked shiftily among themselves and left Bridge bemused.

"What?"

Mrs. Peters gave her husband a nudge and he said, "Oh? Eh…yes. We thought you could go and ask her, Vicar."

"Are you kidding me? I'm the last person she would want to see, far less the right person to get her to agree to something."

Quade quickly stepped into the conversation. "The vicar's right.

Ms. Kane has come to Axedale looking for some peace and space, after a difficult time in her life. From what I've seen, she's not in the frame of mind to help us."

Bridge saw her friends' excitement dissipate. She could understand it would have been a real treat to have a famous magician involved with the village show. But the woman couldn't even apologize to her.

Mr. Winchester's frustration didn't allow him to keep quiet any longer. "Do we really have to involve a non-local in our winter show? Especially someone like Finnian Kane. She is not the right sort of person to be involved in a family show."

Bridge's hackles were immediately raised. She leaned forward and said sternly, "Oh? What kind of person is that then, Mr. Winchester?"

He leaned back and folded his arms, looking as pompous as ever, and smirked. "I think we both know the answer to that question, *Vicar*."

Instead of biting back as he wanted, Bridge put on her best smile and turned to Mr. Butterstone. "If I get the opportunity, and Ms. Kane is feeling more amenable, I will of course ask her. Who could be better to direct our little village show than our resident celebrity?"

Bridge knew it would never happen. Finnian Kane didn't even want to mix with the village, far less help them, but the look on Mr. Winchester's face made her promise worth it.

❖

Finn had been holed up in her cottage for a week. She didn't see or talk to one soul in that time. She didn't want to, as she was struggling to come to terms with everything that had happened with Bridget.

Finn stood in front of her completed painting. She had never completed a piece so quickly and it had changed with her changing mood over the week.

She had been trying to cope with so many feelings and emotions, and they were hard to process. So Finn painted and painted, pouring all her energy into her work. As Finn painted, her conversation with Bridge played over and over in her mind.

At first, she felt nothing but simmering anger. No one had ever called her out like that. She was used to being on the front foot in every social situation or conversation, being ten steps ahead, and leading people psychologically to wherever she needed them to go. Bridget

Claremont was different to anyone she'd met. She was a high femme who wouldn't be led.

Bridget had a different energy, an exciting energy. She was the kind of woman who, with just a look, could make you drop to your knees and crawl, just to be given the privilege of kissing her heels.

As Finn's anger dissipated, Finn realized that her intense response to Bridget was her reaction to meeting someone who represented faith, a faith that sent her world into chaos, and someone who confused her emotionally and mentally. Because despite everything that she was feeling, intense grief, sorrow, and sadness, these past few days she had replayed their last conversation, and the most vivid memory was how fast her heart had beaten as she chased after Bridge, and not her pain.

When Finn recognized that, her dark abstract painting took on new life, and she began to paint something she hoped would please Bridget. Finn picked up the canvas from the easel and moved it to the workbench to wrap it up. Bridget had told her to come back when she could apologize properly, and she would.

❖

After a quick shower, Finn dressed and strapped the painting to the back of her Harley, then drove in the direction of the vicarage hoping Bridget would be there, but she wasn't. Her housekeeper told her Bridge was at the church.

She just had to be, didn't she? It seemed like every road was leading her back to the church, and for an atheist, that was a confusing place to be.

Finn picked up the painting and walked towards the church door. She took a deep breath and went in. The church looked quite different with no congregation, and despite her reservations about its purpose, it was a beautiful building.

She spotted Bridge in the front pew, looking as if she was in the quiet contemplation of prayer. Finn gulped hard. This was so difficult for her on so many levels, and yet she had felt compelled to come in here last week, and compelled to come back and seek out Bridget.

She took a breath and walked down the aisle. When she got to Bridget's row, she stood quietly, not wanting to disturb Bridget's contemplation.

A few seconds went by and Bridget said without opening her eyes, "Can I help you?"

Why wouldn't Bridget look at her? She had been so keen to welcoming her to the village, and now she wouldn't even open her eyes.

*Because you hurt her.*

What she had rehearsed in her mind to say deserted her completely, so she simply said, "I'm here to apologize the way you asked me to."

Her sentence acted like magic words. Bridge's eyes opened and she turned her head to give Finn her complete attention.

"Sit down, Finn."

She had done it, gotten Bridge's attention, and now it was time to eat some humble pie. Finn sat next to her on the bench and put the painting on the floor.

Finn didn't know any way to start except to dive head first. "I'm sorry I tricked you."

"How did you get that information on me?" Bridget asked.

"I didn't. It was simple cold reading. I had no idea I would bring up someone who would cause you so much pain. I thought maybe an elderly aunt or something, not someone like—"

"My friend Ellen," Bridget finished. "How could it be cold reading? The information was too perfect."

Finn swivelled around, so she was looking at Bridge. "It's what psychics do, and so easy to learn. I set up the reading with a bit of showmanship, taking your watch, and from then I asked standard questions to get what I needed from you."

Bridge shook her head. "But the box of photographs was so specific."

"You would think, but it's not. If you think about it, every house has a box of photographs somewhere."

A smile crept up on Bridge's bright red lips. "I suppose you're right."

"And even if you'd said no, I could say, well the spirits say your childhood home had an old box of photographs, and I'm sure I'd get a hit."

Bridget laughed. "You're right. I never thought of it that way. I thought cold reading would be deep psychology."

"No, it's a lot simpler than you think, because usually the sitter wants to make the information from beyond the grave fit with them."

"But how did you get Ellen's name?"

"You told me it, Vicar. I only gave you a letter. The letter *E* that is the most prevalent in the English language. I'm quite certain one relative or another would have an *E* in their name. You did all the work."

Bridget turned slightly and inched closer to Finn. "You know, I had completely forgotten I had given you her name."

"That's because ninety percent of a magic trick is how you remember it afterwards, or how you tell others about it. You always make it more astonishing in your own mind, because you don't like to think you have been fooled that easily."

"Is that so, Magician?" She saw a flicker of something in Finn's eyes when she said that. What it was she couldn't quite tell.

"Was Ellen someone really close to you?" Finn asked.

Bridge looked down at her clasped hands on her lap and said simply, "Someone I loved, who was taken too soon."

Out of the corner of her eye she saw Finn's hand begin to reach for hers, but she pulled it back quickly.

"Anyway, I'm sorry for that, and for the way I tried to apologize the last time."

"It's all right—I suppose I was a bit forceful in my welcome. I was a bit annoyed that you seemed to be different with Quade."

Finn sighed. "Vicar, I came here to get away from magic and to get away from what you represent."

"Then you come here and I constantly try to herd you up like a little lost sheep."

Finn raised an eyebrow at that comment. "I suppose."

"I know you've been through a terrible time, Finn, and if you ever want to talk or let the village and me under those walls you've erected to protect yourself, just let me know."

"I'm not ready, okay?" Finn said brusquely. "I'm sorry, I didn't mean that. Here." She picked up a parcel wrapped in brown paper and handed it to Bridge. "I painted this for you." Finn stood, looking as if her panic had returned.

"Finn, wait—"

"I'm not ready, Vicar. I need to be on my own. I'm sorry again."

Bridge stood quickly but Finn marched off before she had the chance to stop her. Bridge opened the wrapping to reveal the painting, and found an abstract black and grey background with a shining bright cross in the foreground. It was beautiful, and sad, but hopeful at the same time.

"You are a troubled little sheep, Magician."

Bridge was certain Finn wanted to be helped, wanted to make a human connection, but she'd done the best she could today, then ran away. Bridge's job as shepherd of the flock was to be here when Finn wanted to come back into the fold.

❖

*Finn held tightly to her sister's hand. She had been in and out of consciousness all day, murmuring, and talking about random things that made no sense. The hospice nurses said she could have only hours left, and Finn felt like she could hardly breathe. She was trying to be so strong and calm on the outside, lest Carrie would pick up on her negative feelings.*

*Suddenly Carrie's eyes opened, and she looked terrified. "Finn? Finn?"*

*"I'm here, Carrie, I'm always here, and I'm never going to let go of you."*

*"I'm scared, Finn."*

*Finn pulled her chair closer to the bed and stroked her sister's brow trying to calm her. "Don't be scared when I'm by your side, Carrie. You trust me, don't you?"*

*She nodded. "That's why I'm scared. What if you're right, Finn?"*

*"Right about what?"*

*"What if there is nothing? I'm frightened of dying and there's nothing. I think you were right, I'm scared, I'm scared."*

*Carrie started to gasp and the machines started to beep wildly. "Nurse?" Finn shouted. "Carrie, Carrie, I was wrong. Don't be scared, please—"*

*The nurses rushed into the room and she knew Carrie was leaving her. Finn dropped to her knees and repeated over and over through her tears, "I was wrong, Carrie, I was wrong. Don't listen to me."*

Finn woke up gasping and ran to her bedroom window to get some air. She opened it with trembling hands and then leaned on the sill, breathing in cold, calming breaths. "Carrie, I'm so sorry."

She couldn't keep going on like this. Some days she felt so much pain and guilt that she wanted to die herself, and some days her anger at the world made her someone she didn't like.

*I'm an atheist who has lost her faith. Pathetic.*

Finn lifted her head and looked out. Her bedroom window gave her a good view over the whole village. In the distance was the imposing Axedale Hall, and over to the left of the village square was the church and its spire. The thought occurred to her that the only time she hadn't felt such deep, terrible pain was with Bridge, and at the church with her. Maybe that was something that could take her mind off things.

## CHAPTER SEVEN

The next day Bridge made her way to Mrs. Castle's house for her afternoon walk. Mrs. Castle was Axedale's former cook and Harry's surrogate mother, and normally, Harry, Annie, and Bridge took it in turns to take Mrs. Castle out for a breath of fresh air. Otherwise, she would be completely housebound, so while Harry and Annie were away, Bridge took charge. It was no burden—Mrs. Castle was a lovely woman, and Bridge always enjoyed their talks.

Bridge knocked twice then walked into the cottage. "Hello? Ready to hit the road?"

"In here, Vicar."

Mrs. Castle was sitting in her armchair, already kitted out in jacket and headscarf.

"Afternoon, Martha. Lucy got you ready for me?" Lucy was Mrs. Castle's nurse. When Harry gave up her post at Cambridge and made Axedale her permanent home, she went about fixing all her mistakes and taking on the responsibilities that she had before shunned. One was providing Mrs. Castle with a private nurse to care for her.

"Afternoon, Vicar. Yes, she's not long gone. Honestly, she fusses around me like a little chicken."

Bridge chuckled. "You love her really. Okay, let's get you into your wheelchair."

She put the wheelchair to the side of Martha's armchair and helped her up onto her weak legs. "Put all your weight on me, remember."

Once she was safely settled in the chair, Martha said, "Can you not find more sensible shoes for walking, Vicar?"

Bridge leaned over her and gave her a peck on the cheek. "There's nothing you can't do in heels."

Martha just laughed and shook her head. "Look at the lovely picture postcard I got from Harry."

Bridge walked over to the mantelpiece and lifted a picture of Harry, Annie, and Riley.

"They look so happy, don't they, Vicar? I could never have imagined my little Harry would fall in love and have a family. Annie is just the perfect woman for her."

"She is indeed." Bridget put the card back and, as had happened a few times before, felt sadness that she wasn't likely to ever have that in her life.

"Annie is so kind to me. Did you know that she baked cakes, scones, and evening meals for my freezer before she went? Now all Lucy has to do is take one out and cook it for me later in the day. They are delicious."

Bridge started to push the wheelchair towards the door. "She is very kind, and such a good cook. I'm going to miss my weekly dinner at Axedale while they are away."

When Bridge got her out of the front door, she suddenly stopped dead.

"Something wrong, Vicar?" Martha said.

Bridge leaned over with a sly smile on her face. "Annie left you a stock of cakes? You wouldn't happen to be harbouring one of her Death by Chocolate cakes, would you?"

Martha chuckled. "I might be."

"You know there are people in this village who would wrestle you for that cake, Martha."

"I'll be more than happy to give you some, Vicar. No need for any rough stuff."

Bridget rubbed her hands together with glee. "Just don't tell Quade I got some." Bridge winked at her.

"You're some woman, Vicar. So—where to today?"

"I thought we could go down to the river and feed the ducks for a little while," Bridge said.

"Lovely. I have some stale bread in the kitchen for them."

Bridge ran back inside, picked up the bread, and then they headed out into the village.

❖

As they walked down into the centre of the village, as usual they only got a few feet at a time as every villager stopped them to chat and gossip with Mrs. Castle. Bridge was delighted to see Martha so happy and full of chatter. It was such a contrast to before Harry became countess and fell in love. The whole village had come roaring back to a living, breathing entity.

Coachloads of tourists arrived at the weekends and some even during the week to see Axedale Hall, its grounds, and the picture-perfect village. Mrs. Robinson's tea shop was doing a roaring trade.

Bridget stopped by a bench at the side of the river that flowed through the village, not far from the bridge. She made sure the brake was on the wheelchair and sat down next to Martha.

As soon as Martha pulled the bread from the bag, the ducks and swans started to congregate. The birds that lived on the river had a great life. There was always a line of willing adults and children to feed them.

Martha handed Bridge some bread and they both started to throw it for the birds.

"Well, Vicar. Tell me about this celebrity we have in the village. A magician, so I'm told. Have you met her?"

"Yes, a few times." Bridge thought of Finn in the church, feeling such grief and sadness, and her heart ached.

"Does she have family here?"

"No, she has no one. From what I gather from the newspapers, it was just her and her sister, and the sister died of cancer. I think Finn is here to hide from the press and everyone that wants a piece of her in London."

"How awful," Martha said, "to be a young person with no one else in the world."

Bridget stared off into the distance. "Yes, she's sad and very alone. I think I was a bit much for her at the beginning."

"I bet you were, Vicar. I've seen her on the television a few times. So boyishly handsome in her top hat and ringmaster outfit."

"Yes, she is." Bridge thought of her standing in the living room of the cottage with ripped jeans and bare feet, covered in paint splashes, that interesting blond fringe of hers tied back into a topknot, and felt her heart thud.

She shook away the feeling quickly. *She's not my type.*

"I was in love with a magician once," Martha said out of nowhere.

Bridge snapped her head to the side. "What?"

"Before I met Mr. Castle, you understand. I was eighteen and a kitchen maid at Axedale. In those days, a travelling fair used to come to the village green once a year. You know, coconut shy, hook a duck, palm reading, that sort of thing."

Bridge nodded and smiled, enjoying hearing about old Axedale and Martha's younger days.

"And? Who was he?"

"A young magician had a tent where he would put on shows, and you paid a penny to watch. He wore a top hat too, only more traditional, and had a European accent, very mysterious, and so attractive."

"He sounds like quite a dish," Bridget said.

"Oh, he was. We became close and I fell in love. He asked me to run away with him, and I nearly did, but Cook got ahold of me and knocked some sense into me. Said he was a flash Harry, who would use me and drop me as soon as he was tired of me, but when you're young, you love so fiercely."

Bridge put her hand over Martha's. "That's so sad."

Martha laughed. "Not really. Cook was proved quite right, of course. When the fair came back the next year, they told us he had been put in jail for robbery, leaving his wife and child with no one to support them."

"The scoundrel was married while he was courting you?"

"Yes, but around about then Mr. Castle joined the Axedale staff as footman, and I had the most wonderful life with him."

"God guides us to those who will love us best." Bridge told so many of her congregation that very thing. Trust that God will guide you to the right person. But somewhere deep down, she was frightened that was not true for her.

They were interrupted by the roar of a motorbike as it drove through the village. Bridge's breathing hitched and her pulse increased, knowing there was only one person with a bike.

Finn.

To her surprise the bike stopped by the side of the road next to them, and Finn got off.

"Is that your lost sheep, Vicar?" Martha asked.

Bridge couldn't take her eyes off Finn as she pulled off her helmet and that blond fringe flopped down.

"Yes, that's the magician."

"My, what interesting hair," Martha said.

Finn approached with helmet in hand. "I'm sorry to interrupt, Vicar. I wondered if I could ask you something."

"Of course, Finn. This is Mrs. Castle, part of Lady Harry's family."

"Pleased to meet you, Mrs. Castle." Finn shook her hand, and Bridge was a bit surprised at how polite and open Finn was being. She hadn't seen Finn since she gave her the painting, but something was different. Instead of running away, she was coming to her.

"I've seen you on the television, Ms. Kane," Martha said smiling. "You are very good."

Finn smiled bashfully. "Thank you, Mrs. Castle."

Martha turned to Bridge and said, "Vicar, who was the magician in the Bible? I forget his name."

"Simon—"

Before she got the chance to finish, Finn said, "Acts 8:9. *But there was a certain man, called Simon, which beforetime in the same city used sorcery, and bewitched the people of Samaria, giving out that himself was some great one.*"

Again Bridge was surprised at Finn's biblical knowledge. She obviously knew her Bible very well, unusually well, especially considering she had no faith. She was sure there was so much more in Finn's history than she knew.

"Indeed. Simon the sorcerer. How can I help you, Finn?"

Finn looked down at her boots, almost resembling a little lost boy. *Lost.* That's exactly what she saw in Finn. Whether she was displaying her cocky arrogant side, or this, beneath it all she was lost. If only Finn would let Bridge help her find her way.

"I wondered if I would be able to set my painting things up in the churchyard. I'd like to paint the church."

Bridget was more than a little lost for words. Finn had spent her whole career lampooning the Church, and she wanted to paint one? "The...church. You want to paint the church?"

"Yes, its medieval architecture is beautiful. I think it would make a nice subject."

"I thought you were painting abstracts at the moment."

Finn ran her hand through her hair, sweeping it back. "I think I need something more than that now."

"Why do you need my permission anyway? The churchyard is only locked up last thing at night."

The corners of Finn's mouth threatened to rise into a ghost of a smile. "I think after everything, I *need* your permission, Vicar."

The way Finn had said *need* was shooting off all sorts of bodily responses. *Don't even go there. That's all in the past.*

She took a deep breath and said, "Then you have my permission, Finn."

Finn's eyes dropped down to Bridge's legs, as they had every time they had met. "Thank you." Finn said goodbye to Martha, and then said to her, "I'll see you around the churchyard then, Vicar."

As Bridget and Finn regarded each other, there was a fresh new energy between them, something Bridge couldn't quite put her finger on, but it was there, hanging between them with intensity.

"Yes, I'll see you around, *Magician.*"

She was sure she saw a sparkle in Finn's eyes when she said that, and when Finn walked back over to her bike there was a confident swagger in her step. Bridget watched with envy as Finn sat astride her big Harley-Davidson, and almost wished she was on it too, holding on to Finn's waist.

"Vicar? Are you listening?"

"What?" Bridge had almost forgotten Martha was sitting next to her. "Sorry, I was miles away."

"I can see that, Vicar." Martha gave a knowing smile. "She's a very intense young woman, isn't she?"

Bridge nodded. "Intense, complicated, confused, lost, all of the above."

Martha patted her knee. "You are just the woman to sort her out, Vicar."

❖

As it happened, Bridge wasn't in the church for the next couple of days. One day a week she drove around to visit some of the more remote farms and houses just beyond the village of Axedale. It was difficult for them to get to church, so she went to them. Then the next day was her monthly interfaith meeting in the local town.

In a way it was a good thing she wasn't near the church, as she was determined not to overwhelm Finn, and frighten her away, as she had done when they first met.

Bridge arrived bright and early to catch up on all the emails and paperwork that had built up in her absence. There was no sign of Finn at that time in the morning, but she hoped she might see her later in the day.

After spending the morning getting caught up, she was finally nearing the end of her correspondence when Jan knocked and came in.

"Sorry to bother you, Vicar, but Mr. Winchester is here to see you, and he's a little steamed up."

Bridget sighed. "Of course he is."

Mr. Winchester had a huge chip on his shoulder and did not like women in positions of power. To him having a woman vicar was bad enough—but having a lesbian vicar was beyond the pale. He just about kept his loathing under control while Harry was there as head church warden and chair of the church council, but on his own he was obnoxious and problematic.

In fact, Bridge was sure Mr. Winchester was the one who'd told the bishop about her wedding service for Harry and Annie, in the church. No one else would have had a motive.

"Let him in then, Jan, and we'll see what he has to moan about today."

A few moments later Mr. Winchester strode into her office like a whirlwind, took off his hat, and threw it down on the desk.

"Good morning, Mr.—"

She didn't have a chance to complete her greeting as he immediately launched into a tirade.

"What do you think you're playing at, Vicar?"

Bridget clasped her hands and forced a smile on her face. "It depends on what game you're talking about, Mr. Winchester."

He placed his hands on her desk and leaned over in a threatening manner. "I'm talking about the bloody ungodly heathen sitting in my churchyard, painting."

Bridget did not let anyone dominate her, especially a little weasel like Winchester. She stood up and looked him right in the eyes. "Sit down, Mr. Winchester. Now."

Her eyes never left his until he dropped his gaze and took a seat.

"Now maybe we can talk more civilly." Bridge sat back down.

"That bloody woman is a scourge to our faith, a demon sent to confuse and make people distrust their faith. Tell her to leave the churchyard."

"Don't be so melodramatic, Winchester. She's a magician who

calls out those who try to deceive or gain money in God's name, and our church is open to everyone. Every faith, creed, sexuality"—she saw Mr. Winchester flinch at that word—"and to atheists. How else are we to spread God's word if we only allow those who think the same as ourselves in the church?"

"You're a fool, Vicar." He stood up and put his hat on. "This will come back to haunt you. You can be sure your sins will find you out."

He stormed out, and Bridge said under her breath, "Bloody idiot."

Jan popped her head around the door. "Everything all right, Vicar?"

She sighed and said, "Just his usual bluster. Nothing to worry about."

"Okay, would you like tea and cakes? I went to the baker this morning."

Bridge had a thought. "Thank you. Could you make enough for two? I have some missionary work to do."

❖

Finn was sitting in the churchyard, which was filled with the graves of all the former residents of Axedale. She had set her easel up by a bench next to some of the oldest graves. It gave her a good angle of the front architecture of the church and some of the atmosphere of the graveyard. She had spent the first few days sketching out her painting and now was starting it in earnest. Finn found it very peaceful in these surrounds, much better than to be cooped up in her summer house. Although she was disappointed not to have seen Bridge again. After their brief chat by the river, she had thought maybe they could start again, but perhaps she had just pushed her away too much and now the vicar was avoiding her.

Finn felt herself shiver, and was compelled to look up. *It's her.*

Bridge came walking across the churchyard towards her, and Finn stopped breathing for a few seconds. Bridget was a beautiful, striking woman, and those legs and heels did things to Finn. The vicar's garb had at first annoyed her, and was everything that she thought she hated, but now it only added to her sexiness. Everything about Bridget Claremont was so wrong, but oh so right.

Finn hadn't felt excited by a woman in such a long, long time, and she guessed that was because Bridget didn't want to please her, but somewhere deep down inside, Finn wanted to please Bridge. She was different to any femme she had ever met, and she excited her so much.

"Hello, Finn. How is the painting coming?" Bridge said.

"Early stages. I've just sketched the outline, and starting on paint today."

"Excellent. I brought you tea and cakes. I remembered that you forget to eat when you're painting."

Finn raised an eyebrow. "How did you know that?"

Bridge laughed. "Don't worry, I'm not psychic or anything, Magician. When we met on the hill, the first time, you'd forgotten to eat."

"You remembered that from our conversation?"

"Of course." Bridge handed her tea.

"Thanks. I always lose myself when I paint. My sister—" Finn stopped suddenly. Why was she talking about Carrie? She did not want to talk about her to anyone.

"It's okay, you don't have to talk about her, and I'm not going to minister to you about grief."

But somehow this time, Finn wanted to tell Bridge. Her heart told her that she was safe with Bridge. "It's okay, I was just going to say that Carrie always made sure I ate, when I was painting."

"Did you two live together?" Bridge asked.

"Yeah, I bought us a nice house in London, once I made enough money, and we looked after each other." Finn was frightened of any other questions about her sister, but surprisingly Bridge didn't delve any deeper.

"Here, eat your cake then."

"Tea and cakes with the vicar? My manager would never believe it," Finn joked.

Bridge chuckled and took a sip of tea. "My deputy church warden thinks I'm letting the enemy in through the church gates."

Finn's eyes followed Bridge's stockinged legs as she sat back and crossed her legs. "Do you think I'm the enemy, Vicar?"

To her surprise, Bridge put her manicured fingernail under Finn's chin and lifted her head up to meet Bridge's eyes away from her legs. "You know what they say, Magician? Keep your friends close but keep your enemies closer."

Finn was embarrassed to have been caught looking, but she couldn't not look. Then she remembered what Bridge had said to her at the cottage.

*You're not my type, Magician.*

That had hurt Finn's ego. She was *always* a woman's type, and women always wanted her, but this vicar didn't.

Finn noticed that Bridge was focused intently on her hair. "What? Is there something wrong?"

This morning Finn had decided to walk down to the church with her backpack and canvas, rather than bring the bike, so she had elaborately styled her blond fringe into almost a Mohawk on top of her head.

Bridge's gaze felt like a caress. "Nothing wrong, your hair is just so—interesting, and different every time I see you."

Finn laughed. "I like to keep things interesting. When you wear a helmet, it kind of limits your hair self-expression, but I left it at the cottage today."

"Your bike is gorgeous. A Harley-Davidson?"

"You like bikes?" Finn said.

"Bikes, leather, buckles, you don't know the half of it, Magician," Bridge said with a seductive tinge to her voice, and Finn was instantly turned on, so much so that she knocked over the forgotten cup of water that she'd set for her brushes next to her foot, and water sloshed over Bridge's shoes.

Bridget gasped, and Finn jumped up immediately. "Fuck! I'm so sorry."

Finn grabbed her painting rag and went down on her knees to try to dry up the puddle she had made on Bridge's shoes.

"It's okay, Finn. It's just water," she heard Bridge say, but she was determined to fix her mess.

Luckily the water didn't seem to have splashed onto Bridge's stockings, just her shoes. Finn slowed and deliberately dried every drop of water from them. She held Bridge's ankle gently and realized her fingers were caressing Bridge's calf. Finn looked up and was met with what she could only describe as a hot, smouldering look that made her burn.

Finn's mind was already imagining caressing and kissing all the way up Bridge's beautiful legs, and those legs wrapped around her head as she kissed Bridget more intimately.

Her thoughts were interrupted by Bridge pulling her foot away and standing up quickly. "That's fine, Finn. No harm done. I...I need to go back in to work."

Before Finn got a chance to reply, Bridge's heels were clattering on the pavement as she hurried away.

Finn stood and let out a long breath. "Jesus Christ."

She'd had lots of sex in her life, and lots of beautiful women, but nothing had turned her on as much as kneeling at Bridge's feet and touching her. Finn put her face in her hands and rubbed it vigorously. After a few warning shots, her libido was back with a bang. She felt immediately guilty, because she wasn't supposed to be feeling good and enjoying life while Carrie wasn't. She was grieving.

She started to pick up her things and pack them away. She needed to get away from this church and take a long ride on her bike.

"A vicar? Why a bloody vicar, of all the things in the world," Finn said with frustration.

Despite her confusion about her feelings and what they should be, there was one thing she was clear about. The vicar Bridget Claremont felt the attraction too. When their eyes met, she knew Bridget was feeling the same sorts of things she was.

Finn laughed to herself. *I knew I was your type, Vicar. You know it, and I know it.*

❖

Bridge's day went from the confusing to the ridiculous, when her bishop telephoned her. Bridge tried in vain to massage her temples with her fingers to dissipate her stress, but it wasn't working.

"Yes, My Lord. I fully understand, but there is no harm being done here."

"There is harm being done. It is upsetting your parishioners, and they are unhappy about it, and I received a phone call today from a concerned parishioner," Bishop Sprat said.

Bridge sighed audibly. "And I can just guess who. Ms. Kane is here in Axedale to try to recover from a personal tragedy. She is not here to cause trouble, and if it brings her comfort to paint the church, then I will let her."

Bishop Sprat retorted, "I understand your village is on the liberal fringes, Claremont, but letting an atheist run amok in your church is a step too far."

"Run amok? She's painting at an easel, for pity's sake." Bridget was on the verge of losing her temper.

"You would do well to remember who you are talking to, Claremont. I'm not Bishop Lovejoy, and your well-connected family won't protect you forever. One day they will not be able to save you."

"Is that a threat, My Lord?" Bridget knew full well Sprat would do anything to get rid of her.

"Simply a statement of facts. I will be watching, Claremont. Make no mistake about that."

"I'm sure. Good day, My Lord." Bridget slammed the telephone down. "Bloody old fool!"

She got up and started to pace. Today had been a roller coaster of emotions. Earlier in the churchyard, Finn brought out yearnings, longings that were usually well under control, but the sight of Finn at her feet set her body on fire. Putting out that fire was impossible for her, so it would have been better if Finn wasn't going to be there in her churchyard every day.

Bridge should be keeping her distance, giving Finn a huge wide berth. Instead she was protecting her, no matter the cost to herself. Her predictable, safe world was becoming chaotic, and Bridge didn't like it.

❖

The early evening gloom was descending onto Axedale House, as Sam McQuade drove her Land Rover out of the stable block and onto the main driveway. As she drove, she noticed the vicar standing over at the Roman villa site on the grounds. She parked up and walked over.

"Bridge, what are you doing up here?"

"Oh, I was just checking on Willow and thought I'd have a walk through the grounds."

Quade was sure she could sense something was wrong. Bridge was always laughing and joking, up for a good conversation, but tonight she appeared pensive and tense.

"Is everything all right?"

Bridge put her hands into her biker jacket pockets and forced a smile onto her face. "Of course. Tip-top as usual, Quade."

Quade decided to let her off the hook for the moment, walked onto the Perspex that covered the Roman villa floor, and stood beside her friend. "Beautiful, isn't it? It's amazing something like this has been under our feet all this time, and we never knew."

"I think it was meant to come to the surface when it did. It was Harry's sign," Bridge said.

"Her sign? How so?" Quade asked.

Bridget sighed and kicked some gravel off the Perspex surface with her shoe. "I once told Harry, *To everything there is a season, and a time to every purpose under the heaven.* God sends us what we need, when we need it. Harry was at a crossroads. Inside she knew something had to change in her life. She needed her Goddess of love, and God sent her Annie."

Bridge indicated the Roman ruins. "This was the proverbial kick up the backside to make her realize that."

Quade smiled. "Annie certainly weaved her magic on this village, so I quite believe she is a Goddess. What about you, Vicar?"

Bridge snapped her head around. "What do you mean?"

"What's your sign? Is there a time for you to find someone, and me?"

"I'm sure God has his plans for you, Quade. A handsome butch needs to win the heart of a pretty lady."

Quade noticed that Bridge hadn't answered her question. "And you?"

"No. No signs for me," Bridge said rather too quickly. "It's hard enough being gay, with a homophobic bishop breathing down my neck, without having a relationship to complicate matters. My career is too important to me."

Quade was not convinced by that answer. When they'd talked in the church hall, after Harry and Annie's party, she'd sounded like she had hope that there was someone out there for her, but now she sounded defensive, worried, and tense.

Changing the subject completely, Quade said, "How's your lost sheep coming on, Bridge?"

"She's not mine. I barely talk to her."

That quick and blasé comment made Quade's ears prick up. "Oh? I heard at the pub that she was painting at the church."

"Yes, she asked if she could. Why an atheist wants to paint a church I'll never know. Anyway, can you give me a lift back to the vicarage?"

There was something, some sort of tension, going on between them, and Quade was going to find out what.

"Your carriage awaits, Vicar."

❖

Finn sat at her dining table, a half-eaten sandwich discarded at the setting opposite her chair.

She held her sister's dousing crystal by the chain and watched it spin. Carrie, unlike her, believed in everything about the spiritual world, up until the end, at least. She was heavily into New Age beliefs in crystals, auras, and angels. They jokingly bickered, but Finn never made too much of their different perceptions. That was Carrie's way of coping with a difficult childhood. They were both brought up in the strict Charismatic Christian world. Finn was pushed towards atheism and Carrie to the New Age movement.

Finn kept her eyes on the swinging crystal and said, "I'm sorry I made you doubt your beliefs. I'm sorry I made you scared."

She felt tears threatening to spill out of her, and she hated to cry. "I should have just performed my magic and kept my big mouth shut. There's this woman, Carrie, a vicar of all things, and she made me feel something other than sadness."

The crystal started to noticeably spin faster. "It felt good, like this big load was lifted off me, but then I remembered you, and how scared you were, and I felt so guilty."

Finn sat bolt upright when the crystal started to spin even faster. It was unnerving. She started to look around the room quickly.

"Carrie? Carrie? Are you here?"

There was a loud knock at the door and Finn jumped in fright. "Jesus fucking Christ."

She dropped the crystal in the middle of the table and tried to calm her hammering heart.

Whoever was at the door knocked again. Finn quickly pulled herself together and walked over to the door to open it.

It was Sam McQuade. "Evening, mate."

"Hi."

"I was just wondering if you'd like to come to the pub quiz on Saturday night. My team is short on numbers with Harry and Annie out of the country."

Everything inside Finn was screaming *no*, but she tried to say it politely because Quade was a nice person. "I'm sorry, Quade. I don't think I'm up to socializing yet," Finn said.

"Come on, mate. It would do you good. It's just me and Bridge.

Everyone else will be too occupied with their own teams to bother with you."

Finn's ears pricked up at the mention of Bridge's name. "The vicar?"

Quade nodded, and Finn had a hot flashback from today. The sizzling look that was shared between them made Finn want to prove to Bridge she was her type. She shook the thought away and told herself she had more to be worried about than some deviant fantasies about a vicar.

"I'm sorry, Quade. I can't—"

"Oh, go on. Just for a little while? I'm on my own too, mate. I know how lonely life can get, how you can start to go crazy looking at four walls all weekend."

Finn leaned against the door and sighed. "Okay, just for a while. I'm not good company at the moment."

"Great! I'll see you at seven thirty at the pub. Night, Finn."

Finn shut the door and rested her forehead against it. "Why did I agree to that?"

It was so hard to keep up the distant façade when people like Quade were so nice and welcoming, and she didn't want to think too deeply about the excitement she felt when Bridge's name was mentioned.

She walked back to the dining table to pick up her sister's crystal and put it away safely, but panic gripped her heart when she couldn't find it where she'd left it.

"No, no, don't tell me I've lost it," Finn said to herself frantically.

She looked under the table and then back on top, and spotted it at last. It was over at the other end of the table, lying on her sketch pad.

"How the hell did it get over there?"

When Finn picked it up, she realized just how much weirder it was. It was sitting on top of her sketch of the church.

*Are you trying to tell me something, Carrie?*

## CHAPTER EIGHT

B ridge was on her way to the pub. Quiz night was always something she enjoyed. There was laughter, good company, and good cheer, exactly what she needed after a disconcerting week. And the most unsettling thing was the way her body had reacted to Finn. The passion she had felt surge through her while Finn knelt at her feet had shocked her in its intensity and was something she thought she had left far behind her in the past. The bishop's phone call only served to remind her how difficult it would be to ever experience that with someone again. Her faith and her vocation were too important to her, and she wouldn't ask a lover to sneak around or openly defy her bishop.

Bridge had kept away from Finn as much as she could the rest of the week, and sent Jan out to her with tea and cakes.

Her thoughts were interrupted by Mr. Butterstone calling after her, "Vicar? Could I have a word?"

"Of course. How can I help?"

Mr. Butterstone was a slightly flamboyant gentleman, never without his bow tie and highly polished shoes.

"We had our first planning meeting for the winter show last night, and—well, to say we were short on ideas is an understatement."

"You know I always pitch in with painting and moving sets, but I'm not big on theatrical ideas, Mr. Butterstone."

He started to rub his hands together nervously. "Well, we thought that since Ms. Kane is warming up to you that—"

"Who said she is warming up to me?" Bridget said far too sharply. "I'm sorry, but why do you get that impression?"

"Everyone says she's painting at the church every day, and we just assumed…anyway, we thought she might be more open to helping with the show. Have you had the chance to ask her yet?"

Bridget sighed. She'd completely forgotten about her promise to the church council. "I don't know whether she is warming up to me or the village or not, but I do know she doesn't want to do magic or perform again."

Mr. Butterstone looked down sadly. "Oh well, it was worth a try."

Bridget started to feel guilty now. "If I feel the time is right, I'll ask her, but I won't make any promises."

Mr. Butterstone grabbed her suddenly and gave her a big kiss on the cheek. "Thank you, Vicar."

They walked into the pub together, and Bridge looked around to see where Quade had gotten them a table. Her eyes met someone else first—it was Finn sitting beside Quade in the corner.

What was she doing here?

She never thought Finn would want to spend time at a noisy quiz night. Bridge almost considered walking back out, as she did the first time she saw Finn in here, but she couldn't. It wasn't Finn's fault that she was so obviously attracted to her, and she shouldn't be. *Finn is not your type.*

Despite that fact, Bridge couldn't deny the hooded checked shirt, ripped designer jeans, and that infuriating hair made her look boyishly handsome. She walked over to the table and both Quade and Finn stood. "Look how polite you both are."

"Evening, Vicar. I persuaded Finn to come and make up our numbers, otherwise our winning streak would be over."

Bridge smiled. "Nice to see you, Finn."

"You too."

There was an awkward tension hanging between them.

"I'll get the drinks in," Quade said, breaking the ice. "Usual, Vicar?"

"Yes. Thanks, Quade."

Once she left, Bridge put her leather jacket over the chair and sat down.

"I haven't seen you much at the church this week," Finn said.

Bridget tapped her fingers on the table, considering her answer. She had thought maybe she was blowing everything she had felt all out of proportion, but now back in Finn's company, she couldn't deny there was something there. An energy between them.

"No, I've been quite busy. Church issues, paperwork, you know the sort of thing."

Finn gave her a suspicious look. "You haven't been avoiding me, have you?"

Bridget quickly bit back with, "I think it's you who have been desperately avoiding me since you got here."

Finn opened her mouth to reply, but Quade arrived back with the tray of drinks, a sheet of paper, and some pens.

"I got us signed up for the quiz." Quade handed Finn a pint of lager and a pen.

"And a Campari, gin, and vermouth for you, Vicar."

"Thanks." Bridget took a sip to calm the unsettling feelings.

She tapped her fingernails on the side of the glass and caught Finn watching. "Is there something wrong, Magician?"

"Nothing wrong with me," Finn said defensively.

Quade looked back and forth between them, clearly sensing the tension. "I'm glad we've got you, Finn. Usually with Harry and Annie, our team has a good balance. A Cambridge don, a food and baking expert, and of course Bridge is our religious expert as well as an old Cambridge grad."

Finn laughed and shook her head. "You went to Cambridge, Vicar? Straight from boarding school, I bet. Cambridge and Campari. Why am I not surprised?"

Bridget was really getting annoyed now. "What's wrong with that? Are you an inverted snob, Magician?"

Luckily the pub quiz MC began to talk and started the quiz. Bridge grabbed her pen and the answer paper.

"I'll write the answers—that's if you provide any, Magician."

Bridget knew she was being a bitch, but there was something about Finn, her attitude and very presence, that was getting under her skin.

"Don't worry, despite my inferior education I'm sure I can provide some answers you can't."

Finn reached in the top pocket of her shirt and pulled out and started to shuffle her cards.

Even though Bridge didn't return her look, she could feel Finn's eyes on her. Since the last time they spoke, Finn had regained some of her arrogance, but again not when speaking with Quade. Just her.

Keeping her focus on the answer paper, Bridge said, "Are you going to show us a trick, or pull a rabbit out of a hat? I thought you didn't perform magic any more."

"For you I'd be willing to make an exception, and maybe saw you in half."

Bridge's head sprang up, then she leaned over and said, "I'd rather chain you up, lock you in a sack, and see if you could escape."

"Okay, everyone"—Quinn's voice halted their taunts—"the first question's coming. Get ready."

❖

Quade sat back and watched Bridget and Finn bicker over a question. It had become a bit of a competition between them, and Quade found it more amusing to stay silent and let them slug it out. She'd had a hunch there was some sort of spark between them when she spoke to Bridge at Axedale, and she'd been proven correct.

They behaved differently around each other. Finn was not the grieving, lonely, sad person she'd had a pint with, or the person she had persuaded to come out from the safety of her cottage to quiz night. She was full of energy, confident, and revelling in her verbal tussles with Bridge. Finn reminded Quade of a little schoolboy pulling a girl's pigtails to try to get her attention. Bridge, on the other hand, was assertive to the point of being haughty and dismissive. That wasn't the Bridge she knew.

At the break, Finn excused herself to go to the bathroom, and further annoyed Bridge when she bumped into the back of her chair.

Quade shook her head, and once Finn was away said, "What's going on, Bridge?"

"What do you mean?"

"You seem really pissed off with Finn. Did she say something to you?" Quade asked, knowing she probably wouldn't get a truthful answer.

"No. Nothing at all. Well, apart from being an arrogant little brat," Bridge said.

Quade was now sure there was some sort of chemistry going on. "Why do you say that? She seems a nice enough person to me."

Bridge closed her eyes and let out a breath. "You're right. I've just had a difficult week. I'll go and get another round in." Bridge lifted her handbag to get her purse, and found nothing there. "My purse is missing. I—"

Bridge then looked down at her wrist. "And my watch—that bloody magician."

Just then Finn appeared back from the bathroom and dangled Bridge's watch and purse over Bridge's shoulders. "Looking for these?"

Bridge grabbed for them. "Keep your little trickster hands off my things, Magician." Then she walked off angrily to the bar.

Finn sat back down beside Quade and laughed. "She hates it when I do that."

"I see that, mate. It's maybe not the best idea to rile Bridge. She can be scary," Quade warned.

"That's what makes it so fun."

This was the first time Quade saw Finn smiling and light-hearted and it was all centred on the vicar.

Interesting.

❖

At the end of the evening, Finn held open the door and Bridge walked outside. As Finn went to follow her, Bridge said, "Why are you following me, Magician?"

"Quade asked me to walk you safely home."

"I don't need to be walked home like a damsel in distress. I'm a thirty-six-year-old woman and perfectly capable of walking myself home." Bridge stopped and turned to look at Finn. "How old are you anyway, Magician?"

"Twenty-seven."

Bridge laughed. "No more than a boy. I've got a whip at home older than you."

Finn gulped hard. She'd never met anyone that could turn her on with just her words. Bridge was elegant and beautiful, and the more dismissive she was to Finn, the more she turned her on.

"May I walk you home, Bridge? I promise not to steal anything from you. Can we call a truce?"

Bridge started to walk off and said, "Keep up, boy."

Finn felt a surge of excitement and ran a few steps to catch up. They walked in silence for a few moments before Finn said, "I'm glad I came out tonight. I didn't really want to, but it was nice to be around other people."

"I thought you wanted to be left alone."

"Not by you—and Quade of course. I missed seeing you at the church the past few days."

Bridge didn't respond to that thought, but Finn was sure they were both thinking about the incident in the churchyard.

"You have a great deal of biblical knowledge. Where did that come from?"

Finn had answered all the biblical questions in the pub quiz correctly, much to Bridge's annoyance it seemed. She looked up at the starry night sky and sighed. "I was brought up in the Charismatic Christian world. My father was a pastor, faith healer, and all-round charlatan. You know the sort—if you pledge enough money to the pastor for his new car, boat, house, you'll receive God's blessing."

Bridge stopped and turned to look at Finn. "Really? I'm not surprised you have difficulties with faith in that case." That kind of thing was so far removed from the word of God, it was unreal. Bridget wanted to ask her so much, but was frightened of scaring her away.

They walked down to the vicarage in quiet companionship, and when they reached Bridge's garden gate, Finn said, "I better go then. Goodnight, Vicar."

Bridge felt Finn tug at her heartstrings. She looked lost and Bridge knew she had nothing to go home to. Against her better judgement she said, "Do you want to come in for a drink or coffee?"

Finn nodded quickly. "Yes, that would be great."

Bridge led Finn into the kitchen and put on the kettle. "Take a seat. Coffee?"

Finn sat the kitchen table. "Please. This is a beautiful old house you've got."

"Old is the word," Bridge said as she got the milk out of the fridge. "Old and draughty. I have Mrs. Long, my housekeeper, but she goes home at night."

"I feel like I might be struck down, just being here in a vicarage," Finn joked.

Bridge brought the coffee over and sat next to Finn. It was a strange sensation having Finn here, like it was wrong, taboo, but it gave Bridge a thrill. She hadn't felt these urges in so long, and now they wouldn't go away around Finn.

"How could you be struck down, Finn, if there's no God to do it?"

"Touché, Vicar." Finn took a sip of coffee and then stared down into the liquid. "I'm not sure of anything any more. Not after Carrie—"

Finn stopped mid-sentence and looked ready to run. Bridge immediately put her hand over Finn's to soothe her. Finn lost her bravado when talking about her sister, and then the hurt and confusion came rushing to the surface.

*You've lost your faith*, Bridge thought. Some things about Finn started to fall into place. She was an atheist who was losing her faith. Was that why she wanted to be so close to the church by painting it?

Bridge squeezed her hand. "You don't have to talk about it, but if you ever do, then I'm here, and I promise not to minister to you."

Finn nodded. "Something happened that made me question everything that I believed in, but I don't want to talk about it."

They both looked down at their clasped hands, and broke apart. Finn immediately took out her cards and started to shuffle them. Bridge noticed she did this when she was obviously feeling stress.

"Will you show me a trick, Magician?"

Finn smiled at the use of the name that Bridge used to annoy her. "I don't practice magic any more."

"It's just me. Show me something." Finn looked reluctant so Bridge tapped her red-painted fingernails on the table, drawing Finn's attention, and said, "Show me."

"I think you like telling people what to do, Vicar."

Bridge chuckled. "Maybe."

"I'll show you one if you tell me your story."

"What story?" Bridge asked.

"How a beautiful, passionate woman like you could become a vicar," Finn said.

Bridge sat back in her chair and crossed her legs. "How do you know if I'm passionate or not?"

Finn split the deck into two and shuffled them together, now regaining that hint of cockiness. "You forget—I'm an expert on reading people," Finn said.

Bridge moved closer to Finn and leaned on her hand. "And what do you read in me?"

Finn inched closer as well and looked her directly in the eyes. "I read that you keep passion tamped down so hard, that you keep that side of you at bay, because maybe you don't want to face it, and you use that dog collar as protection from some hurt that came into your life."

Was she that transparent, Bridge wondered. "My story is simple. The Claremonts have always been eccentrics of sorts. Explorers, adventurers, sportsmen and women, conquering new worlds and lands. My mother was an actress and model—"

"Wait." Finn held up her hand. "Your mother isn't Cordelia Claremont? The Bond girl that half the Western world had a poster of on their walls?"

Bridget was used to that reaction when they realized who her mother was. "Yes, that's Mama. I can tell you it was highly embarrassing to see that picture of your mother everywhere."

Finn had a far-off look in her eyes. "In that swimsuit, with the gun on her thigh…It's iconic."

"Hmm, but hard to see. I knew I didn't want to go down that route, although my brother did."

"Do you get on well with her?" Finn asked.

"Oh yes, even after I changed my degree to theology, she was behind me. We always had it drummed into us as children that Claremonts could achieve or do anything, but in a nice way. We like to blaze a trail."

"What about your father?"

"Papa was a great outdoorsman, an explorer and adventurer. He passed away five years ago."

"I'm sorry to hear that," Finn said.

Bridget smiled despite the subject matter. "It's okay. He died after a bad fall. He was training for a return climb to K2. He passed away doing what he loved, what brought him happiness, and that brings me comfort."

"I'm glad you have that," Finn said softly.

Bridge could hear the hurt in Finn's voice, and had to stop herself from taking her hand. She had to change the atmosphere between them before she did something she would regret.

"Show me your trick then, Magician."

Finn smiled. "I'll show you the first card trick I ever perfected." Finn shuffled and fanned the cards out for Bridge. "Take a card, and look at it. Remember which one it is."

Bridge did as asked, and placed it back into the deck.

"Okay," Finn said, "I'll shuffle to make sure the deck is really mixed up."

Bridge watched her hands carefully as they whizzed through a few shuffles. It was hard to keep up with the speed of Finn's fingers and hands. Once the cards were back in a neat pile, Finn held the deck in one hand, the other waiting above the deck at head height.

Finn flicked the top of the deck and caught the card in her other hand, up above.

"The king of clubs. Is that your card?"

"Yes!" Bridge said with amazement. "How did you do that? I saw you put it into the deck and shuffle. How could it possibly get to the top of the deck?"

"Watch again. Take one card," Finn said.

They repeated the same process, but this time when she put Bridge's card back in the deck, she said, "You shuffle this time, Vicar."

She did, and handed them back. In a few seconds, Finn did exactly the same, and flicked Bridge's card up into her other hand. "This your card?"

"Yes." Bridge chuckled. "That was amazing, Finn—you really are good."

Finn winked and said, "That's nothing. I can turn water into wine if you want, Vicar."

Bridge raised an eyebrow. Finn's overconfident streak was back with a bang. "Don't even go there, Magician. Thank you for showing me."

Finn put her cards away. "No, thank *you*. I enjoyed showing you. The past few years my illusions and tricks have been so elaborate, I've forgotten what it was like to do a simple card trick. Carrie used to love them."

"I suppose these simple tricks are the reason you fell in love with magic," Bridget said. Finn nodded, and Bridge continued, "When you started doing your big arena shows things changed?"

"I had to keep making things bigger and better, and at some point, it became more about Finnian Kane the character, than the magic."

"The character I saw on your YouTube channel is a little different to who you are in Axedale," Bridge said.

"Yeah, well, that Finnian Kane was an illusion, just like my tricks. Besides, all I had to worry about then was which nightclub I was going to after the show, and which woman I was taking back to my hotel room."

"You must have been popular with girls, a cocky young boy like you, with all your conjuring and mystique. They must have been eating out of your hand."

Finn rubbed the back of her head bashfully. "Yeah, I've never had to work hard to get a woman's attention." She looked up and connected with Bridge's gaze. "All except you, but then I'm not your type."

"No…I suppose not," Bridge said.

She shouldn't be, but Bridge couldn't deny the attraction and energy between them. Finn was confident and cocky, but sweet and vulnerable, and Bridge had seen her reaction when she deprived Finn of her attention. She was so trainable, and that was such a lure to Bridge.

*If I had gotten hold of you before I became a woman of the cloth, I would have had fun training you, boy.* Bridge chuckled to herself.

Bridge couldn't afford to think like that, so she changed the subject. "I was thinking—you would enjoy our cards night. We have it once a week at Axedale with Harry, Annie, and Quade. It's always a lot of fun."

Finn raised a quizzical eyebrow. "You know how to play poker?"

"Of course. My grandfather played poker with King George IV."

Finn shook her head. "You are the most unusual vicar I've ever met. You have read your Bible verses about coveting money, haven't you?"

"Oh, shush! We play for matchsticks. It's about fun and conversation. So, will you come?" Bridge asked.

"I don't play poker," Finn replied matter-of-factly.

Bridge sat back in her kitchen chair and crossed her legs. As usual she saw Finn's eyes flit up and down, trying so hard to appear as if she wasn't staring at Bridge's legs but failing miserably. It had been a long time since she'd felt so appreciated for being a woman, for her femininity, rather than being seen as just a vicar. Despite the revealing and sexy way she liked to dress, the dog collar tended to cancel out what she wore.

Finn saw the woman, and that thought made her feel a flush of heat deep down in her stomach.

"You don't play poker? What do you mean?"

Instead of answering. Finn took out her cards again, shuffled, then dealt two hands out onto the table. "Turn over your cards."

Bridge turned over the cards and found a full hand of twos. Finn turned over her hand and she had four aces.

That cocky smile was there again. Finn said, "When I can deal you any hand I like, it wouldn't be fair to anyone I play. I'm unbeatable."

"Oh, you are, are you?" Bridge tapped her nails on the table. She was itching to bring her arrogance down a peg or two, but now wasn't the time. She had just gotten her lost sheep to talk, and she wasn't going to frighten her away so soon. "Well, we'll see."

# CHAPTER NINE

Finn woke up the next morning eager for the day ahead. That hadn't happened for a long, long time, and it was because of Bridget. There was something about her that both excited and intrigued her. Finn wanted to know more.

She arrived at the church, ready to paint, to find Quade and Bridge talking very closely at the church door. Finn got off her bike and pulled off her helmet. When she turned back around she found Bridge with both hands holding Quade's face, and she felt an immediate stab of jealousy. It came out of nowhere and surprised her.

Finn had never seen or suspected anything between Bridge and Quade, but what if there was? Finn stopped herself. *What am I thinking?* Not only didn't she have any right to feel jealous, she shouldn't even be thinking of anything else but Carrie, and again her guilt set in.

She was just about to put her helmet back on and get out of there when she heard Bridge shout, "Finn? The very person."

She couldn't leave now, so she put on her best false smile as Bridge and Quade approached. As Quade got closer to her, she noticed how tired and drawn she looked. "Is everything okay?"

"Yes and no," Bridge said. "Quade lost a few of her cattle during the night and a couple are still sick."

Quade tried to rub the tiredness from her eyes. "Yeah, and I need to get back to them. Three fell down an embankment last night, and one is pregnant."

Finn couldn't believe she'd felt jealous at all. Bridge was just comforting Quade, who clearly cared a great deal about her animals.

"I'm sorry," Finn said.

"I need to sit with her until the vet says she's out of the woods, but

I had promised to help Bridge pick up the costumes and equipment for Witch's Night at Axedale Hall."

"Is there anything I can do?"

"Would you mind helping Bridge? There's quite a few heavy boxes that need to be brought back to the church for rehearsals."

Finn opened her mouth to answer but Bridge did it for her. "Of course she will. How else will she expect to grow up to be a rugged butch like you, Quade, if she doesn't do some heavy lifting?"

"I'll lift anything you want me to, Vicar," Finn snapped back.

Bridge grinned. "You see? I'm well taken care of, Quade. Off you go."

Quade looked at them both, her eyes narrowed with suspicion, but she nodded in agreement. "Okay then. I'll leave you to it."

Once Quade was in her Land Rover, Finn said, "What did you say that for? I'm strong enough for anything you would ever need, Vicar."

Bridge turned and walked back towards the church door with a sway in her hips that made Finn ache inside. "Oh, shush. You're nothing but a boy."

Oh God. Finn groaned internally. How did Bridge always manage to say things that were both so dismissive, bordering on offensive, that made her angry but turned her on at the same time?

*I want her. I want to show her how good I am.*

"Hey, I thought we were going to Axedale, Vicar. Jump on my bike."

Bridget stopped before she walked around the back of the church and looked back at her. "I love motorcycles and leather as much as the next girl, but if you think I'm going on your bike in a Chanel skirt and Jimmy Choos, then you've got another think coming. I'll meet you up there—we have a church van."

When she walked out of sight, Finn leaned onto her bike and let out a long breath. "Jesus Christ. That woman is—"

Finn couldn't think of a way to describe her, but Bridge's description of her skirt and heels painted pictures in her mind of those legs that tormented her wrapped around her bike and her waist. Bridget Claremont could top her, and Finn would enjoy every minute of it.

A van with *St. Mary's Church* written on the side came out of the church car park, and Bridge signalled her to follow. This ride was going to be torture.

❖

Bridge pulled up in front of Axedale's entrance and gathered her shoes from the passenger seat. There was no way she could drive in heels. As she turned around to open her door, she saw Finn walk towards her with helmet in hand and hair flopping across her face. *You are so delicious, I could eat you all up.*

But Bridge could think of at least five reasons why that was a bad idea. Finn was too young for her, she was grieving, she wouldn't be around for long, she was an atheist—one of the most renowned in the country, and a relationship would give her bishop his perfect reason to get rid of her. The intensity of the feelings she had experienced in the graveyard had frightened her, and the bishop's phone call had compounded the matter. Trying to stay away from Finn didn't work— she was her lost sheep and she needed to help her. Bridge resolved to pray for strength and God's guidance when she returned to the church.

Finn opened the door and looked at the pair of heels in Bridge's hands. "May I?"

*Not again.*

"No, it's okay—" Bridge couldn't stop her taking them from her.

She watched as Finn knelt and put on her shoes with great care and reverence, and had the biggest urge to reach down and run her fingers through that long blond fringe, grasp it roughly, and pull Finn up for a kiss.

A verse from Proverbs kept running through her mind. *Lust not after her beauty in thine heart; neither let her take thee with her eyelids.*

Thankfully Beverly, Axedale's housekeeper, interrupted them. "Vicar, nice to see you."

Finn jumped up and back, and Bridge slid from the van. "Bev, how are you today?"

"Very well. You here for the Witch's Night paraphernalia?"

"Yes—oh, this is Finn. She's new to the village and here to help me."

Bev's face lit up. "Oh, the magician? Mrs. Castle told us all about you—I think she was quite taken with you."

Bridge watched Finn's cheeks turn red. Adorable. "Yes, I've heard Mrs. Castle has a thing for magicians. You better watch out, Finn."

It was strange the way Finn seemed so bashful about such little comments of praise, and yet when she was taking the applause of an arena, she was confident and dazzling.

Beverly left them to get on while Bridge led them into Axedale's grand entrance hall. "Oh my God," Finn exclaimed as she walked into the middle of the hall. Finn looked up at the painted ceiling and walked backwards with her arms open. "This space is just—wow!"

Bridge stood by one of the stone pillars, arms folded, and smiling at her reaction. "Not bad, is it?"

"Not bad? It's amazing. Your friends really live here?"

Bridget nodded. "Most people have this reaction when they walk in here."

"How old is Axedale?" Finn asked.

"The Knight family has been here since 1115, I believe, although they first had a castle a few miles away from here, but they built the manor in 1485 or thereabouts, after they backed the winning side in the War of the Roses. But it has been rebuilt and remodelled many times. It's one of the finest houses in the country."

Finn stuffed her hands in her pockets and strode over to Bridge. "I don't know about you, Vicar. Cambridge, Campari, that accent, and best friends with a countess, shouldn't you be skiing in St. Moritz or partying in an exclusive London nightclub, and not preaching sermons on Sunday? You never really told me your story."

Bridge never moved an inch from her position against the pillar, and looked unflappable. "I told you about my family, and honestly, darling, I'm not as interesting as them. As for the clubbing and skiing? I've done more than enough for one lifetime. Now I just want to help people and praise God. Let me show you around first."

There was a part of Bridge she was hiding, or maybe not facing up to, Finn thought. She was sure it was to do with the mysterious Ellen. Something must have made her turn her back on her socialite life to go into the Church.

Bridge had walked off and Finn had to run a few steps to catch up. "You know, when I was just starting out as a magician, I used to do pubs, clubs, and restaurants, some of them really exclusive. Maybe I saw you there sometime."

She saw Bridge's body language tense up subtly. Most people wouldn't have noticed but she did.

"I doubt it, Magician. I went to a particular kind of exclusive club, which I don't think you would have frequented," Bridge said without turning around.

Now Finn was really intrigued. She had been in some dives in her time as well as some private members' clubs and started to rhyme off a few. Bridget never replied, but stopped momentarily when she mentioned one club. "Red's? I worked there a lot one summer doing close-up magic. Interesting place."

"Can we get on? I'll show you the drawing rooms, the library, and the ballroom before we go up to the attic."

*Red's.* She'd hit the nail right on the head. *I knew there was something kinky about you, Vicar,* and the things she'd seen while working there were definitely kinky.

*I'm going to find out your secrets, Bridge.* Finn wasn't just being nosy. She needed to find out about the woman who was constantly in her thoughts.

❖

Bridget showed Finn all the places she was sure she'd find interesting, and going by her reaction to the house, Finn did appreciate it. First, she took her to the grand ballroom.

"This is one of the most impressive rooms in the house."

"It's beautiful." Finn pointed up to the painted ceiling and asked, "Who painted that?"

"Antonio Verrio. He's responsible for a great many ceiling paintings in the grandest estates."

Finn walked over to the large ballroom windows that looked out over the estate grounds. "Everything about this place, this village, seems idyllic. There must be more to it than meets the eye."

"How so?" Bridge asked.

Finn turned around, "A darker side. This Witch's Night festival, for example. What's that all about?"

"Witch's Night is a lot of fun, and it's a celebration. Back in the early eighteenth century, Axedale and the surrounding villages had many wise women or white witches, as they called themselves. They were well-loved by the villagers because they handed out natural medicines and potions to the poor who couldn't afford a doctor. Anyway, one of our wealthier landowners, the Winchesters, had a tragedy. His only son was struck down with a fever. He blamed a local woman, Ethel Fletcher, who did nothing more than help, giving out painkillers, sedatives, things like that. The boy was near the end and his mother went to ask for her help, after the village doctor could do no more."

"He died? And this Ethel got the blame?" Finn said.

Bridge nodded. "The boy was beyond help, in that era anyway, and his father took out his grief on Ethel Fletcher. Whipped the village men into a frenzy, and they demanded her death—by fire."

Finn sighed. "That's barbaric. What about the lord of the manor here at Axedale? Were they on this guy's side?"

Bridge walked to her, a smile on her face. "Oh no. Not at all, and that's where the hero of Witch's Night comes in to it. The lord of the manor at that time was Harry's most wonderful ancestor, Lady Hildegard. She was everything a woman wasn't meant to be, a butch in eighteenth-century clothing, sword fighting, riding horses, all that tough stuff."

Finn smiled. "Sounds like an amazing woman."

"Even more amazing was that she managed to live here with her"—Bridge made air quotes—"female companion, Katie, as a wife. She really was remarkable. Anyway, Hildegard rode to the rescue and saved Ethel Fletcher. It's a longer story, but I can tell you all about it when you come to Witch's Night."

Finn's smile dropped away. "No, Bridge. I'm not ready for something like that. I'm all right with you and Quade, but a whole village—no."

"Come on, Finn. It's fun," Bridge said.

"No," Finn said sharply, and then closed her eyes, regretting it straight away. "I'm sorry. I'm just not ready." Then she walked off to the door. "Can we get on now?"

"Of course," Bridge said. Bridge led her into the blue drawing room, the awkwardness between them at least temporarily set aside. The blue room got its name from the dark blue theme running throughout the room, from upholstery and wall hangings to the sky-themed fresco on the ceiling.

"The painting and the architecture are beautiful, Bridge. I would love to paint here," Finn said.

"I'm sure that can be arranged." Bridge walked over to the card table by the window. "This is where we play cards every week."

Bridge watched Finn walk over to the large card table and take a pack of cards from the dispenser. "You just can't resist when you see a pack of cards, can you?"

"No, they're part of me. I've had cards in my hands since I was ten years old. We moved from place to place a lot when I was a kid, so I never made friends. There was always a new church to perform at for my father and, as he grew more successful, his own shows—or as he would call them, healing ministries. It was easier to make my own entertainment than make friends."

It was no wonder Finn was such a complex human being. A nomadic life and isolation were so difficult for a child to cope with. "So you taught yourself magic?"

"You could say that. Each new school I went to, I could win over the bullies and impress the girls."

Bridge walked over to Finn and took the cards from her hands. "Oh, I just bet the girls liked you. That swagger and cocky attitude would certainly impress most girls."

Finn took a step into her personal space. "But not you, apparently."

Bridge jabbed her index finger in the middle of Finn's chest and pushed her back. "I see confidence and swagger rather differently to most. I like to see it and then bring it into check."

Finn crossed her arms and raised an eyebrow. "Really? Well, I have confidence in my skills and abilities, like cards and card games, so I doubt that could be done. As I said, I'm unbeatable."

Bridge laughed and walked around Finn slowly and purposefully, as if she were inspecting her. She could hear Finn's breathing quicken under her close inspection and that gave her a thrill.

*You've still got it, Bridge.*

"An arrogant little thing, aren't you? Well, how about we have our own little game of cards, here, at this very table, tomorrow night?"

"Vicar. I never lose at cards, but if you're determined to go through with this charade, let's make this more interesting. The stake is your clothes," Finn challenged.

"My clothes? Strip poker, you mean?" Bridge said.

Finn's eyes sparkled with delight. "I'm going to strip that dog collar off you, Vicar. I want to see the woman underneath."

*Oh Finn, Finn. I'm going to enjoy this.*

"You can certainly try, but I doubt you'll get that opportunity. I agree to your terms, with two stipulations. I'll bring the cards, and I'll deal every hand. Clear?"

Finn's jaw tightened momentarily but she replied, "I can beat you with any pack of cards, Vicar. You have a deal."

They shook hands. "Tomorrow night, pick me up on your motorcycle at seven thirty."

"You're going to ride on my bike?" Finn almost squeaked with excitement.

"I am, and I'm looking forward to it." Bridge leaned in close to Finn and whispered, "It's a long time since I've had something as powerful between my legs." Bridge was sure she heard Finn groan. "Let's go to the attic and get what we came for." She started off towards the door and added, "Make sure you wear some sexy underwear, Magician, because I'm going to see it."

❖

The damp, cold Axedale attics were a perfect antidote to Finn's raging hormones. When Bridge was talking to her in the blue drawing room, she was wet and ready for anything Bridge wanted to do with her. It was insane. She'd worked with some stunning women on tour, some who were willing to do anything to sleep with the star, but that was boring and humdrum compared to Bridget Claremont, and she was going to have so much fun stripping her down tomorrow night.

As much as it thrilled Finn to please Bridge, she was not going to lose at cards, especially not to a vicar.

"It's just up the next set of stairs," Bridge said.

They climbed the unfinished wooden stairs and found themselves in a large attic, almost as big as the ballroom downstairs. There were boxes, dusty chairs, and other creepy items all around the walls, and shelving with tableware, silverware, and china. On the sloping roof there were a few windows letting in much-needed light.

"This place is straight from a horror film, Bridge."

She laughed. "I know. It used to both terrify and intrigue us when we were children. We played here a lot."

"Did you spend a lot of time here as a kid?" Finn asked as she walked around looking at the china on the shelves.

"Yes, once I met Harry at boarding school, we'd be with my family at the holidays for a part of the time, and then come here. Harry's father didn't much care what we were up to, so we pretty much had the run of the place."

Finn saw paintings, tapestries, books, and antiques as she looked around. "Some of these dusty items must be worth a fortune."

"Probably. Harry has never gotten around to checking through the lot yet. There's a lot of unusual things—come and see this."

Finn followed Bridge over to the corner where there was a gold birdcage on a stand. When she looked in, she jumped in fright. "Jesus fucking Christ!"

"Tut-tut. No swearing, Magician." Bridge laughed at her fright.

Inside the cage was a skull and a collection of smaller bones. "What are they?"

"They've always been kept in that birdcage as far as we can tell. Harry's grandfather remembers them being here when he was a boy. There's a rumour that they could be a Roman burial that a previous occupier of the estate dug up in the grounds. There are a lot of Roman remains all over Axedale."

"That is creepy—" Finn's words died in her throat when she spotted a teddy bear on a chair in the corner. Just like Carrie's. She walked over and picked it up with trembling hands.

"What's wrong, Finn?" Bridget said.

Finn didn't answer. She checked the label and found it was a Steiff bear. It looked the same in every way. She felt Bridge's hand on her arm, and she started to calm her hammering heart. Bridge always made her calm.

"Finn? What's wrong?"

"This bear. It's exactly like Carrie's. She always loved teddy bears and soft toys. She had a lot of inexpensive ones she'd collected over the years, but she always wanted a Steiff bear. I promised her that when I made it big, I would buy her one."

"And did you?"

Finn nodded and felt the tears coming to her eyes. "I always kept my promises to Carrie."

"What happened to her, Finn?" Bridge asked.

"She came to me eight months ago, after a show, to tell me she had terminal cancer." Now she had said it out loud, and tears rolled down her face. "She died and I couldn't help her, not with any money, any trick, nothing could save her."

Bridget tried to take Finn in her arms but Finn pushed her away. "No, don't comfort me. I don't deserve it."

"Why? You loved her. Of course you do."

"Because of me she died a frightened little girl." Finn stormed off to the other end of the attic.

❖

Bridget was certainly not expecting Finn to open up about her sister on a walk through Axedale's dusty attics, but she had often noticed that it was the little things that sometimes broke the dam of emotions after a loved one died. She approached Finn gingerly, trying not to scare her away.

Finn rubbed her face vigorously and turned around. "Let's get the stuff you wanted and get out of here."

Bridge placed her palms on Finn's chest, hoping her touch would calm her. "No, don't run from this. Tell me. I promise—"

"All it will do is make things worse—then one more person will know what a hypocrite bastard I am."

She thought she might never get this kind of moment again with Finn. Alone, out of the way, and on their own, with Finn showing some vulnerability. Bridge tried a different tack.

"Listen, tomorrow you think you're going to strip me out of my dog collar. I think if we are both prepared to get naked together, then we can trust each other. You think?"

Bridge was sure she spotted the tiny beginnings of a smile on Finn's face, so she took a chance and led Finn over to sit on a couple of boxes. "Now I want you to talk because I'm not getting my Chanel skirt dusty for nothing."

"You're like a rabid dog, Vicar. You never give up."

Bridge took Finn's hand and held it between her own. "I will never tell anyone what you tell me. Think of this as a confessional."

Finn looked at the boxes and back to Bridge. "I don't think a Catholic church is set up quite like this, and you're the wrong sex."

"I prefer to think of myself as the right sex. Now shush with your stalling tactics and talk to me."

Finn sighed. "When my dad left, and I got us out of that religious world, we each reacted differently to being free from that dogma. I was already on my way to becoming an atheist before we left. The things I had seen my father do, how he twisted God's words to benefit himself, how he tricked people with his apparent healings, it all just turned me against God and spirituality."

"But not your sister, I take it?" Bridge said.

"No, not Carrie. She went heavily into the New Age movement. Angels, crystals, meditation, and spirituality. She believed in God and a higher power, all that peace, love stuff. We had a few arguments when I was younger and headstrong."

"You mean you're not that now, Magician?" Bridget joked.

Finn smiled. "Believe me, when I was seventeen, I was even more impressed with my own importance. After a while I realized that everyone has their own coping methods for a dysfunctional childhood, and that was hers. I went off to prove everyone and everything wrong, while she sat quietly on the sidelines with her own beliefs, but always loving me, supporting me, and taking care of me in all her little ways."

"Who was your father?"

Finn immediately looked fearful, and got up from the box. "No one knows, except my manager. If the public ever found out, I would never work again, not that it matters much any more. When Carrie and I started our new life, I chose Kane as our family name, and Finnian suited the illusion that I wanted to project."

Bridge realized Finn was struggling with the truth of who she was, and she didn't need that burden, not now anyway. She walked over to Finn and cupped her cheek. "I don't need to know. Tell me when you've worked it out in your head, okay?"

Finn nodded and leaned into her hand as if she was desperately trying to find comfort in her. Finn closed her eyes and covered Bridge's hand with hers so she wouldn't move. "Carrie looked up to me. She thought I was this kind of hero who gave us a good life and took care of her, but I was no hero. I couldn't even help her to die with peace in her heart. In her last days, she was full of morphine and rambled about the past, about who would be waiting for her on the other side, about our mother—but then on her last day, she had some clarity, talking to me. She started to say, what if there was nothing, what if I was right and there was nothing but death. In the end, she believed all the shit I talked all these years."

Finn opened her eyes that were full of pain, and said, "She died scared, terrified, and in so much pain because she believed me. I caused that."

Bridget's heart broke for Finn. "Please don't think that, Finn. She would have questioned her beliefs in any case. I've been by the bedside of many people as they come to the end of their lives, and everyone feels panic. They question everything simply because they fear death, and in the final moments even more so."

Finn stood up and walked back over to the teddy bear. "But she always looked up to me, and if I hadn't wasted my life trying to debunk every spiritual phenomenon people took comfort in, she might have believed and not been scared."

Bridget went over and grasped Finn gently by the arms. "Finn, what happened to make you lose your faith in everything you believed in?"

Finn seemed to be about to speak, but they were interrupted by Julie, one of the housemaids, and they jumped apart.

"Oh, sorry, Vicar. Bev asked me to come and give you a hand."

"Oh, thank you, Julie."

Finn retreated, and Bridge cursed her bad luck. She nearly had Finn's story, she'd nearly opened to her, and now Finn was back in her shell.

Bridge pointed to the boxes in the corner full of costumes and some props, and said, "That's them. Let's get them down to the church van."

# CHAPTER TEN

The next evening Finn drove her bike down to the vicarage. She had been waiting for this moment all day. After such an emotional yesterday, and some bad nightmares last night, the only thing that seemed to give her solace was being near Bridge.

It was strange to think that she had ridiculed people of faith her whole career, and found faith to be a frightening thing, only to find that the only person who could lead her out of the dark, and the darkness of her thoughts, was a vicar, a woman of the God she had gone between hating and insisting didn't exist her whole life.

There must be a reason she was destined to come here, and maybe Bridge could help her find the answers. She also wanted to solve the mystery about Bridge and her connection to Red's private members' club. When she got home yesterday, she contacted her publicist, Allegra, and asked her to make enquiries about Bridget Claremont and her past. If there was information out there, Ally would find it out.

Finn slowed to a stop outside the vicarage and tooted her horn, as Bridge had told her to, and dismounted to retrieve the second helmet from her backpack. She heard the door open, and turned around quickly.

Finn gasped. Instead of her usual black skirt, Bridge had on a pair of skintight leather trousers and the highest heeled boots she had ever seen. "Oh my fucking God," Finn said under her breath.

She said nothing as a smiling Bridge approached her but her body was reacting loudly. Her heart thudded wildly, her mouth went dry, and her sex throbbed. Finn felt the instinct to drop to her knees and praise Bridge at her feet, but resisted the urge.

"Good evening, Finn. Do I fit the biker chick bill?"

Finn imagined those leather-clad legs wrapped around her bike and had to stop a groan escaping from her mouth. "Oh yes. You look great, Vicar." Finn saw her dog collar peeking from under her biker jacket. "I'm glad you left the dog collar on. I'm going to enjoy getting you out of it."

Bridge shot her an imperious look. "I'm not worried, Magician. I hope you wore your best jockey shorts for me...or are you the lacy thong type?"

"I think it's quite clear I've never worn lace in my life." God. This woman wound her up so tight, she didn't know if she was just angry, or turned on, or both. She thought about the last time she'd had sex, with two of her dancers. She had been simply going through the motions, and couldn't wait till she could get out of there.

But in this moment with Bridge, she was more excited and turned on than she ever had been. She noticed Bridge gazing at her hair. Finn ruffled it, thinking she must have helmet head. "Is there something wrong?"

"No." Bridge reached out and ran her fingers through her long fringe. "I simply find your hair so very interesting, Magician."

The only other woman to touch her like that was Carrie, but she didn't mind. With Bridge she was safe. When Bridge's manicured fingernails trailed down the shaved left side of her head, she gulped hard and jumped. "We better make tracks."

Her skin was so sensitive and all she could think of was Bridget's nails dragging down the back of her head and neck.

"Do you have a helmet for me?"

Finn handed it to her and held her hand out to help Bridge onto the bike. As she watched her mount, Finn knew she would never get that image of Bridge's leather clad legs wrapping themselves round her bike out of her head.

Bridge smiled. "Hurry up. I want to see those jockey shorts, Finnian Kane."

Finn got on and revved her engine. "No chance. No woman vicar is ever going to beat me at cards."

She was entirely confident in her card skills, even though she wouldn't have control of the deck or the deal, but still she was the best in the business with cards, and she wouldn't be beaten.

Bridge wrapped her arms around Finn's waist, and she felt her thighs against her own. *Jesus, I've fallen in lust with a do-gooding Christian vicar. Just my luck.*

❖

Bridge and Finn sat in the blue drawing room around the card table. The lights were dimmed, the cracks and snaps of the fire burning in the fireplace giving the room a warm atmospheric glow.

Bridge had asked Beverly to leave them a selection of snacks and drinks for the evening, before going home. The snacks were set up on a table beside them, with bottles of lager for Finn and one of Harry's bottles of red wine for her.

Bridge took a sip of wine from her glass and started to open one of two packs of cards she had brought.

"Wine, Vicar? I thought your drink of choice was a Campari?"

"It is one of my favourites, but I prefer red wine. Unfortunately, The Witch's Tavern doesn't have as good a choice in wines as Harry's wine cellar."

Finn picked up her bottle of lager and said, "Cheers, then, Vicar. Here's to getting you out of your dog collar."

"Good luck trying."

Finn burst out laughing when Bridget's attempt at a shuffle ended up with the cards all over the table. "Good start, Bridge. Why don't you let the expert shuffle them for you?"

*Cocky little bugger.* "I don't want your trickster hands anywhere near these cards. This is going to be a fair game."

"Then less talk, and deal," Finn said.

She did and carefully studied Finn as she perused her hand. She didn't need to look at her own hand to know it was poor.

"Two cards please, Bridge."

She handed them over and took three for herself. It looked like the best her hand was going to be was king high, but no matter.

Finn put her cards down and smiled. "So if I win the hand I get to choose what you take off?"

"You do," Bridget replied.

"Let's not waste any time then." Finn swept her cards out into a fan face up. "Royal flush."

Bridget turned hers over. "King high."

Finn rubbed her hands together with satisfaction. "See? I told you I don't need any tricks to beat you."

Bridge sat back in her chair with her wine, and crossed her legs nonchalantly. "So it would seem. What do you wish me to take off?"

Finn's eyes travelled all over her body hungrily. "I think since it's the first hand, I'll let you off lightly. Take off your earrings."

Bridge smiled, unclipped them, and set them in the middle of the card table.

Finn picked them up. "These are some sparklers."

"They were my grandmother's. She had a thing for diamonds."

"You must be the most expensively dressed vicar in the country," Finn said.

Bridge didn't like the way that sounded, and wanted to put Finn right. "Finn, I'm not a greedy person. I like nice clothes, and I would say that's my only indulgence or vice. It's not my fault I have a trust fund to live on, but I do live frugally, and I distribute my salary as a vicar into three different charities—a children's programme, a charity for the elderly, and an LGBT youth group. I try to give back."

Finn held her hands up defensively. "Hey, I didn't mean anything by it. I never, ever thought you were greedy. You're a good caring person, I know."

"Let's get on with it, shall we?" Bridge said.

"Absolutely. It's lucky the housekeeper left a roaring fire for you, Vicar. You're going to be chilly really soon."

Bridget chuckled. It was going to give her such a thrill to put this uppity boy in her place. "Listen, if you're so confident about winning, let me add one more stipulation."

"Name it."

"Whoever ends up with the most clothes on wins, and if I win, then you come to Witch's Night and a church service sometime."

Finn gave her a serious look and took a long swig of lager. "Why do you want me, the most famous atheist in the country, to come to church services?"

"Well, for one, as I told my friend Harry a long time ago, church is about more than praising God. It's the hub of the community, the place where you feel like you're an important part of that community, where we come together in love and friendship. And two, I'd like to show you why faith can be a cause for good, and bring comfort to your soul, not like the crazy version of Christianity you were brought up in."

Finn was silent, and looked unsure of herself.

"Surely you're not frightened of losing?" Bridge challenged.

Finn leaned over the table towards Bridge. "Bring it on, Vicar. You have a bet. Get ready to lose that dog collar."

"Excellent." Bridge dealt another hand, and this time took more care as she looked over her cards. As she waited on Finn's request for cards, she said, "You seem to have an unhealthy interest in defrocking a vicar, Finn."

"I love all women's bodies, but a beautiful vicar would have an added excitement."

*She thinks I'm beautiful.* Bridget felt a thrill to think she could still attract someone like Finn, so young and vibrant. "Surely you've done more exciting things. You must have lots of little groupies who follow you around. What's Finnian Kane's exciting love life like?"

Finn sighed. "I don't have a love life. I just have a sex life, and you're right, there's an abundance of sex on offer. Three cards, please."

She dealt Finn her cards and returned her attention to her own. "You don't sound as if you find that very exciting."

Finn shrugged. "It's not. I've been bored for a long time. I thought I'd lost my sex drive until—well anyway, they all want Finnian Kane, sexually confident taker, in control of everything and anything around her, the illusion that I made. I'm tired of it."

*You're perfect.* Ten years ago, Bridge would have had so much fun showing Finn how exciting sex could be. Her body throbbed with anticipation at the thought of whipping Finn into shape, but those days were long gone. Now, with Bishop Sprat in charge, all she could do was to comfort her soul.

She took two cards for herself and sorted them into the correct order. "Who is beneath the illusion?"

Finn gave a hollow laugh. "A geeky attention seeker who used magic to try to make friends and fend off bullies at school."

"You forgot, with such an interesting hairstyle," Bridge joked.

"Very true. At school, everyone knew who my father was and I was labelled the freaky Bible-bashing kid," Finn said sadly.

"Your sister saw the real Finn, and you've shown me that person." Bridge popped a couple of olives from the snack plate into her mouth.

"You're different," Finn said quickly.

"Why?"

Finn slid her cards into a neat pile and tapped the top of the pile. "I don't know. You're Bridge. I feel safe with you, and I like talking to you."

"Why do you feel safe?"

Finn let out a breath. She looked nervous talking like this. "Because I can't read you very well, I can't be ten steps ahead of you, and I don't know what's coming next."

"That's a good thing." Bridget smiled seductively. "Anticipation is part of the excitement. Show me your cards, Magician."

Finn smiled and fanned out her cards. "Read them and weep, Vicar. Two queens and three tens."

Bridge gave a big exaggerated sigh and said, "What a shame. I've only got three kings and two aces."

"What?" Finn said with horror.

Bridge reached over the table and dragged a fingernail down Finn's forehead, nose, and lips, before grasping her chin lightly. "Pride comes before a fall. Get ready to fall, boy."

"That's not even possible. I can't be beaten."

Bridge sat back and considered which article of clothing to take off her first. "I think I'll start big. Get your T-shirt off. I want to see those arm and ab muscles."

Finn reluctantly pulled off her T-shirt, leaving her in a sports bra, and giving Bridge a great view.

"Are you ready for round three?" Bridge said.

Finn looked furious. "Deal the cards. You've made me angry now, Vicar."

❖

Finn smashed her cards down on the card table, while Bridge laughed at her. Since winning the first hand, which had obviously been a set-up, she had lost every single hand, despite some sleight of hand and a few extra cards in her jeans pocket.

This had never happened to her. Finnian Kane never lost at cards. Now here she was in the blue drawing room of Axedale Hall, with only two items of clothes left to take off. Her jeans and sports bra.

"I don't know how you did this. You must have a loaded deck. I never lose."

Bridge threw her head back in laughter. "You don't trust a woman of the cloth?"

She had been played, and by a vicar. "How did you learn to play poker?"

"My grandfather learned to play cards from Houdini. Grandpa taught me all his tips and tricks."

"Houdini? You've got to fucking be kidding me."

"Watch your language, boy. I told you my family were eccentrics and trailblazers. Claremonts are taught to never take a bet without knowing you can win."

Finn hung her head in defeat. "Just put me out of my misery, and tell me what you want me to take off."

Bridge tapped her chin and considered carefully. "I think your jeans. Get them off."

Finn stood up quickly and started to unbutton her jeans, but Bridge said, "Stop."

For one minute Finn thought Bridge might be letting her off the hook, but then Bridge simply refilled her wine glass and sat back. "Slowly, I want to enjoy this."

Bridge winked at her and said, "Take them off."

Finn felt heat spread all over her body, like Bridge's gaze was burning her skin. This was different, exciting, even though she'd lost. She slowly took off her jeans and threw them on the chair next to her.

An intoxicating smile spread across Bridge's face. "Oh my, look at those thighs. No wonder the girls love you. And those tight jockey shorts? Delicious."

All Finn could think about was how much she wanted Bridge to touch her, and how hard it was to hold back from going over there and begging at Bridge's feet.

"I thought I wasn't your type," Finn said.

Bridge smiled enigmatically and stood. "You say that a lot, Magician." She started to walk over to her. "Does it bother you? Do you want to be my type?"

Finn's heat and frustration were turning to anger. "I couldn't care less, Vicar. I can get any woman I want."

Bridge laughed and then walked slowly around her, making Finn feel very exposed. How she was remaining still, she would never know. Any other woman, she would be kissing and taking by now.

The sound of Bridge's heels as she walked around her made her even more excited than she was. Then Bridge stopped behind her, and she felt Bridge's breath on her ear.

"You might be the professional mentalist, but I can read you so easily, Finn."

Finn's breathing shortened. *Touch me.* "I doubt it."

"You've gotten things far too easy for too long. Women have been too easy for you to get. You crave something different, you want to work for it, and it annoys you that you don't get that attention from me."

Finn clenched her hands together tightly to stop her turning around.

"You can have anyone you want, you always win at games of cards, you control every conversation, you lead people where you want them—" Bridge walked around to the front and ran her fingernail down Finn's arm, leaving a trail of goosebumps in its wake. "You might have all your magician hocus-pocus on your side, but you can't use mind tricks on me, and you can't seduce me because I have God on my side, and I know which I'd rather have."

Finn couldn't speak. She was confused, unsure, and Bridge had her where she wanted her. "Bridge—"

Bridge smiled and said, "I beat you, so you're coming to Witch's Night, and coming to church. Consider yourself taken down a peg or two, boy."

With that Bridge walked off, and said, "Get dressed and take me home."

Finn grabbed her jeans, and said, "Just one thing."

She turned around and raised an eyebrow.

"You're forgetting one thing, Bridge. I know the way you looked at me in the churchyard." Finn grinned. "You want me."

Finn felt her confidence returning. Bridge just walked on and shouted back, "In your dreams, boy."

# CHAPTER ELEVEN

*T*he lights flashed brightly, and the music thumped in Red's. Bridge watched from the side as dancers gyrated together on the dance floor, some with collars and chains, but all in PVC or leather of some kind. The atmosphere was heavy with sex and excitement. She watched Harry, two women draped over her and vying for her attention. Bridge smiled and shook her head. Harry didn't come clubbing with her often, but when she did, Bridge hardly saw her as she acted like a Pied Piper for the single women.

Bridge looked at her watch again. She was late. Really late.

A deep voice beside her said, "Time is going to stand still if you keep staring at that watch of yours."

It was Harry. "I thought you'd have retired to the playroom by now, with your lovelies."

"No, I'm here to spend the evening with my friend. There's plenty of time for that later."

Without thinking, Bridge checked her watch again.

"Bridge, would you relax? Let me get us another drink."

"She's over an hour late."

Harry sighed and put her hands on Bridge's shoulders. "Bridge, you need to stop this."

"Stop what?" Bridge asked defensively.

"Stop waiting and putting your life on hold for someone who is never going to feel that way about you, not unless you grow some other equipment."

Bridge shrugged out of Harry's grasp. "You have got no right to say anything. You seduce straight women all the time."

"Seduce, yes, not fall in love. You want Ellen to love you, and that's never going to happen, Bridge."

Bridge picked up what was left of her drink and downed it. "I can't move on. She's the perfect woman for me, and I love her. No one has ever made me feel so hot and out of control. She's all I've ever wanted, Harry."

"Bridge, you're beautiful. Look around you."

She did and she saw eyes from all over the club on her.

"You're so busy concentrating on one woman who can never love you that you're missing all the ones who would give their right arm to be kneeling by your knee-high boots. Go and live your life, Mistress Black. Ellen will always be your friend."

Just as Harry's words were starting to make sense, her phone beeped with a text. "It's Ellen—she wants me to meet her upstairs. I'm going to tell her how I feel tonight. I'm going to tell her I love her."

"Bridge—"

Bridge set off upstairs to the bar, full of excitement and determined to finally tell Ellen what was in her heart. She spotted Ellen, who wasn't dressed in her usual PVC outfit. Ellen ran over to her excitedly, throwing her arms around her.

"I'm sorry I'm late, Bridge, but I have an excuse, and super-exciting news."

Bridge smiled and tenderly brushed the hair from Ellen's face. "Don't worry about it, darling. You're here now. Tell me your news, and then I'd like to talk to you about something important."

"You know I was staying at Mummy and Daddy's?"

Bridget nodded and a small knot of worry started to form inside her. She grasped Ellen's hands, and her stomach sank when she felt a ring that hadn't been there before.

Ellen carried on, overflowing with excitement. "Well, they invited Miles to one of their dinner parties and—"

As soon as Ellen said Miles, her stomach dropped. He was an ex of Ellen's who had driven her to cry on Bridge's shoulder more than once, but whom Ellen's parents were in love with.

Ellen lifted her hand and revealed an ostentatious diamond ring that completely summed up Miles.

"I'm getting married!" Ellen squealed.

Bridge felt like all the air had been stolen from her lungs as she struggled to keep the tears from her eyes.

Ellen must have noticed her shock, because she said, "Bridge? You are happy for me? I know Miles and I have had our ups and downs, but I think he's changed, and I think it's time to settle down."

*Bridge managed to croak through the crushing pain in her chest, "Of course I'm pleased for you, darling, if that's what you want."*

*"I do. I love him so much, I always have."*

*There was a long silence, because Bridge just couldn't verbalize anything positive when her heart was being crushed.*

*"I can't stay, Bridge. We're going over to his parents' house. I just wanted to stop by and tell you my news."*

*Ellen kissed her on the cheek and said, "Bye, Bridge. Tell Harry my news and give me a call during the week."*

*"Goodbye, darling." Bridge knew inside that this truly was goodbye. She couldn't bear to be around Ellen when she was excitedly planning for a wedding.*

*Ellen ran off, leaving Bridge's heart broken. Then Harry's arms were around her, comforting her. "Let's go downstairs. This was always going to happen. You deserve someone to worship you, not someone who gives you scraps of attention between boyfriends."*

*She turned around and found Harry wasn't there any more. Instead she was in Finnian Kane's arms.*

*Finn didn't say anything, but led her downstairs and on to the dance floor. They were dancing slowly, seductively, and Bridge was getting hotter by the second. Then Finn looked her straight in the eye and smiled. "You want me, Mistress. Let me worship you, Mistress."*

Bridget woke from her sleep gasping and covered in a light sheen of sweat. She hadn't dreamt about Ellen for such a long time. She swung her legs over the side of the bed and grasped for the bottle of water on her bedside cabinet. She took a long drink and her heart started to calm.

"Why now?" Bridge said out loud, and why was it different?

Her nightmare always ended with Harry trying to comfort her and keep her from running to confess her love to Ellen, but tonight it had been Finn, and her hurt had changed to wanting and hunger for Finn on the dance floor.

Bridge looked at her bedside clock and saw the date. October 2. The anniversary of Ellen's death. She felt immediately guilty that she hadn't remembered until now.

Bridge had been so caught up with helping her little lost sheep that she had forgotten about her long-standing pain. Last night Bridge had her fun putting Finn in her place, but their evening did more than that—it unlocked that passionate part of herself that she had vowed to keep locked inside since that fateful night. She had vowed never to let someone close to her heart, because Ellen had very nearly destroyed her.

Finn had been right. Bridge did want her, and last night it had been so hard not to act, as she had walked around Finn. The old passionate lustful side of herself had always been relatively easy to keep locked down, but there was something about Finn that made it so hard.

When she'd first met Finn, she assumed their energies would clash, but instead of that they appeared to not only mesh, but reacted to each other and heightened her sexual needs and wants. Mistress Black, her former persona, was closer to the surface of her being than she had been in years, and she had to do something about it. Bridge could not afford to let that genie out of the bottle, not in her religious life.

She went over to the wardrobe and took out her box of pictures, and held the picture of Harry, Ellen, and herself. It had been four years since Bridge found out Ellen had died on this very day, and it always brought back the bad memories and hurt.

"I'll never forget you, darling."

Prayer, Bridge thought. Prayer was what she needed and what always soothed her soul.

Just as she stood, her phone rang. It was Harry.

"Hello, Harry? Is everything all right?"

"Hello. Yes, everything's fine. Are you all right, Bridge? You sound a little upset."

Bridge closed her eyes and took a deep breath. "I'm absolutely tip-top. You know me, Harry."

"Yes, I do know you, and I also know what day it is. I wanted to call and check you were all right."

Harry never forgot the day. Despite her own struggles dealing with emotions, she always understood Bridge's love and the broken heart that Bridge still carried to this day.

"I'm okay."

"Bridge—"

"No, honestly, I'm fine. I've been really busy with the church and the village."

"Martha says you have a celebrity in the village. A handsome young thing, with extraordinary hair, in her words. I called her last night."

Bridge laughed softly. "Finn, Finnian Kane, yes."

"Riley is unhappy she missed her. She loves her shows."

"Finn's not really the magician you're used to seeing on TV. She's recently lost her sister, and come to the country to recuperate. A little lost sheep in need of guidance."

"And you are just the vicar to do it."

"What? No. I hardly see her," Bridge said defensively.

There were a few seconds of silence before Harry said, "Are you sure everything is okay, Bridge? You—"

"Believe me, I'm absolutely okay. How are Annie and Riley?"

"Wonderful. They are loving visiting Italy. Riley has her field notebook with her everywhere we go. It's wonderful sharing it with them."

"You're one lucky countess, Harry," Bridge joked. "And the dig?"

"Not going quite so well. The weather has been dreadful, and it's made everything slow up. We're thinking about shutting down and waiting till next season."

"That's a shame."

"Yes and no. It's given me much more time with Annie and Riley."

"My, you have changed, your ladyship."

Right on cue she heard Annie say to Harry, "Tell Bridge we love her."

Bridge heard a little sigh, and then Harry said, "Apparently we love you, Bridge."

Bridge laughed and played along, teasing and making Harry feel more uncomfortable. "Love you too, honey bunny."

"Grow up, Vicar. Seriously, keep your chin up today. Oh, and I sent you something. You should receive them soon."

"Thanks, Harry. Enjoy the rest of your stay. Bye."

When she hung up the phone, Bridget heard the crunch of gravel in the driveway. She looked out and saw a florist's van pulling in.

"Oh, Harry."

❖

Finn's feet pounded the road as she ran through the village. She passed the vicarage and saw Bridge standing by her front door receiving a big bunch of flowers from a delivery driver.

*Who is sending you flowers?* Finn thought enviously. Did Bridge have someone in her life?

She put her head down and ran up and out of the village. On both sides of her were fields filled with cattle and sheep. She had been running for about forty-five minutes now, music pumping in her wireless headphones.

She'd had a fitful sleep last night, and had awoken with an intense ache and hunger, deep inside her, and not even painting would soothe it. Last night Bridge had pulled the rug from under her world. She had beaten her physically and mentally, and wound her up so tight that she was ready to fall at her feet.

Finn had never experienced that before meeting Bridge. She had always done the running, been the one to seduce a woman into bed and take control. Bridge had been right in what she said—women had been too easy, but Bridge was not, and Finn found that intoxicating.

Finn pushed herself as she ran uphill, hoping to release some of this energy she felt. She took Bridge home last night and was left burning for her, and the touch of her own hand was never going to make her feel better.

Despite her physical discomfort, there was one thing that was inescapable. In Bridge's company she didn't feel the depths of grief that had been tearing at her heart. No, Bridge possessed some quality that brought calm to her soul, and made her feel alive after so many months of feeling dead and angry inside.

This morning colours were brighter, sounds were sharper, and she didn't feel as guilty for feeling better about the world.

Up ahead she noticed Quade by the fence, in the field on the right. She was wrestling a broken post out of the ground single-handed.

*Bridge was right. You really are rugged.*

She ran over to her and pulled her earphones out. "Hey, Quade. Having trouble?"

Quade threw the broken post to the ground and wiped her brow on the back of her heavy work gloves. "Morning, Finn. It's just part of the never-ending battle to keep the fence in one piece. Either the animals break it or, like this one, a fallen tree takes it down. You're up and about early."

"Yeah, I felt like a run. Can I give you a hand?"

"If you don't have anything better to do, sure. Thanks, mate."

Finn jumped over the fence and said, "What can I do?"

"Can you get me a new post from the back of my truck?"

Quade's pickup truck sat behind them. "No problem."

Finn carried the post over to Quade and helped her fit it. She helped with a few more posts, enjoying the physical labour. Half an hour later they were finished, and Quade invited her back to the farmhouse for a cup of tea.

Quade took her into a warm, cosy farm kitchen. "Take a seat and I'll put the kettle on."

"Thanks, how are your animals?"

Quade brought over a packet of biscuits and two big mugs of tea. "Much better, thanks. I hate to lose any of my animals, but thankfully I got to them in time. Thanks for helping Bridge with the Witch's Night stuff for me."

Finn put sugar into her tea and stirred. "No problem. I was happy to help. You've all been so kind to me since I've come to Axedale, despite how hard I've tried to keep everyone away."

"It's not surprising, mate. You've been through hell."

Finn looked deep into her cup of tea, and said, "The whole world has been black and grey for so long, but here in Axedale I've started to see colour again."

"Are you going to stay with us or—"

"I haven't been able to think that far ahead, but I can't see how I can go back to my old life. Who knows how long it'll be till the press find where I am, anyway."

Quade patted her on the shoulder. "Don't worry, mate. We'll keep them away as long as possible."

"How long have you lived here, Quade?" Finn asked.

"Since I was seven. My mother died and my aunt and uncle took me in."

"I'm sorry about your mother." Finn saw clear emotion on the tough farmer's face, and Quade gulped hard.

"Thanks, I know how it feels to lose everything and start a new life. The pain never goes, but if you just keep working hard, you get through it, if you have the right people around you."

Finn immediately thought of Bridge. "Did you?"

"Yeah, my aunt and uncle were like a mother and father to me. I lost them a few years ago, but everyone in Axedale has been a great support to me."

"Has Bridge?" Finn asked gently.

"Oh yes, Bridge is a wonderful woman—frightens the life out of me sometimes though," Quade joked.

Finn smiled. "I can imagine. I've never met a woman like her, and I've met a lot of women. Has there been anyone in her life?"

Quade blew out a breath. "Not as far as I know. I know she finds it quite difficult with her new bishop. Her old one was really gay-friendly, but this one is not and would love nothing more than an excuse to get shot of her, but Bridge has powerful friends."

"Like Lady Harry?" Finn asked.

"Amongst others. Her family is very well connected, and in fact her aunt is a bishop, but she's still under a lot of pressure."

Finn wondered if that was why Bridge pulled back from her when they connected passionately.

Quade continued, "She gave Lady Harry and Annie a blessing in the church for their wedding, and she's had hell to pay with him."

It sounded like Bridge was under more pressure than she was showing, and all the time she was feeling it, Finn was pushing her away and being dismissive.

There was one thing she'd known for certain this morning when she woke up. She wanted to know Bridge better—no, she needed to know Bridge better, and to prove to her that despite her protestations, Finn was her type.

## CHAPTER TWELVE

Finn left Quade's farmhouse, ran home, and got showered and changed quickly, eager to get on with her day and see Bridge again. She stood styling her hair in the living room of the cottage, and realized it was the first time since Carrie died that she cared what she looked like. The first time that she wanted to look good for someone.

The top hat that she performed in caught her eye on the coat hook. She lifted it down and ran her fingers along the brim. The steampunk hat represented the character she presented to the world, Finnian Kane, the confident ladies' woman who was in control of every person and situation she was in.

As she held it in her hands, she didn't believe she could ever return to that life. How could she, when she felt like a hypocrite? She had arrogantly smashed down other people's beliefs, and now she had her own doubts. The truth was that deep inside her soul, she did believe that Carrie was looking down on her, and that reinforced what a lie her life had been.

Finn put the hat back and could only think of one thing to help her confusion—Bridge. She got her painting equipment and began walking down to the church. Finn stopped off at the village bakery to pick up some sandwiches and cakes to—she hoped—share with the vicar. As she was waiting to be served, she noticed a little boy and girl in school uniforms, pulling at their mother, whispering and pointing to her.

She heard the mother say, "No, you've heard what your friends said, she doesn't do magic any more."

Great. She had successfully frightened off little kids now.

Once she was served, she added two candy lollipops from the

sweets selection. As she went to leave, the two kids were eyeballing her, no doubt somewhat fearful and somewhat in awe of the magician they had seen on TV.

Finn stopped dead and looked down at them, gave them a quizzical look, then knelt.

She said to the little girl, "I'm sorry, I couldn't help but notice you had something stuck in your ear."

Both children looked up at their mother nervously. Finn gave their mother a quick wink and put her purchases down on the ground. She held up her two empty hands in front of them and waved them around, mystically, before pulling a lollipop from the back of the girl's ear.

"See, I told you. Must have been the fairies that left it there for you."

Both kids gawped at her open-mouthed, astounded at magic.

She turned to the little boy. "Do you think they left one for you—what's your name?"

"Josh," he said in a small voice.

Again, she showed her empty hands, but this time she said, "You have to say the magic words, Josh. Say *I believe in magic*."

"I believe in magic."

Again, she pulled a lollipop from behind his ear. "See? You've got to watch those fairies."

"Say thank you to Ms. Kane," their mother prodded them.

"Call me Finn."

"Thank you, Finn!" they squealed.

Finn smiled and stood with her bags. "No problem. See you around."

When she walked out of the bakery, she experienced the feeling she had when she showed Bridge her magic. The joy of a simple magic trick, and the look of wonder in the children's eyes. It was the kind of magic she had done in restaurants and the pubs and clubs of London. As her shows had gotten bigger and more spectacular, somehow she had left the joy of simple face-to-face magic behind, and instead got her kicks from exposing frauds and fakers.

Feeling good, Finn started to walk to the church. As she approached the gates, a man she hadn't seen before was coming out of them. He looked like your stereotypical country gent in a tweed suit and deerstalker.

When he looked up, she saw a scowl on his face. "Just the person

I want to see." Whoever he was, he wasn't happy and in fact sounded downright hostile.

"Do I know you?" Finn said.

"No, you don't, but you bloody well do now. My name's Winchester and I'm deputy church warden. I don't know what you're trying to pull here but I won't allow it."

Winchester? Wasn't that the family Bridge had said wanted the witches lynched? "I don't know what you're talking about, Mr. Winchester."

"I know what you do—you make trouble, and you make people of faith look like fools, but that will not happen here."

She could not imagine this pompous idiot being one of Bridge's church wardens. "I expose charlatans who take innocent people's money. Nothing more."

"Well, what business do you have sitting in our village church every day, and ingratiating yourself with our vicar? It's bad enough that we have a woman, a lesbian vicar here, without the country's most renowned atheist and troublemaker sitting in our churchyard plotting trouble."

"I'm painting your fucking church. I don't have a camera crew hidden in the trees."

Mr. Winchester's face went red with rage. "If the vicar doesn't listen to reason soon, steps will be taken."

With those words, he walked off leaving Finn puzzled and angry. "Fucking arsehole."

Finn picked up her things and walked into the churchyard. She left her painting things by the bench and started to make her way to the church office.

❖

Bridge sat at her desk staring at her blank notepad and tapping her pen on the desk. She had just had another frosty meeting with Mr. Winchester, and her attempts at writing this week's sermon appeared futile. She held her head in one hand and closed her eyes, thinking inspiration might strike, but only images of her nightmare last night played over and over in her eyes. Her mind kept jumping from the pain of Ellen's memory to dancing with Finn in the club, and feeling intense passion and want. It was wrong, all wrong, especially today.

Normally her morning prayers helped any worries or concerns

she had, but they hadn't helped today. Guilt was the overwhelming emotion that coursed through her body, and it was not conducive to sermon writing.

Janice knocked and popped her head around the door. "Vicar? Ms. Kane to see you."

Bridge sighed. *Brilliant, just brilliant. Finn is the last person I need to see.*

Finn walked in with the biggest smile she had seen on her. Bridge had thought after last night, Finn would be keeping a low profile, but the opposite seemed to be the case.

"Morning, Vicar. I thought I'd return the favour today and bring sandwiches and cake for lunchtime. Could I put them in your church hall fridge?"

It was the sweetest, most open gesture Finn had shown since coming to the village. She should be rejoicing at her progress, but instead all Bridge could feel was guilt and a desire to be anywhere else but here.

"Of course you can, but I'm going out soon, and I don't know when I'll be back." Bridge said that more dismissively than she meant to and saw Finn's smile falter.

"But I thought you'd like to rib me some more about your epic victory. I can wait till you get back."

Bridge got up and started to put her jacket on. The last thing she needed was to feel things for Finn on Ellen's anniversary. "I'm sorry, I haven't got time today. I have the school service and then a few appointments after that."

"What about later? I wanted to talk to you about something that happened to me today."

Bridge placed a gentle hand on Finn's shoulder. "Not today, Finn. Not today."

She saw hurt in Finn's eyes and those walls she had started to breach build themselves again.

Finn grabbed her bags, and said, "Fine, I won't bother you."

"Finn, I didn't mean—"

But it was too late. Finn had left her office and slammed the door shut.

"Well done, Bridge. You handled that impeccably."

❖

Finn didn't bother to set up her painting things in the churchyard. There was no way she wanted to paint the church, perhaps not ever again.

She walked through the village, heading to the loneliness of her cottage. As she walked by a row of cottages and heard a knocking on glass, she turned and saw Mrs. Castle waving from her living room window. She smiled at her and waved back.

Mrs. Castle mouthed some words, and appeared to be beckoning her over. The old woman was nice, but the last thing she needed this morning was chit-chat.

Finn reluctantly walked over to her door and opened it a little. "Hello?"

"Come in, dear."

With a sigh, she entered and, after leaving her things in the hallway, walked into the living room.

"Come in, come in. Sit down. I was hoping I'd see you again."

Finn sat and looked up at all the pictures above her fireplace.

"That's my Harry, her wife Annie, and her daughter Riley. Beautiful, aren't they?"

"They are. Very much so." So that was the Harry everyone spoke of. She did indeed look intense and formidable, but her appearance was softened by the smile on her face, and her arms were around her wife and daughter. Annie was gorgeous—no wonder Harry fell in love with her.

"You'd never think Harry tried her best to run away from Annie as she fell in love with her, would you?"

"No, you wouldn't. They look very happy," Finn said.

"Love can be a terrifying emotion. Anyway, how are you settling in? I've heard you're painting the church."

Finn raised an eyebrow. "Word travels fast."

"There are no secrets in a small village like this."

"So it seems. I don't think I'll be doing it any more," Finn said.

"Oh? Why is that?" Martha asked.

Finn didn't want to say the real reason. "One of the church wardens doesn't like me being there, because of my background, and is giving Bridge a hard time about it. I don't want to make life difficult for her."

"You like the vicar, don't you," Martha said.

The way Martha looked at her suggested she meant more than friendship. "Yeah, I didn't at first. I just wanted to be left alone, but she didn't take the hint."

Martha laughed. "Yes, she's nothing if not persistent, our vicar, but it's just because she cares. She wants to help everyone, even the lost sheep."

"Meaning me? The atheist? The lost sheep?"

Martha was silent for a few seconds. "That depends. Do you feel like you're lost, Finn? Most atheists I've met are very sure about their convictions, and when I've seen you on TV, you seem very sure."

"I'm not sure of anything any more. That's why I'm here in Axedale."

For some reason, it was very easy to talk to this woman. She was comforting, didn't have an agenda, and cared for Bridge.

"You should talk to the vicar. She's not like other religious people who try to push their own ideas on you."

"I have been," Finn said. "I mean, I thought we were becoming friends, but today she didn't—well, she had other concerns today."

Martha sat forward and said, "I don't know everything about it, but I know this date is very difficult for the vicar for some reason. My Harry always sends her flowers on this day, for the past few years."

Flowers. *That must have been Lady Harry sending them.* That changed everything. Maybe Bridge wasn't dismissing her after what they shared over the past couple of days. She had other things on her mind.

God, she was so selfish. Finn was so caught up in her own pain, her own needs to be with and talk with Bridge, she didn't stop to think that Bridge might have her own worries or problems.

Bridge needed some space, and that's what she would give her.

"Thanks for telling me that, Martha." In a move surprising even herself, Finn said, "Would you like me to take you out for a walk in your wheelchair?"

Martha had a huge smile on her face. "Oh, I'd love that. Do you know, I once knew a young magician? He was handsome and boyish, just like you."

Finn flushed. "Well, let's get you ready and I might even show you a trick or two," she joked.

"Oh my!" Martha said. "I can't wait."

## CHAPTER THIRTEEN

Bridge managed to keep away from the church most of the day, but when she did return, Jan told her Finn hadn't stayed around. She had hurt Finn this morning, and just when Finn had opened up to her, but today she just couldn't deal with the feelings being with her brought.

Staying away didn't help much either. Bridge still thought about her, and her thoughts of Finn were drowning out her thoughts of Ellen. She had never thought about anyone else on Ellen's anniversary, and it was hard to sort through those conflicting emotions.

To make matters worse, Bridge had dropped in to Martha's on her way home. Martha told her that Finn had taken her out for a beautiful walk, and it made Martha's day.

The thought was so sweet, it melted Bridge's heart. She was wrong to hurt Finn's feelings this morning, and she wanted to make things right.

Figuring Finn probably hadn't eaten all day since she had rebuffed her attempts at lunch together, Bridge asked her housekeeper, Mrs. Long, to make up enough dinner for two to share. She walked to Finn's cottage, food basket in hand, and prayed that Finn hadn't regressed to hating her. She arrived at her front door and hesitated before she knocked. How could she explain why she had acted as she had today?

She closed her eyes for a second and prayed. *Lord God, give me the strength to make Finn understand, and help me to be strong and not break down.*

Bridge balanced the basket on one knee and knocked on the door. It took a few knocks, but she eventually heard footsteps. The door opened and Bridge caught her breath. Finn looked…sexily tousled. She had on her paint-spattered jeans, a loose white shirt open to the waist, and a sports bra, and that hair of hers was floppy and interesting.

She couldn't take her eyes off those ab muscles of Finn's. She ached to drag her nails across them and make Finn groan.

"Bridge? Is everything okay?" Finn said.

Bridge shook away that thought and said, "Do you always answer the door in a state of undress?"

"There's only two people who come to my door, you and Quade, and I doubt I'm Quade's type."

Bridge nodded. "And me?"

"I'm apparently not your type either, so I must be safe," Finn said.

There it was again. It really did bother Finn that she apparently wasn't Bridge's type, but somewhere between them, they both knew that couldn't be further from the truth. They had such an energy and attraction that Bridge felt compelled to touch Finn.

"Yes, you are safe from my clutches." Bridge played along. "I wanted to apologize for the way I acted today, and hoping you might accept my apology, I took the liberty of bringing dinner. I thought you probably hadn't eaten." Bridge waited hopefully for Finn's reply, and then she saw a smile creep up on Finn's face.

"Okay, Vicar, come on in, and give me that heavy basket."

Bridge handed over her basket and said, "My, my, you are learning to be gallant and charming."

"Well, you did say I needed to work hard to grow up from a boy to be a rugged butch like Quade." Finn winked at her.

"True." Bridge chuckled. "Although I quite like your boyish qualities."

Finn took it and led her into the kitchen. She took a casserole dish out of the basket and peeked under the foil that covered it. "This looks good, and you were right, I forgot to eat and I'm starving."

"Mrs. Long said just to put it into the oven for twenty minutes, and it'll be ready," Bridge said.

"Perfect, I do at least know how to turn the oven on." Finn put it in to heat up and took a bottle of red wine from the cupboard. "Drink?"

"I didn't think you drank wine," Bridge said.

Finn rubbed the back of her head bashfully. "I don't, I just—well, I got a couple of bottles in case you wanted to have a drink with me sometime."

*God, why does she have to be so bloody adorable? You're not making this easy for me.*

"That would be nice then, thanks."

Finn poured her a glass of red and got herself a cold bottle of lager.

Bridge took the wine glass from her and said, "No vodka?"

"No, not any more. Let's go and sit in front of the fire until the food is ready."

They both got comfortable and watched the flames dancing in the fireplace for a while. Bridge was trying to build up her courage for what she had to say, but it was not easy.

"Finn, I'm sorry I tried to push you away this morning."

"It's okay. I probably shouldn't have been bothering you at work," Finn said.

Bridge put her hand on Finn's knee. "No, you should. I like talking to you, Finn, but today is a difficult day for me. It's hard every year."

"I'll listen if you want to tell me."

Bridge took a good sip of wine. This was the hard part. "You keep asking me why someone like me finds themselves in the Church. This is part of the story. It's the anniversary of Ellen's death."

"Ellen? The woman who was brought up in the cold reading?" Finn said.

"Yes." Bridge sighed. "This is the day she died."

Finn held Bridge's hand and it felt quite natural. Bridget looked raw and emotional, and she so wanted to comfort her. "Was she family? A lover?"

"Neither. She went to school with Harry and me. We grew up together, and went to university. While Harry read archaeology, Ellen and I both took physiological and behavioural sciences. I was always interested in the way the human mind worked, like yourself, I suppose."

That was quite true. Despite not having a formal education, Finn was a student of the mind. Perhaps they had more in common than she first thought.

"And what happened? Did you have fun at university?"

Bridge smiled. "Too much fun. Ellen and I enjoyed the same types of…nightclubs, but Harry, not so much. She only came out with us every so often. Harry was more interested in bars, and seducing her way through the entire female population of Cambridge."

It was hard to reconcile the Lady Harry she had seen with her family, in Martha's photographs, with this idea of Harry, but strangely enough, it wasn't hard to imagine Bridge as a young woman enjoying clubbing, drinking, and debauchery. Finn also noticed the reluctance to mention the kind of nightclubs she went to. Finn was sure she meant Red's and other S&M clubs but she didn't want to scare Bridge off.

"You sound like you were perfect for each other," Finn said.

"Yes, I thought so. I'd been in love with her since school. Ellen was all I thought about, she filled up my heart, but there was just one problem."

"What problem?"

Bridge nearly drained her whole glass of wine, and then said, "The biggest problem of all. She was straight."

Finn could hear the emotion in her voice threatening to spill over. "I'm sorry, Bridge."

"Yes, well, I wouldn't give up. Harry kept trying to tell me to move on, and get on with my life, but I wouldn't. I couldn't get her out of my heart."

"That must have been so hard." Finn rubbed her thumb over the back of Bridge's hand, trying to bring her comfort in some way.

Bridge's eyes welled up, and tears ran down her cheeks. Finn grabbed a box of tissues from the side table and handed a tissue to Bridge, who quickly wiped them away. "You can't imagine how hard it was, having the woman I loved cry on my shoulder about every single man she went out with who hurt her, when all I wanted to do was kiss her and make it better."

Finn's heart broke for Bridge. She felt bad enough thinking Bridge had gotten flowers from someone else, far less hearing all that stuff, and Finn wasn't even in love.

Finn's stomach clenched when she thought that. No, she was in lust, that was all.

"It must've been so hard. What happened to Ellen?"

Bridge got a faraway look in her eyes. "We persuaded Harry to come out clubbing with us. I went with Harry and we were going to meet Ellen there. I had decided that was the night I would tell her I loved her. She was late, and it got later and later. I think Harry thought she was with some boyfriend and tried again to get me to move on, but she texted and said she was on her way." Bridge cleared her throat and gulped hard. "I went upstairs to meet her at the bar and—"

"What happened?" Finn moved closer and took her other hand, desperate to give Bridge some comfort, somehow.

"When I met her upstairs, ready to tell her I loved her, she told me she was getting married to one of her good-for-nothing boyfriends."

Finn did what came naturally and pulled her into her arms. Bridge felt stiff at first, but then she relaxed.

"I went off the rails for a while after that, but found solace in the Church. Anyway, four years ago my mother phoned to tell me she had read Ellen's obituary in *The Times*."

"What happened to her?" Finn asked.

"Car accident." Bridge wiped away more tears. "She had alcohol in her system. Things weren't good at home for her, so my mother heard. It hit me hard. Even though the years had passed, a part of my heart still loved her."

"I'm so sorry, Bridge, and I'm sorry I bothered you today," Finn said.

Bridge pulled back and shook her head. "No, don't be sorry, you didn't know, and anyway there was another reason why today was so difficult."

Bridge wiped away her tears, and hesitated before saying, "It was the first year I forgot the anniversary of her death. Last night when we were at Axedale having fun, I never thought of her once and didn't even realize what day it was going to be today, until this morning."

Finn's heart started to beat faster. Could she have taken Bridge's mind away from her pain, the way Bridge did for her with Carrie?

"Why did that happen, do you think?" Bridge inched closer to her. She reached out and caressed Finn's face with her fingernails. Finn felt goosebumps break out all over her body. Her lips parted to match Bridge's and they were getting lost in each other's eyes. They were so close to kissing when the timer on the oven beeped, and Bridge jumped back from her.

"Bridge—"

Bridge had managed to pull herself together. "Go get my dinner, Magician."

And the moment was gone. Finn got up and walked to the kitchen, but before she went through the door she said, "Don't beat yourself up about forgetting your pain sometimes. I never forget that I've lost Carrie, but I forget about my pain for some brief times, times when I'm with you."

Bridge didn't reply, so she walked into the kitchen, a million words left unsaid between them.

❖

"You'll need to thank your housekeeper for me," Finn said. "That was delicious."

Bridge handed Finn her plate and she took it through to the kitchen. Finn returned with the bottle of wine to top up Bridge's glass.

"Are you trying to get me drunk, Magician?" Bridge joked.

"I doubt that would work on you, Vicar." Finn sat back down on the couch with a fresh bottle of lager for herself.

"You're right. I always like to keep firm control of myself and my surroundings."

Bridge kicked off her heels and put her feet onto the coffee table. She noticed Finn's breathing hitch and her fist clench tightly.

Bridge always noticed responses in other people, another skill she'd used in her former existence. It was good to know Finn was attracted to her, but also hard to resist. There was nothing better as a top than taking someone who had such confidence and swagger and putting them in their place, which was usually at her feet. She couldn't help but chuckle.

"What is it?" Finn asked.

"Oh, nothing."

"So, will you finish your story? How did you end up taking holy orders?"

"That's complicated to explain, especially to someone like you," Bridge said.

Finn looked at Bridge and her gaze was open and warm. "Bridge, I'm an atheist in crisis. I don't know what I believe any more, but even if I was certain, I would never disregard your beliefs, which I know you hold sincerely."

Bridge took a sip of wine and cleared her throat. "I went through a really dark time. Harry and my family didn't know what to do with me. Ellen's wedding pictures were in *Hello!* and *Tatler*—impossible to miss a big society wedding. It was so hard to see, and hard to refuse her phone calls and texts. She couldn't understand why I suddenly broke off all contact with her. I even got an invitation to her wedding.

"I did everything to forget my pain—drink, drugs, sex—everything to make me forget the woman I'd loved since I was at school. About eight months after Ellen's wedding, my aunt Gertie, who was a vicar at the time, was leading a protest group to introduce women bishops in the Church of England. I think mainly to try and keep me busy, she asked me to help organize the protest group. I spent a year handing out leaflets, making phone calls, going on marches, and all the time listening to my aunt's speeches about what God meant to her, and why it was important for women to be involved at the head of the Church."

She felt Finn's hand slip closer to her on the couch, until their fingertips were touching.

"I guess that had a big effect on you," Finn said.

"It did. It crept up on me slowly, but through her words I saw and felt God's love, and my pain didn't disappear, but I saw a sunny future for the first time, instead of blackness, and felt God's love filling my heart."

"*My flesh and my heart faileth: but God is the strength of my heart, and my portion for ever,*" Finn said.

"Psalm 73:26. My, you are a mine of Bible quotes." Bridge smiled.

Finn took a long swig of lager and said, "That's what childhood indoctrination will do for you. So you felt hope again?"

"Yes, I had hope in the world and in life again. I wanted to share God's love and word with people the way my aunt did, so I left my life of partying behind me and went back to university to study theology. You can imagine the look on my professor's face when I turned up on the first day."

Finn laughed. "I can imagine. You certainly took me by surprise, Vicar."

Bridge nodded. "I know I'm a little different, but my dearest wish is that people can see faith in God and the world isn't boring and old-fashioned."

Finn was silent for a time, and appeared to be thinking hard.

"What's wrong, Finn?"

"It's funny, isn't it? I started off with a faith in God when I was a kid, and listening to my father preach destroyed my faith rather than strengthen it like your aunt did for you."

"What was your father like?"

Bridge saw Finn stiffen and felt her anger simmer close to the surface. "A failed magician who realized there was more money in selling miracles and fake faith healing than pulling a rabbit out of a hat."

Finn got up quickly and walked over to the fireplace. Her emotions were clearly still raw, and Bridge didn't want to push her lost sheep any more than was necessary.

"You don't have to talk about it, if you're not ready. Come and sit with me."

Finn sat and rubbed her face in her hands. "I'm sorry, you were just so honest with me, and I can't—"

"Finn?"

Finn turned around and gazed at her with such vulnerability that Bridge had to touch her. She placed her fingers under Finn's chin and said, "This isn't a race. You can tell me today, tomorrow, or never tell me at all about your pain, just as long as you let me be your friend and know I'm here for you. Besides, it's nice to have someone listen to me for a change. Vicars usually do all the listening to other people's problems."

Finn grasped her hand and gave her a smoky look. "I'm here for you, Bridge. I'll be whatever you want me to be."

The emotional moment had turned hot and all Bridge could think of was kissing her. There was something indefinable between them, an undeniable chemistry that was so hard to resist, but she had to, for the sake of her heart and her career.

*Don't. Take a breath.*

Bridge pulled her hand away. "I think I better go."

"Please sit with me for a while longer. It's nice to have someone else's company at night."

Bridge couldn't refuse the longing in that voice, so she smiled and said, "Fill up my glass."

Finn smiled and hurried to fill the wine glass. "I performed magic today." She'd wanted to tell Bridge about this all day, as she still wasn't sure how she felt about it.

"You did?" Bridge said.

"Yeah, for a couple of kids in the baker's and for Mrs. Castle."

"Martha would have enjoyed that. I think she's a little bit in love with you. You're lucky she's not forty years younger." Bridge smiled.

"At least I'm someone's type." Finn meant that as a joke, but she saw Bridge's smile falter.

Bridge cleared her throat and said, "How did performing magic make you feel?"

Finn took her cards from her jeans pocket and started to shuffle them. "It felt good, exciting, different."

"Why different?" Bridge asked.

"I had forgotten the simple pleasure of doing one-to-one magic with someone. My act has changed so much since my early days in the pubs and clubs. The more successful I got, the bigger and more spectacular my shows got, and then I got caught up in the TV shows debunking faith healers and psychics. I forgot the pleasure of seeing wonderment on someone's face when they see magic done right in front of their eyes."

"Maybe you need to go back to basics then," Bridge said.

"I promised myself that I wouldn't perform magic any more. Not after Carrie—" Finn closed immediately, and held her cards so tight, her knuckles went white.

Bridget placed her hands on hers, and Finn relaxed considerably.

"What happened, Finn?"

"The day she died, I went home to our house. I drank myself to sleep, but—" Finn struggled. This was so hard to say out loud.

"Tell me, Finn."

"I woke up during the night, and I felt something, someone sitting on the end of my bed. I was crapping myself. So I sat up, and just as I was going to snap on the light, my phone started to ring. It was Carrie's number calling."

Bridge gasped. "Did you answer?"

Finn nodded and tears came to her eyes. "I could hear her voice. She said not to worry about her. She'd arrived safely and it was nice there. My heart was thumping. I was panicking, sweating and shouting for her. That's the last I remember before I woke up."

Bridge scooted closer and put her arm around Finn, and kissed her head. "What did you feel the next day?"

"My logical mind told me it was an elaborate dream, brought on by grief and alcohol."

"What did your heart tell you?" Bridge asked.

"That it was her. The thing that made me believe it even more was Carrie's bear. When I came home from the hospice, I put it in her bedroom, but when I woke up, it was on the foot of my bed. Exactly where I'd felt someone sit the night before."

"It sounds like much more than a dream, Finn."

"Exactly, and I've spent my career debunking people who believed in things like that." Finn shouted, "I'm a fraud and I let Carrie die frightened, because I shattered her faith."

Finn threw her cards into the fire across the room and they started to burn, while she broke down in tears.

Bridge held her in her arms and rocked her back and forth. "Shh. It's all right, Finn."

The pain that was locked inside came tumbling out. She tried to struggle from Bridge's arms half-heartedly.

Then she heard Bridge whisper in her ear, "Dear Lord, our God. You're close to people whose hearts are breaking, those who are discouraged and have given up hope. May you who see their troubles and grief respond when they cry out."

She stopped struggling and gripped onto Bridge tightly, drinking in every ounce of comfort she could give her.

❖

The next morning the sun was just starting to rise in the autumnal sky. This was Archie Winchester's favourite time of the day. There were no villagers or bloody tourists milling about the streets, just him and his dogs, and his thoughts.

He was frustrated after his confrontation with Finnian Kane yesterday. Everything about her disgusted him. A lesbian who looked more like a boy than anything, with an outrageous haircut, and an atheist to boot, who had caused no amount of trouble in the religious community.

*This would never have been allowed when Lady Henrietta's father was earl.*

He slowed to allow his dogs to sniff by the bright red village postbox.

Archie had been good friends with the late earl, and since he hadn't been interested in village matters, he'd let Archie have pretty much a free hand with the church. But since the countess had taken control, he had been sidelined.

He walked a little further into the main village, and noticed the door of Mason's cottage. A woman crept out of Finn's cottage and down the garden path.

*Typical.*

Finnian Kane's scandalous reputation with women didn't disappoint. He wondered who the female was, and then when she reached the gate he saw a dog collar.

"Bloody hellfire. It's the vicar," he said out loud.

He watched Bridge walk out the gate, check around to see if anyone was watching. Then satisfied it was all clear, she hurried off home.

"You've done it this time, Vicar. I'm going to nail you to the bloody wall."

## CHAPTER FOURTEEN

Finn set up her easel in the churchyard nice and early. She had gotten the best sleep she'd had since Carrie's death and awakened not with sadness or more energy than she knew what to do with, but just with contentment and calmness.

Finn hoped she would see Bridge when she arrived at work. This morning when she awoke, she'd found a note from Bridge saying she had left. Selfishly, Finn wished that she would've still been there in the morning, but understood it probably wouldn't look good for the village vicar to be seen leaving her cottage in the morning, no matter how innocent their shared evening had been.

It was funny to Finn that even though nothing happened between them in a sexual sense, their time together had felt more intimate than any sex she'd ever had. Finn was so at ease in Bridge's company. She didn't have to be Finnian Kane the illusion, the creation she had shown the world. No, she could just be Finn, and show her vulnerability without fear.

Finn had cried out a lot of grief on Bridge's shoulder, pain she had kept inside far too long, and Bridge calmed her soul. She was sorry she had thrown her cards in the fire in anger. She'd had them since she was a child, but maybe it was time to let the past go and start a new chapter in her life.

Finn finished getting set up and sat back on the churchyard bench. It was a crisp, bright autumnal morning, perfect for painting. She put in her earphones and started to play her painting playlist. The church painting was more than half done, but there was still some way to go. The stone carvings around the walls were beautiful but intricate, and Finn was determined to capture them correctly, despite her rustiness.

*Maybe Bridge would like this when it's finished.*

Just as she thought that, she became aware of someone by her side. She looked up and saw the woman who made her heart thud and her sex pound with anticipation. *Bridge.*

Bridge said something but she couldn't hear because of her music. She pulled out her earphones. "Sorry?"

Bridge smiled. "Morning, Finn. How are you feeling?"

Finn flicked her hair from her eyes nervously. She was glad she got all her emotions out last night, but it was still hard to face the fact that she'd cried on a woman's shoulder. She couldn't imagine Quade doing that.

"Good. I'm feeling good."

"Did you save any of your cards?" Bridge asked.

Finn shook her head.

"I'm sorry, Finn. I know what they meant to you."

"I'm sorry I broke down like that," Finn said.

"Oh, tosh." Bridge sat down beside her. "Everyone needs a good cry sometimes." Bridge leaned over and whispered in her ear, "Don't worry, I shan't tell a soul. You won't lose butch points."

The feeling of Bridge's breath on her ear sent all sorts of crazy sensations all over her body. Finn tried not to show how much she was affected and joked, "Yes, thanks, because you know I'm saving them, and building up from boy to card-carrying butch, like Quade."

Bridge laughed. "But I do so like you as a boy, Magician."

*God. I want her so much.* Finn stared, transfixed, as Bridge crossed her legs.

Bridge rested her hand on her knee and continued, "I appreciated you listening to me about Ellen. I seldom get to talk about her."

Finn took a chance and placed her hand over Bridge's. Bridge tensed for a second and then clasped Finn's fingers. It was the closest she had gotten to touching those gorgeous legs and she was forcing herself to remember every feeling, every thought.

She took full advantage of her position, to lightly caress Bridge's knee. She heard Bridge gasp, and then shift in her seat, but she didn't stop her.

❖

Bridget cleared her throat. How had she arrived in this position, from simply saying hello?

The sensations her body was experiencing were wrong, so wrong inside her own churchyard, but the setting only made her feel more turned on. An image of herself leaning against her office desk, with Finn on her knees between her legs, flashed across her mind.

She jumped up quickly and said, "I better get on. Remember, a bet is a bet. Set-up for Witch's Night starts at seven. We've only got a few weeks."

Finn stood and took a step too close. "I'll be there, Vicar. I won't see you this afternoon, because I said I'd go and give Quade a hand. Keep myself busy, you know?"

"Sounds like a good idea. I have tea and gossip with the Axedale ladies this afternoon anyway."

"Tea and gossip?"

"Well, it's a women's fellowship meeting that we have every week at the church. We are meant to talk and pray and…it usually descends into tea and gossip, but it's more fun that way. I'm sure you'll be the topic of some of the gossip." Bridge smiled.

"Have fun," Finn said. "I'll see you tonight then."

Bridge looked at her painting and said, "It's really coming on, Finn. You have talent."

"Nah, it's just for fun, but I'm glad you like it."

"I better start my day then." Bridge leaned in to Finn and ran her nails across the back of Finn's hand, and whispered, "Next time, don't take without asking, boy."

Then she turned on her heel and walked towards her office. She had to force herself not to look back or else she and Finn would probably be kissing on the bench.

She made it to the safety of her office and leaned back against the door to catch her breath. *God give me the strength.*

Finn made her feel things she couldn't even process. Finn was cocky, arrogant, and that made the thought of her submitting to Bridge all the more delicious.

Her old persona was creeping out from its restraints every time she was with Finn, and being near her was just going to get harder. What made her feelings for Finn worse was the fact that as cocky as Finn was, she was also vulnerable, and that made Bridge's heart ache. All in all, Finnian Kane was a frightening challenge for someone who was trying to remain celibate.

Bridge rubbed her forehead and thought. "My Bible. I need my Bible."

She went over to her desk and, inspired by all these intense sensations, wrote the week's sermon.

❖

After lunch Finn met Quade and her work crew at the Axedale stables, and headed out into the Axedale woodland in their trucks.

"Lady Harry wants to expand this for the wildlife in the area," Quade explained as she drove them down a single-track road to the edge of the forest.

"It's a wonderful woodland. Like something from a fairy tale," Finn said.

Quade smiled. "It is, isn't it? We used to play in here when we were children. Our parents didn't see us all day, unless we wanted something to eat. You probably couldn't do that nowadays."

"It must have been great growing up here. My family travelled around a lot. Never got a chance to settle and make friends," Finn said sadly.

Quade turned the truck into the edge of a clearing and parked. She patted Finn on the shoulder and said, "You have friends now, mate."

Finn didn't know what to reply. It was a simple thing to say, but meant so much to her. "Thanks, Quade. I appreciate that."

"Right, let's go. We've got trees to plant."

When the rest of Quade's team arrived, Finn helped carry the tools and the saplings over to the planting area. Quade handed her a spade and said, "Start digging there. We're trying to fill up this open space with new oak. The forest was decimated during the Industrial Revolution, so we're trying to get it back to what it was."

"Okay. Sounds good," Finn said.

Quade was digging next to her, and her team each took up an area on the spare ground. Finn enjoyed the manual work. It wasn't something she had done before, but it was certainly helping her deal with all the emotions she was feeling.

As they dug, Quade said, "How are you getting on with Bridge?"

Finn stopped and looked up at her questioningly. "Why do you ask?"

"I'm not stupid. I've seen the way you look at her. You care about her," Quade said.

Finn thought about denying it, but that would just be wrong. Quade was her friend. "Yeah, I do. A lot."

"What does Bridge say?"

Finn speared the spade into the ground and leaned on it. "I think she feels something for me. There's something between us, but I don't know if it's just attraction or something more."

"I thought as much," Quade said. "I'm not very good at reading people's emotions, but when you two are together, there are sparks flying. Just like our friends Harry and Annie. Bridge hoped she would feel that one day, I know."

Finn's heart raced with excitement. If other people could see it, then it must be real. *I want her. I want to know who she is.*

"Thanks for telling me, Quade," Finn said as she took a sapling and placed it in the fresh hole she had dug.

Quade walked a few steps to her. "I like to see people happy, but you be careful, Finn. Bridge has a hell of a lot to lose."

"I know." Finn was frightened that would keep them apart.

❖

Bridge looked around the church hall with satisfaction. Everyone who had signed up to help was there and working hard on costumes and props, and even her lost sheep was over in the corner painting masks for the participants.

Finn had made such progress, Bridge thought. Not long ago she was slamming a door in her face, and now she was taking part in a community event. Bridge was doing her Christian work well. The only fly in the ointment was that she wanted to rip Finn's clothes off, and that posed great difficulties in her role as spiritual leader of the community. The only thing she could do was to keep praying and trust that God would lead her on the right road.

A stream of children kept going over to Finn, asking to see tricks, and luckily Finn was in good spirits and happy to oblige. She noticed a few times Finn's hand went to her shirt pocket by instinct, to take out her cards, and then she realized they were gone. Instead she did some coin tricks that delighted the kids.

Bridge wished there was something she could do to bring them back for Finn, but any new pack wasn't going to have the same history. Then something popped into her head. Maybe there was something she could do, especially with Witch's Night coming up. It was traditional to give a gift to someone who needed it, just like the witch was given her life.

She took out her phone and called her mother. When she answered, Bridge said, "Mama? It's Bridge. How are you?...Wonderful. I'm calling to ask a favour, Mama, but just say if you don't want to do it."

After chatting for a few minutes, she hung up and smiled with satisfaction. Finn was going to love this, she hoped.

Mr. Butterstone approached and said, "Vicar? Good turnout, isn't it?"

"It is indeed. I think we're going to have a great night this year. Bigger and better than usual."

"And you managed to get Ms. Kane to help."

Bridge followed Mr. Butterstone's gaze to Finn, who was showing Sophie, Riley's best friend, a trick repeatedly, and making her laugh.

"Yes, she's doing very well," Bridge said.

Mr. Butterstone was silent and then cleared his throat nervously. "Have you managed to ask her—"

Bridge closed her eyes and shook her head. "No, not yet. She's going through an extremely emotional time right now, and I don't want to push her more than necessary, but I will ask her when I think she's ready."

"That's all we ask, Vicar. Thank you."

He walked away and Bridge watched Finn closely. It was one thing doing some tricks for an old lady and some kids, but pushing Finn to perform and direct a show was an entirely different thing.

Bridge had a need to protect Finn as she stumbled her way through grief and back to life, and pushing her was not going to help. She thought about how much she cared about Finn already, and it scared her.

❖

"Thanks for showing me your cool tricks, Finn," Sophie said. "My friend Riley is going to be so mad she didn't see you. She has all your shows on DVDs."

"I tell you what—I'll sign some things before I leave, and you can give them to your friend, okay?"

"Oh, thanks! Riley will be so happy. I better go and get my mum. See you, Finn."

"Bye, Sophie. Nice meeting you."

Finn got up from the floor and brushed down her jeans. Everyone was starting to pack up, so she gathered up all the masks she'd painted. Her good mood was starting to go downhill when she thought of what she'd said to Sophie. That she would be leaving Axedale sometime. The very thought scared her. She just couldn't imagine going back to her life in London, and being alone. If she did that, all there would be was lonely grief, and the illusion of Finnian Kane.

At least here she had two friends, Quade and Bridge, the woman who dominated her thoughts. Watching Bridge stride around the church hall tonight, clipboard in hand, keeping everyone on task, only served to remind her how much she wanted Bridge.

It was a passionate need that was building with each passing day. Her atheist acquaintances would laugh at her predicament of being in lust with a vicar, but there was more than that. Bridge made her feel safe, calm when her soul was in torment, and cared for, just as Finn cared for her.

All this was in Axedale, and in London her old life lay in wait. She had bought her way out of the last few shows in her contract, but she still had commitments. People who relied on her. Her PR, her management team, all waiting on Finnian Kane to return, but she didn't think she could be that person any more.

Bridget walked up to her smiling. "Would you like to walk me home, Magician? I might even let you buy fish and chips."

"Oh God, now you're talking. Just let me clean up."

❖

Finn waited in line at the smallest fish and chip shop she'd ever been in. As she looked around, Bridge said, "Not quite London, is it?"

"I think it's great. Very quaint. I didn't think you'd have a fish and chip shop in Axedale."

"It's not been open long. Mrs. Robinson who owns the village tea shop thought the new tourists would like an alternative to her tea, sandwiches, and cakes at the Axedale tea room, something a bit less formal, so she rented this little stone building from Harry and has her son run it. It's been a roaring success, with the locals too."

"Sounds like Lady Harry has brought a lot of money and jobs to the village. Quade was telling me as much today."

"Yes." Bridget sighed, then looked right into Finn's eyes. "And all because she let love into her heart."

Finn felt those words were directed at her, and they stood gazing at each other until the server said, "Can I help you?"

They had come to the front of the queue without Finn noticing. Time spent with Bridge seemed to do that.

"Yeah, sorry. Um…" Finn looked up at the menu on the back wall quickly.

Before she had the chance to answer, the server said, "Are you and the vicar together?"

Finn looked back at Bridge, who appeared a little unsure, but somewhere inside herself, Finn knew. She winked at Bridge and turned back to the man at the counter. "Yes, we're together. Could we have two large fish suppers with mushy peas, lots of salt and vinegar, and two pickled onions."

When the server went off to get the food, Bridge sidled up beside her. "Did you just order for me, Magician?"

*Oh God.* The very sound of Bridge's voice when she reprimanded her made Finn shiver.

"I did. You did say I could buy you fish and chips and walk you home."

Bridge smiled. "I suppose I did. Very well, but I am not eating mushy peas."

Finn gave her a mock look of shock. "That's an essential part of the perfect fish and chips, but I forgot you were so posh, Bridge."

"Oh, shush." Bridge gave her a swat on the behind and set off all sorts of excitement in her body.

They got their food and walked slowly along the river. Finn suggested they take a seat on one of the benches to eat. It was getting dark in the evenings, but the streetlight gave them enough light to see each other and their food.

Bridge said, "It's maybe not London calibre, but still very tasty."

"I don't know. London is all tempura batter and trying to improve something that doesn't need improving." As they ate Finn said, "You know this is like a first date, Vicar."

"How so? I've never been on a date. My past social interactions were a bit more intense, but no dates," Bridget said.

"Neither have I, but from what I've seen on TV and what Carrie told me, they usually consist of sharing food, talking, and sometimes long walks."

Bridge smiled. "I see, well we have three points already. What else do people do on dates?"

Finn shrugged. "Find out the things you like, food, colour, drinks, music. Then you can use the information on your next dates, if you're lucky enough to get any more."

What had started as a joke for Finn was now a way of testing out Bridge's feelings. Luckily Bridge appeared happy to play along.

Bridget wrapped up her remaining food and sat it to her side, then opened a bottle of water.

"Well, we have to follow the rules on our pseudo date. You already know my drink preferences…so, food? I would say ice cream. I have an ice-cream fetish, but unfortunately, we don't have a good ice cream parlour. I like the kind of place where you walk in and are faced with fifty different choices, along with sprinkled nuts, hot fudge sauce, the whole shebang."

Finn dispensed with what was left of her food and moved closer. "What flavour's your favourite?"

"Hmm, praline or raspberry ripple," Bridge replied.

Finn only wished it wasn't a pseudo date but a real one. Then she would plan something special with that information.

"And your favourite colour?"

"That's easy, but again I'll choose two." Bridget moved closer, and said with a flirtatious smile, "Red and black."

Finn gulped. She could imagine Bridge in all sorts of red and black outfits that would make her wild. While Bridge was so close to her, Finn said, "And your favourite song?"

Bridge's gaze searched her eyes and face slowly, and then Bridget brushed Finn's fringe away from her eyes, and said in almost a whisper, "'Can't Help Falling In Love.'"

Finn stopped breathing and Bridge waited a beat before saying, "By Elvis Presley."

Their lips came together softly, slowly, small kisses at first, and then Finn felt Bridge's fingers thread through her long fringe. Their kiss deepened and Bridge's nails scratched down the short-haired back of her head, and dug in slightly at the nape of her neck. Finn groaned and slipped her tongue into Bridge's mouth. Her body was thrumming, and she wanted to taste every part of her.

Bridge suddenly pulled back and the intense moment they shared was over. "I'm sorry. I can't." They sat in silence for a moment or two, and Bridge said. "Shall we walk back?"

"Sure," Finn said with sadness. Bridge couldn't or wouldn't face what was between them, and it was making her heart hurt.

❖

Bridge could not believe she had kissed Finn. Something in Finn was pulling her like an unstoppable force, and she felt almost powerless against it. Not a sensation that Bridget liked. All the prayer and pleas to God for help with these feelings were not helping. She was sure Finn was just as interested, but it would be doomed to failure.

They were a few minutes from the vicarage, and they had both been mostly silent, until Finn said, "Why Elvis?"

"What? Oh, my grandmother was a huge fan, and she and my grandfather spent a weekend with him at Graceland—"

Finn started laughing hard. "Of course they did. Is there anything the Claremonts haven't done?"

Bridge played along. "Hmm, not really—oh, go to the moon. We've still to do that."

"I'm sure one of you will, one day. So, Elvis?"

"Oh yes, I grew up hearing his music, but that song just always melted my heart, and 'Always On My Mind' always made me cry."

"Bridget Claremont cry over a song? Never," Finn joked.

"I have a softer side, Magician."

She felt Finn's fingers caress her own. "I know that, Vicar."

Finn suddenly stopped and looked behind quickly.

"What's wrong, Finn?" Bridge asked.

Finn scanned around her in all directions. "I don't know. I just had the feeling someone was watching us. I'm probably just being paranoid. Let's keep going."

They got to the vicarage gate, and Finn said, "So do I merit a second pseudo date?"

Bridge felt like Finn was only half joking, and she had to make things clear. "Finn, you know what I told you about my position in the Church? We are *supposed* to remain celibate within a gay relationship."

"But I thought it was a don't ask, don't tell kind of thing."

"Unofficially it is, and those colleagues in my gay Christian group respond to that in different ways. Some have a normal sex life but are discreet, while some are not discreet believing that more militant protests will bring change more quickly, and some keep their vow of celibacy to the Church, hoping that change will come soon. The first two types of clergy I mentioned risk losing their jobs, their homes, their church, their vocation every single day, depending on the attitude of their bishop. My last bishop wouldn't have cared, in fact he would probably have encouraged me, but this one—to put it simply, to have a sexual relationship, I'd have to risk losing my job every day. I'm not sure I'm ready to make that choice. It wouldn't be fair to anyone to ask them to give up a sex life to be with me. So, dates or pseudo dates are not a good idea."

Finn shook her head in disbelief. She couldn't understand Bridge living like that. "Bridge, how can you live like that? You're such a passionate woman. If someone cares about you, why would you give up on that?" Finn said angrily.

Bridget snapped. "Because I love God, something an atheist could never understand."

"Well, if some have the courage to be open about it, I can only conclude that I was right in what I said when I first met you. You're hiding behind that dog collar, frightened that you might possibly feel love and get your heart broken and rejected. Maybe no one will ever be good enough for a place in your heart like Ellen was."

Bridget's face went stony. "Goodnight, Finn."

Before Finn could reply, Bridge was gone up the path to the vicarage doors. "Why did I say that? Idiot."

It might have been better left unsaid, but Finn was convinced it was true.

As she walked home the guilt started to set in. If someone had mentioned Carrie in the way that she had used Ellen's name, she would be both angry and hurt. It had just been such a good day, and they were becoming so close. That's exactly what Finn wanted, to be close to Bridge, because when she was she didn't feel pain, and when she did think of Carrie she remembered only good times, and how well Carrie would have gotten on with Bridge, the only two women who could put her in her place.

When she got to her cottage door, her phone rang. She was used to screening her calls at the moment, but when she saw it was her publicist, Allegra, she answered. "Hello, Ally."

"Hi, Finn. How are you?" Ally sounded reticent. The last time they had spoken, Finn hadn't been in a good way.

Finn walked through the front door and locked it. "I'm much better, Ally. This break in the country is really helping."

"Wonderful! I knew it would. I can't guarantee how long the press will leave you alone. They're trying everything to find you."

Finn went to the kitchen, took a bottle of beer from the fridge, and sat at the kitchen table. "I'll just have to deal with it when it happens. What can I do for you?"

"It's what I can do for you. I have the information you wanted on Bridget Claremont."

"You do?" Finn took a drink of lager.

"Yes, and it wasn't easy, believe me. The clientele of Red's nightclub and the others like it in London do not like to talk. I made up a file and emailed it to you."

"Thanks, Ally." Finn couldn't wait to look at it.

"Who is this woman to you anyway, Finn?"

"A friend I'm curious about, that's all. I'll be in touch. Thanks, Ally. Bye."

Finn hung up the phone, then hurried through to the living room to grab her tablet. She sat on the couch and opened her mail.

The subject line of the email read, *Bridget Claremont: Mistress Black.*

❖

Finn could hardly believe her eyes as she swiped through picture after picture of Bridget, or Mistress Black, as she was labelled in the pictures. They had been taken on special nights at Red's—Halloween, Christmas, spring balls.

Red's was an S&M club, not as hardcore as some, but the patrons had lots of fun, as she remembered from her days performing there.

Bridge looked gorgeous in her outfits—black leather, PVC, and one outfit that consisted of a military style jacket with brass buttons, and only fishnet stockings on her legs. And of course, her designer heels, the one vestige of Mistress Black that remained to this day.

"How can she keep this part of herself locked up inside?"

Finn thought back to her first gig at Red's. She was a cocky twenty-year-old full of swagger and attitude. Carrie had been a bit nervous about her performing there, but she had laughed it off.

The jovial attitude soon gave way to nervousness as she walked through the club. The club's atmosphere was what she would describe as sexual. The music had a heavy beat to match the excitement, the décor similar to a Victorian gentlemen's club. Her nerves started to turn to excitement the longer she was there. The women were sexy, and she longed to be part of the group that sat around dressed up in leather, collars, and chains that she performed to at the tables.

*If only I'd seen Bridge there.*

Finn finished her last drop of beer and a smile emerged on her face. She looked at one of the pictures and said, "I'm going to tease you out to play, Mistress Black, because you are a huge part of her, and I want to know all of Bridget Claremont."

## CHAPTER FIFTEEN

Bridge sat at her dressing table, applying her make-up for the village's Witch's Night. For the past week, since she'd kissed Finn, Bridge had kept a low profile around the village and Finn had avoided the church. She had texted Bridge, apologizing for what she'd said about Ellen, and she had accepted Finn's apology, but it wasn't so much what Finn had said that made Bridge want to keep her distance. It was that kiss by the river, that gentle, loving kiss that she couldn't get out of her mind.

Bridge applied her make-up carefully, focusing on her lips, and all she could think about was Finn's kiss. She touched her lips with her fingertips and closed her eyes remembering every moment of it.

Bridge had never kissed anyone since accepting God into her life and going to theological college. But from the last time she had seen Ellen to the day she acknowledged her calling, she'd indulged every carnal excess. She opened her eyes and gazed at her reflection as shame bubbled in her stomach. The kisses she had then weren't soft, they weren't even passionate. They were all about losing her pain in someone else, no matter who.

Her gaze dropped to her dog collar, her shield, her armour against pain and losing control. Finn said she used her faith as an excuse, so that she didn't have to try and care about someone again. Was that true? She did feel something for Finn. She wanted to help Finn, care for her, show her that she could believe in life again, even if she could never go back to the beliefs of her childhood, but most of all she wanted to kiss Finn again and make everything okay.

Then she thought of the heat between them and banished her feelings of shame, turned it to aching want.

Bridge's phone rang. It was Finn. She hesitated for a few moments then answered. "Hello, Finn."

"Hi, I—" Finn hesitated. "I wondered if you still wanted to go to Witch's Night with me, after what I said—"

"Of course I want to come with you. Who else would explain our quaint village customs to you? The other matter is all forgot."

There was a period of silence, because they both knew the kiss was not forgotten.

"Great, I'm with Quade just now. I've been helping her and the estate staff set up the barn for dancing, and then we're going to light the bonfire."

"My, my, we are being quite the helpful magician." Bridget shook her head. They so easily slipped back into the flirtatious banter that characterized their relationship. So easy to do and hard to resist.

"I'm trying to be helpful. Where will you be?"

"I'm going down to the church hall to coordinate everyone taking part in the parade."

"Of course you are, Vicar. You're never happier than when giving out instructions," Finn joked.

Bridget chuckled. "Very true. Why don't we meet at the pub at six? We can get a quick drink before the parade starts?"

"Perfect. See you later."

Bridge ended the call and clasped her hands in prayer. "Dear God, help me make sense of these growing feelings I have, and guide me to my purpose and destiny, whatever that may be. Amen."

As Bridget finished her prayer, she thought, what if Finn was her purpose? What if she was meant to save her and bring her back to the fold, and make her feel loved?

But that would conflict with the Church's position on same-sex relationships. Deep down, she knew that one day she'd have to make a choice—to follow the Church's archaic position or follow her heart and what she believed God was leading her to.

❖

Finn pocketed her phone and smiled. There might still be so much unsaid between them, but things were better after her stupid comment. Bridge felt like a shining light in the darkness of her life, and she wanted to be near that light as much as possible.

*And I want to see if Mistress Black is still hiding under the surface.*

In fact she didn't have to wonder, she knew, and Finn so wanted to meet her.

"Finn," Quade called out. "Everything okay?"

She had stepped out of the barn to make the phone call, and Quade probably wondered why there was now a smile plastered on her face instead of the nervous tension she'd been displaying all morning.

Finn jogged over to Quade at the Land Rover and said, "Yes, everything's good." She had told Quade about unintentionally upsetting Bridge, but not about what or, crucially, the kiss.

"I'm going to meet Bridge at the pub before the parade."

Quade handed her a couple of cases of lager to carry. The back of the truck was full of alcohol from the pub, for the dance.

"Great. I'm glad to hear it. You've both looked upset by the situation this week."

Quade grabbed a few cases of wine and spirits and they both started to walk to the barn.

"Have you seen Bridge this week, Quade?"

"Yeah, a few times. She comes up to Axedale to feed Riley's horse. I usually bump into her there if not in the village. She seemed quite preoccupied."

Finn just nodded. Bridge was no doubt trying to come to terms with the kiss, just like she had. Finn hadn't experienced anything like that soft gentle kiss before. She'd wanted to kiss Bridge more than anything, but she hadn't expected that kind of kiss.

Finn knew she was in lust with Bridge, but when her lips touched hers, she felt something very different from lust. It was heart-achingly beautiful, and it felt like Bridge was healing parts of her broken heart with every touch of her lips.

"Finn? Finn? Can you hear me?"

She shook herself from the memory. "Sorry."

They put the cases of alcohol on one of the tables in the barn. People buzzed about sweeping the floor, putting up witch and gothic decorations, and setting up food.

"You were a million miles away. Is there something going on between you and Bridge?"

"Yeah, well…we got closer and she pulled away. I got frustrated and said something I shouldn't have, but it's okay now."

Quade sighed. "Finn, you remember what I told you? Bridge has a lot to lose if she pursues something with you. You need to follow her lead, and if you can't, then maybe you should walk away."

Finn felt a sense of horror imagining herself leaving Axedale, leaving Bridge. "I can't, Quade. I feel—I care about her too much."

"Well, in that case, you need to talk to her, and tell her how you really feel," Quade said.

Finn placed her case of lager on the table and said, "I'm working on it."

❖

Bridge was waiting for Finn by the bar in the pub. There was standing room only as everyone tried to get a few drinks in before the parade. Bridge was nervous. It felt like she was waiting on her date. How she wished Finn was her date. She made her yearn for things she didn't think she could have any more.

The pub door opened and Bridge's heart fluttered as Finn walked in and smiled at her. Her hair was elaborately styled into a fauxhawk and made her look just adorable.

*My beautiful boy.*

"Evening." Finn leaned in and kissed her cheek, and Bridge's heart started to race. It had been a long week without seeing her.

"Good evening. I got you a drink." Bridge handed Finn a pint of lager.

She took a sip quickly. Unusually for them, there was an awkwardness in the air. Bridge was sure it was because they both felt this was a date.

Finn finally broke the silence. "So tell me how this night works. It's so busy out there."

Bridge put her drink down and explained, "We basically recreate the night Ethel Fletcher was taken to be hanged and then burned."

Finn nearly choked on her lager. "And this is a celebration?"

"Yes, because she was saved, and good won the day. The relatives of Ethel Fletcher play her in the parade—this year Diane Fletcher takes over from her mother—and usually Harry plays Lady Hildegard, but since she's out of the country, I persuaded Quade to play her." Bridge looked at her watch. "Oh, bugger. I didn't realize the time. We better get to the start of the parade. I need to say a prayer. Drink up."

❖

Finn watched with amazement at this quaint, weird village custom. They were standing outside the church, while one of the villagers, playing the part of Ethel Fetcher, was brought from the church, dressed in a white smock, and was placed on a horse-drawn cart. Quade, along with a few others, were on horses around the cart, dressed in eighteenth-century clothes, with swords on their hips. They formed a guard around the cart.

Bridge stood in front and said a few words of blessing.

Villagers lined the street down to the start of the river, each holding a fiery torch like some lynch mob from an old movie.

Bridge rejoined Finn and was now carrying a torch. She handed it to Finn and said, "Carry this for me, please. I don't want a smoky smell on my Chanel."

"Perish the thought," Finn joked. "And what about my clothes?"

Bridge raised an eyebrow and looked her up and down. "As much as I love your boyish apparel of sexy jeans, hooded shirt, and of course those motorcycle boots, I don't think they are as prone to smoke damage as Chanel. And besides, you're supposed to be chivalrous. Haven't you been learning anything from Quade?"

Finn held the torch away from them both and leaned into Bridge. "Oh, don't worry. I always follow your instructions."

She was sure she could see Bridge shiver and then stand a little straighter. *She does want me. I know it.*

"That's what I like to hear," Bridge said. The cart started to move off, with Quade and her friends following.

Finn followed Bridge walking behind the cart. The crowds that lined the way started to follow as soon as the cart passed them.

"So this is what it was like all those generations ago?" Finn asked Bridge.

Bridge nodded. "It must have been a terrifying ordeal for Diane's ancestor. If you can imagine, the crowds wouldn't have been as supportive as today. Some were for the witches, and a lot against. Those sympathetic didn't like to make their feelings too well known, or they might have drawn suspicion on themselves."

"I take Mr. Archie angry Winchester doesn't come along to Witch's Night?"

Bridge laughed at her description of him. "No, he stays away. It's a little bit awkward when your ancestor is the villain of the story."

"I don't think angry Archie would mind his ancestor being the villain—in fact, he's probably proud."

"I hope he's not proud that his family nearly got an innocent woman killed. I've always loved Witch's Night since I first came here, because we're not only remembering a dark chapter of the village, we're celebrating the goodness and kindness that one human being can show another, and those that took part in saving the goodness of this village should be celebrated."

Finn squeezed Bridge's hand. "You're right. It is a celebration."

They followed the cart down to the banks of the river at the bridge in the village. Quade got off her horse and approached the cart while the crowd clapped.

Bridge raised her voice to try and be heard over the noise. "Lady Hildegard, or Quade, helps the witch down from the cart, and tells her to be ready for rescue. Which means that Hildegard and her men meet the boat downstream and as soon as the boatmen leave the prisoner in their care, one man rides off with her to a safe house along with Hildegard's lover, Katie, and a dummy is mounted on the pyre."

"She sounds like a real hero, this Hildegard," Finn said.

"Yes, she was, and Harry's idol. She loves to play hero on the night, but Quade is doing a good job."

Finn had a thought. "Does Martha not like to come? I could have pushed her wheelchair."

"That's a sweet thought, but the crowds and noise are a bit much for her."

They followed the barge down the river, and when it went out of sight, all the villagers made their way down to the bonfire at the barn.

## CHAPTER SIXTEEN

The barn was bouncing with music, laughter, and dance. Finn poured herself another pint from the keg of Quade's Axedale Ale, and watched Bridge make her way around the room, sharing a joke, listening, and most of all being available to whoever wanted to talk to her next. She was Finn's perfect idea of what a person of God should be, nothing like her father.

Finn hadn't seen a lot of Bridge since they got to the barn dance, but her eyes always managed to seek her out in the crowd and gaze longingly at those legs that tormented her.

She jumped when someone tapped her shoulder. "Dance with me," Bridge said. She'd gotten lost in her lusty thoughts for a moment and hadn't realized Bridge had walked up behind her.

"What? I don't really—"

"One dance and then I want to talk to you outside, in private."

"Very mysterious," Finn said. "Give me a second."

Finn ran over to the band and asked them to play Bridge's favourite song, then hurried back.

As the strains of the Presley classic started, Bridget said, "Very nice, Magician."

Finn took Bridge into her arms to dance, and said jokingly, "Are you sure you're going to let me lead?"

"I might like to give out instructions, Magician, but I'm still a lady. Lead me."

"Yes, Mistress," Finn replied with a smile.

She could see the fire in Bridge's eyes after that comment, a fire that Finn wanted to consume her.

Finn didn't say anything for the rest of the dance, and neither did

Bridge. They didn't need to. The way Bridge felt and fit in her arms and the words to the song said more than Finn could admit to Bridge—at the moment.

❖

After the dance, they walked outside the barn for some fresh air and found the bonfire grounds just as busy with people. Everyone was standing around the fire enjoying conversation, drinks, and laughter.

"This way." Bridge led them around the back of the barn, where they found one young couple in a heated clinch. They jumped when they saw the vicar, and quickly rearranged their clothes.

"Sorry, Vicar, we—" the young man said.

"Shush now, go and find somewhere a little more discreet, Toby." Finn laughed as they ran off. "Poor kids."

"I know," Bridge said. "There must be nothing worse than coming face-to-face with a dog collar when you're feeling so passionate."

Finn took Bridge's hands and manoeuvred her against the side of the barn, where the young people had themselves been so passionate.

"Oh, I don't know, Bridge. I find you in your dog collar a huge turn on."

Bridge placed one finger in the middle of Finn's chest and pushed her back. That was one of the most intoxicating things about Bridget Claremont. Finn might have had more strength and muscle than her, but Bridge could control or subdue her with a touch or the merest look.

"Now, now, Magician. I came out here to give you something special, not to act like a horny teenager."

"Are you sure, Vicar?" Finn lifted her hand and placed kisses all over the palm. How was she supposed to survive Finn's time in the village without touching her and kissing her? Finnian Kane was intoxicating, but Bridge had to regain control of this situation, and the few drinks that they'd shared were not helping.

On instinct, she gently grasped Finn's infuriating blond fringe and pulled her head up. "Behave, I told you, boy."

That only seemed to increase her sexual arousal, so Bridge fished her gift out of her biker jacket quickly. "This is for you, Finn, from me."

Finn looked confused. "For me? Why?"

"Another tradition of Witch's Night is to give someone who is in need a gift. Just like Hildegard gave the witch the gift of freedom. So I got you this."

"Bridge, I don't know what to say."

"Open it. It won't bite. Not like me," Bridge joked.

Finn smiled and opened the small box. Inside was a pack of cards with a bow tied around them. "Bridge?"

"I wanted to make you feel better after losing your cards, and I thought of these. They are special, and I'm sure you alone would treasure them."

Finn took them out of the box and untied the ribbon.

"Look at the signature on the pack."

Finn gasped. "It can't be."

Bridge nodded. "These have been sitting in my family's collection at our London house for years. Houdini gave my grandfather his own pack of cards and signed them."

Finn's eyes were now full of a torrent of emotion. "Bridge, I can't accept these. They're a family heirloom."

"You can. My mother was more than happy to send them when I told her about you, and my brother thought it would be a wonderful thing for the famous Finnian Kane to use the Houdini cards from our collection."

Finn went to speak but couldn't. She turned away from Bridge and paced to where a few bales of hay were stacked by the barn wall and sat down, staring at her gift.

"Finn, are you okay?"

Was she okay? Finn wasn't quite sure. Thoughts of her past life kept playing over and over in her mind.

Bridge sat down beside her, and Finn said with emotion in her voice, "I can't say thank you enough. When I was young, I was always made to feel bad about my love of cards and magic. My dad—"

Finn covered her face with her hands and shook her head, the cards sitting on her knee.

Bridget put an arm around her. "What about your dad? You can trust me, Finn. Surely you know that."

Finn nodded, and opened the cards, shuffling them and getting a feel for the deck, and she felt the calm that had been missing since she'd destroyed her last pack.

"My dad always made me feel ashamed of my love of magic. He said it was from the devil, and only sinners practiced magic. He caught me with a magic book and cards and he burned them right in front of me. I didn't know then why he was so prejudiced against it, but I did later in life. Anyway, I bought another pack, and Carrie always kept them hidden for me. Dad never bothered her the way he did me. He hated me."

"I'm so sorry he did that to you. Why would he hate you?"

Finn cleared her throat and continued, "When I was young I thought it was because of what I was. I was always drawn towards my masculine side—short hair, jeans, playing sport—and never playing with girls' toys. I thought I embarrassed him. In that Charismatic Christian world, being like that is not a good thing, especially if you were the daughter of—" Finn hesitated.

Bridge brought her hand to the back of Finn's neck, and caressed her. "Who was your father?"

Finn looked up at her and said, "My real name is Judith Maxwell."

Bridget appeared as if she was thinking hard, the name meaning something. "Maxwell, Maxwell," Bridget murmured. Then she was still and turned her face to Finn. "You're the daughter of Gideon Maxwell, the TV evangelist?"

Finn nodded. Everyone knew the name Gideon Maxwell. He'd filled the newspapers for a few years.

"Yes, I'm the daughter of the fake faith healer and preacher who conned thousands and thousands of people out of their hard-earned money and was sent to jail for attempted murder. You can see why if anyone found out what my real name was, my career would be over."

Bridge nodded, and instead of pulling away from her like Finn though she might, she stroked her cheek and said, "Why don't we walk back to your cottage and have a quiet drink."

❖

Bridge had taken Finn's hand when they left the festivities at the barn and had never let go. She didn't care what it looked like to the villagers they passed in the street. Her lost sheep was sad, and she needed to make her feel anchored and safe.

Every so often, Finn would stop briefly and look behind them.

"What's wrong, Finn?"

"I've just got the feeling we're being watched—I've felt that a lot lately," Finn admitted.

"Don't worry about it. You always feel like you're being watched in a small village, and remember God is always watching. Especially troublesome boys like you."

Finn laughed and the tension appeared to be gone.

"Keep going. It's good to get it off your chest," Bridget said.

Finn let out a breath. "I never knew my mother. Gideon told us and everyone who asked that she was dead. My first memories were sitting by the side of the stage with Carrie holding my hand, watching my father not only preach God's word, but heal people and make them overcome with joy and God's love, *slain in the spirit* as they call it. People literally threw money at him for his miracles. I thought he was a superhero or something, someone special God had chosen to channel his power. I believed it all, every word the Bible said, and when Gideon would chastise me for looking like a boy, and I realized I liked girls, I felt like God had forsaken me."

"I've seen the way those so-called miracle workers sweep people into their grasp, and it's so alien from the God I know."

"You're right. Sometimes I think I'm just like him. I can command an arena and show them miracles in return for money."

"That's not true, Finn. You don't promise people otherworldly miracles and take their money in exchange for false hope. In fact you've campaigned against these charlatans."

Finn laughed ruefully. "That's not what the public and press would say if they found out who my father was."

"When did you find out he wasn't a man of God?" Bridge asked.

"I think it was around age ten or eleven that I started to have doubts about him. We travelled around a lot, all over, Britain, Europe, America, Canada. He played to huge arena sized churches, a bit like my shows today. Anyway, I was always moving schools as we went around the world. We were in America, the South somewhere, and I made friends with this boy who was really into magic. We were inseparable, but when I left, as we always had to, he gave me a book on magic and a pack of cards."

"The ones that your father burned?" Bridget said.

"Yeah. Well, as I read and learned everything I could from it, including sleight of hand, cold reading, and suggestion, I started to notice similar tricks in Gideon's act. I became more and more disillusioned, and then one day I went backstage and watched his right-hand man, Simon, reading information from the sign-up sheets all the audience fill out as they come in, and speaking into a headset. It didn't take much to work out what the earpiece in Gideon's ear was for. I felt like God, my whole belief system, was ripped from under me."

"I can imagine," Bridget said. "It must have been so shocking. Did you confront him about it?"

Finn nodded. "He tried to explain to me that God's miraculous works can be difficult to see in everyday life, so he was just helping things along. It was all right to do as long as it brought people close to God."

"What did you do?" Bridget said.

"I learned everything I could about magic so I could understand what he was doing. I told Carrie, and we both began to try to find out everything we could about his past. Turns out he was a failed magician from the performing circuit who found more money in turning to the dark side of faith healing and messages from God."

Bridget looked shocked. "You mean he had no faith?"

Finn shrugged. "Maybe he lied so long that he began to believe his own lies about being called by God, I don't know, but he definitely didn't practise what he preached."

They arrived at the cottage and Finn let them inside and poured Bridge a glass of wine. Finn leaned against the fridge with her bottle of lager and continued with her story. "It's funny, though, even though Carrie knew he was a fake, she never lost her faith in God or the afterlife."

"Belief in God isn't tied to one sect of the Church, or one religion or another, Finn. All you need is a personal relationship with God. When I'm alone with my own thoughts is when I feel him the most."

"Bridge, I was brought up thinking I was wrong—I was made wrong and that there was something bad in me, because of the way I dressed and who I was attracted to. Then—"

Finn clammed up and Bridge walked right up to Finn and put a hand on her chest. "Then?"

"I found out he had been lying to me. One day I opened the door to his dressing room and found him fucking John, his assistant. Can you believe that? He made me think there was something wrong with me, that God didn't love me enough to change my feelings when I prayed for it, and he was gay the whole hypocritical time," Finn said, fury in her tone.

"Shh, it's okay. I know how much hurt you must have inside you."

Finn pushed away from Bridge. "No, you don't. You praise the God that let me think I was broken, that I was evil."

Finn stormed off into the living room, and Bridge found her holding her sister's photograph. Bridge touched Finn's shoulder, and Finn said, "I was fifteen when that happened and I promised myself that I would save all the money I could, and get Carrie and me away from him."

"When did you leave?"

"Around sixteen or seventeen. The authorities were sniffing around my dad's whole set-up. He was preoccupied by an impending fraud investigation, but I still didn't have enough money to go, so I got hold of a bank card for one of his everyday accounts—he kept a few thousand there. I emptied it out and we ran. I've been taking care of Carrie ever since. I don't have anyone to take care of any more."

Bridge turned her around and cupped her face. "Maybe you need someone to take care of you for once in your life."

"You, Bridge?"

Bridge started to speak but couldn't say what was in her heart. She turned away from Finn so that she wouldn't weaken. "You know I can't take that place in anyone's life, Finn. As a friend—"

"Stop hiding who you are, Bridge. You know what's between us. It has been since we first met."

Bridge said nothing. She couldn't turn around or face Finn now. If she did, she might lose control. The woman Bridge had kept locked under her armour for so long was fighting to get out.

Without turning she said, "I need to leave," and headed to the door.

Finn was behind her in a second and put a hand on the door to stop her. "Stop running away from what you feel. That's what you've been preaching to me all this time. I have to face what I've lost, and you have to face who you are."

"And who am I? You seem to know so much, Finn. Who am I?" Bridge said angrily.

"Mistress Black, a passionate woman who knows what she wants and takes it. You are hiding a huge part of yourself behind your faith just so you have the excuse not to love anyone."

Bridge looked furious. "You forget, Magician. You're not my type."

"Then prove it," Finn raged. "Kiss me like you did the other day, and tell me I'm not your type."

"Don't be so ridiculous," Bridge said.

Finn moved to within inches of Bridge's face and said, "Prove it, Mistress. Prove that I'm nothing to you, or are you too frightened?"

Bridge felt such an upsurge of fire, anger, and desire that she responded by kissing Finn with a passion that shocked her. Finn responded, and she felt Finn's hands all over her. Bridge realized as she kissed Finn that she had never felt so much for any one person before. Not even Ellen. When she started to push Finn back onto the couch, she knew the part of her that was Mistress Black would not easily go back into the bottle, not while Finn was around.

Finn lay with Bridge on the couch, and her right hand went straight to those gorgeous legs. She ran her hand up Bridge's leg and grasped her thigh. She remembered Bridge's legs around her on the motorbike, and she got even more turned on. Her hips started to naturally thrust into Bridge beneath her, nothing had ever felt like this, nothing was ever Bridge, and Bridge was everything. Finn was losing herself to the lust she was feeling. She wanted to be inside her, filling her, being everything that Bridge needed. She moved her hand further up Bridge's skirt and felt her silky underwear. She was about to touch Bridge more intimately when she felt her head pulled back by her fringe and her hand slapped.

When Finn came back to her senses the woman looking up at her was the woman Finn had seen glimpses of at their poker night and in the churchyard. It was Mistress Black.

Bridge said, "You're going to have to learn that we don't just take without permission, boy."

Finn groaned out loud. "I knew you were in there, Mistress. Please let me touch you."

Bridge gave her a sly smile. "Oh no. It's not that easy. You pushed me to this, Finn, and no one pushes me."

Finn didn't think she could get any more turned on but she was. She had never considered enjoying being dominated before, she was always the one in control, but with Bridge it was different. Everything was different with Bridge.

"I'm sorry that I pushed you, but I wanted to see what was inside of you."

"Up," Bridge ordered.

Finn did as asked and was surprised when Bridge straddled her lap and started to scratch her fingernails down the sides of her shaved head.

"You think I need to face what's between us, and who I used to be?"

Finn nodded. "Yes, I can help."

"Maybe that's true. Maybe there's some part of me that I haven't come to terms with, but if I have to face it, then you have to face God."

Finn did a double take. "God? Why?"

"You know you're being pulled to church, pulled to God, since you came here. Although you promised me you'd come to church one Sunday, you've been putting it off with excuses. I know in my heart, you feel the need to have the comfort of faith in God that you had as a little girl before your father destroyed it."

Finn was defiant. "I'm Finnian Kane. I do not believe in God, and I don't need him."

Bridge leaned into her and whispered while she ran her fingers through her hair. Finn was turned on, confused, distracted. Every nerve in her body was on fire.

"What about Judith Maxwell?" Finn froze. "What does she believe, and what does she need?"

Finn opened her mouth and nothing came out. She thought back to her childhood, about being that little girl watching her father preach of miracles and wonders of God. She remembered being scared, but knowing that she would never be alone because she always had God on her side. Losing that feeling didn't seem to matter when Carrie was there, and she was surrounded by people while she worked, but now with Carrie gone, and her career on the brink, she had nothing but herself. An emptiness that she wanted Bridge to help her fill.

She took her time and said, "Judith wants to know if there is more, because she believes she spoke with her sister that night and the consequences make her scared."

Bridge softened her touch and rested her forehead against Finn's. "Come to church then. Face what you fear, face what you don't understand any more, and I will face my own past."

Finn nodded and said, "I will if you come out with me for one night and show me the real you. The one that's not a vicar, frightened of what her arsehole of a bishop would say. Mistress Black, let me see her, see you." She felt Bridge stiffen. "If you do, Bridge, I'll never ask it of you again, but we need to explore this. Please—I will be completely discreet. I promise, and you are in charge."

Bridge smiled at that comment. She let out a breath and said,

"Okay. You're right. I need to explore this, but I don't know how it can ever work."

"Don't worry about that just now. Worry about writing a sermon that's going to knock my socks off."

That broke the tension and they both laughed. Bridge slipped off Finn's lap. "I better go."

"Bridge, I had the best time today. Thank you, and thank you for the cards. They mean the world to me." *And so do you.*

Bridge kissed her sweetly on the forehead, and replied, "You're welcome, Magician."

They got up and walked to the door. It was awkward. Finn didn't know if she should kiss her goodbye so she joked to ease the tension. "Next time you give me a present, can I have a signed poster of your mother in that swimsuit?"

Bridge smacked her on the shoulder. "Behave. I don't want to think of you having lustful thoughts about my mother, thank you."

Finn rubbed the back of her head bashfully. Aching to have one last touch, she pulled Bridget into a hug.

"Goodnight, Bridge. Thanks for everything."

"Goodnight."

Finn opened the door and was startled by a flash. "Something wrong?" Bridge said.

"Just thought I saw something. It's nothing."

When Bridge walked away down the path, Finn had the feeling of being watched for the second time that day.

*If there is a God, I hope he wasn't watching me with my hands all over his vicar.*

# CHAPTER SEVENTEEN

The next morning Finn felt sick with nerves. She was stepping back into a church after all these years, and it wasn't easy.

She straightened her tie and splashed on some aftershave. It was a long time since she had worn a suit, and she didn't feel comfortable, but Bridge told her to be smart, and she was learning she would do anything for Bridge.

"Why did I agree to this?" *Because you want to please her, and face your past.*

She walked over to her bedroom mirror and put wax in her hair before combing her fringe back into a top knot. Finn thought that was the smartest she could make her hair. She looked over at the picture of Carrie and her, backstage at one of her shows, and said, "I bet you're laughing your head off at me, Carr. Making myself look smart and going to church."

Then it hit Finn what she thought. She was now assuming Carrie was somewhere else, somewhere better. Was it just wishful thinking?

Finn shook her head and was disgusted at the way she used to patronize people's need to believe in a spiritual world after a loved one's death, but the feeling was palpable. She still felt connected to Carrie as if the tethers of love and family were unbroken. She took a few seconds and closed her eyes. In her mind's eye she could see a smiling Carrie standing beside her, with her hand on her shoulder.

"I love you, Carrie."

Finn felt a ripple of cold air. She snapped her eyes open, turned around, and saw her bedroom curtain move. "Carrie?"

She nearly jumped out of her skin when someone banged the cottage door. "Jesus fucking Christ!"

Finn hurried downstairs and opened the door to find a smiling

Quade there. "Morning, mate. Bridge said you were going to church this morning, and I thought we could walk together."

Finn raised a quizzical eyebrow and said, "More like she sent you to make sure I get there."

"Well, whatever. I'm glad of the company and it's best to do what Bridge says, in my experience," Quade joked.

"Okay, give me a second." Just before Finn went back in to get her wallet, and her pack of cards for her top pocket, she realized that Quade had on jeans, boots, but a smarter shirt and blazer. "Wait, we can wear jeans? Bridge said I had to wear a suit."

Quade smiled. "It's a country parish, very informal. If you've been up since half past four, looking after animals, you're lucky the farmers get washed and put on a smarter shirt, far less a suit."

Finn let out a sigh. She would have been so much more comfortable in jeans, but if that's what Bridge wanted, then fine.

Finn and Quade walked through the village enjoying the early morning sun and crisp, cold air.

"So," Quade said, "did you enjoy Witch's Night?"

"It was great. I guess things like that make living in a small village something special."

"Yeah, you could say that. I love life here, though it would be even better to share it with someone," Quade said with a sigh.

"The farmer wants a wife, eh?" Finn joked.

Quade laughed and pushed her hands into her jeans pockets. "Something like that."

"You need to get out of Axedale for a night or two with me and visit some gay pubs and clubs in London. The women would love a strong farmer like you."

Quade looked terrified at the thought. "Um...thanks, but I doubt sophisticated city girls would much like the life of a farmer's wife. Anyway, what happened to you and Bridge last night? You disappeared."

Finn got nervous suddenly, remembering Bridge on her lap kissing her, and making Finn want her like no one had before. "We just went to talk."

Quade put a hand on her chest and stopped her. "Finn, did something more serious happen?"

Finn sighed. "It's complicated."

"Isn't it always." Quade pointed to the bench by the bus stop and said, "Sit."

As kind and as friendly as Quade was, she was big and tough, and looked intimidating when she wanted to.

Finn sat and Quade stood over her. "Is this the part where you threaten me with bodily harm if I hurt her?"

"Something like that. Bridge has made a good life here, and the church and her friends are her life. You know the position she is in, and the homophobic bishop she has breathing down her neck. So if you care about Bridge, you take it at her pace and be discreet. Especially considering who you are."

"I know what she has at stake, Quade, but we have to explore what's between us. She is the most wonderful and infuriating woman I've ever met, and she's helped me so much. I promise I will go at her pace—besides, no one tells Bridge what to do."

"Very true." Quade laughed and then held out a hand to help Finn up. "Bridge means a lot to the people of the village, Finn, and remember—we're country people and farmers, so we have lots of shotguns and lots of land to bury you on."

"Very funny. Get me to church, or the vicar will have a fit."

Quade started to stride forward. "Yeah, keep up. I don't want her to bring that whip out. It's not my thing."

"Wait. What whip?" Finn jogged to keep up with her.

Finn's heart thudded and her palms were sweaty, as she and Quade sat in church waiting for the service to start. The church organ music played in the background, and only made the knot in her stomach worse. *You're doing this for Bridge.*

Then everyone stood, and Bridge walked out to the pulpit. Her worry floated away as she listened to Bridge welcome everyone and start to give out some parish notices. This was Bridge, and there was nothing to worry about when she was there.

The Church of England service was very different to the ones she had been involved with as she grew up. There were no flash tricks, loud music, or people being whipped into unnatural excitement. It was reflective and calming almost, and Bridge had been right about church being more than praising God. She felt like an important part of the community here.

As Bridge spoke, Finn couldn't help but remember Bridge sitting on her lap and kissing her. It was entirely wrong to be thinking these thoughts, but they made her feel even more excited.

They sang a hymn together and Bridge prepared to start her sermon. "I've taken for my reading today the parable of the lost sheep."

Bridge looked at her then and gave her a small smile. Finn could only smile back, and thought, *I'm falling in love with you.*

Once the service was over, everyone filed out of the church, shaking Bridge's hand at the church door. When it was Finn's turn she squeezed her hand, and said, "I loved the sermon, Vicar. Very appropriate."

Bridge smiled. "Did I knock your socks off then?"

"You always do, Bridge." They gazed at each other a little too long and Quade gave Finn a soft nudge in the back.

"Sorry. Will I see you later, Vicar?" Finn said hopefully.

Bridge nodded. "Go to the pub with Quade, and I'll join you there soon. We usually have Sunday lunch at Axedale but since Harry and Annie are away, we thought we'd have a pub lunch. I need to pop into Mrs. Castle's on my way."

"See you soon."

Finn wandered down to the church gates to wait on Quade, and Mr. Butterstone approached her. "Morning, Ms. Kane. It was wonderful to see you in church this morning. Has the vicar asked you yet? She must have done, since you've come this morning. You must be feeling a lot better."

Finn hadn't a clue what he was talking about. "I'm sorry, Mr. Butterstone. I'm not quite sure what you mean."

"Our winter show. When you came to the village, we on the parish council thought it would be wonderful if you could perform and maybe direct our village show. We'd love to see your magic performance, but the vicar insisted we wait until she got to know you a bit better, and then she'd ask you to do it. I know it's just a little village show, but it would keep you well practised before you return to your big shows in the city."

Finn's heart sank at the reminder that there was another life waiting for her back in London. A life where the illusion of Finnian Kane took people's money for cheap magic tricks, just like her father, and a life that would pull her away from this tranquil little village where she could be herself. And away from Bridge, the woman she was falling in love with.

"Excuse me, Mr. Butterstone," Finn said and hurried out of the church gates, emotion and confusion threating to spill over.

❖

Bridge looked in the pub, and asked around if anyone had seen Finn. When she'd seen Mr. Butterstone talking to Finn, she just knew he was going to say something about the village show.

She finally spotted Finn on the bench where they had shared their first kiss. She walked up and said, "May I sit?"

"It's a free country," a moody Finn replied.

Bridge sat and sighed. "I'm sorry, Finn. I—"

Finn turned on her quickly. "Is my show the only thing people will ever see, Bridge?"

"I don't believe that, darling," Bridge said.

Finn held her face in her hands and said, "I'm a con artist just like my father. I use the illusion of Finnian Kane to take people's money, just like him."

"Do you really believe that, Finn?" Bridge said.

Finn let out a breath and stared down at her feet. "No, not really, but you know I'm not ready to perform. It's one thing showing you and some kids a few tricks, but performing in a show? I can't be that person I am in London, and in the media. I just don't know if I have that in me any more."

Bridge took a chance and grasped Finn's hand. "I know that, Finn. I just kept putting Mr. Butterstone off, but he was too eager and said something to you. I would never put you in a position where you feel uncomfortable."

"If I did something like that, the press would find me. I just can't."

"I'm sorry if it upset you," Bridge said.

Finn squeezed Bridge's hand. "For one split second, I thought maybe this wasn't real, maybe what I've found here is an illusion."

"No, Finn, this is real. Trust me?"

"Always." Finn stood and pulled Bridge up into a hug.

They lingered awhile and Bridge said, "We better get to the pub. Poor Quade will be waiting."

When they walked off, they held hands and neither made comment on it.

## CHAPTER EIGHTEEN

The next week dragged slowly, as both Bridge and Finn were looking forward to their night out in London. Bridge had been feeling the excitement building all day. It was just like all those years ago, a time when going out and having fun were the only things she had to worry about.

She put her bags in the boot of Harry's car, and the thought of what was inside made her shiver. Before her dog collar, Bridge's kink outfits were her costume and her armour. Kink expressed that big part of her personality so perfectly, but was she really ready to face it?

Bridge stopped and leaned against the car, as doubt and fear started to spread through her.

*I could lose everything.*

Her home, her career, the safe life she had built up for all these years.

Fear and the memories of those dark days after Ellen broke her heart started to grip her body.

"I can't do this." Bridge let out a breath, pulled out her phone, and looked up Finn's number.

If she cancelled, she ran the risk of losing Finn forever, and hurting her the way Bridge had been. She would also be saying goodbye to this part of herself, the part that was Mistress Black, who was screaming to get out. She thought about her bishop and what he would do to her if he ever found out.

*But I'm falling in love with her.*

Bridge's finger hovered over Finn's number. *Safety or...*

Then a feeling of righteous indignation came over her. Why should she be put in this position? Why should she have to choose? This was part of who she was.

She slammed down the boot of the car and said, "Claremonts don't run and hide."

Finn was right. She had to recognize and explore this part of herself again, and even if it was just for tonight, this was for her, her chance to be totally true to herself, and she would not feel guilty about it any more.

She walked around to the front door of the car, and reapplied her deep red lipstick in the car door mirror, then took her sunglasses from her biker jacket and slipped them on.

Her outfit of figure-hugging black jeans, tight black rollneck cashmere sweater, and black heels very much suited her mood today. The black sunglasses only finished off the look.

Bridge smirked at herself in the mirror. "Welcome back, Mistress Black. We have a magician to put on her knees."

The black Aston Martin suited the energy she was feeling completely. If only Harry could see her.

❖

Finn sat on the couch waiting on Bridge picking her up. Bridge said she'd commandeer one of Lady Harry's cars. Finn shuffled her cards nervously.

"Why did I get myself into this?" When she had suggested this night out, it seemed like the most exciting idea in the world, and it still was, but she was also nervous. What if when she saw the Mistress Black side of Bridge, she didn't like it? It was one thing finding Bridge and her dismissive top attitude different and sexy, but what if in reality she didn't like being with the dominatrix that was Mistress Black? She had always been the one who did the running, the demanding, the leading. Maybe this was a step too far? And that would be tragic, because she was sure she was falling for Bridge in a big way.

Her phone beeped with a message. *I'm outside.*

Finn let out a breath and put her cards away safely in her bag. "Well, this is it, Finn. You wanted this."

She threw her bag over her shoulder and said to Carrie's photo, "Wish me luck, Carrie."

When Finn opened her front door, she gasped. "Bloody hell."

Bridge leaned against a black Aston Martin, looking a lot like one of the Bond girls her mother played, arms crossed, in tight black jeans, black sweater, an extremely high pair of heels, and black sunglasses.

Bridge had clearly left the vicar at home. She was standing taller and carrying herself with more confidence. This was Mistress Black.

She lowered her sunglasses along the bridge of her nose and gave Finn a smoky look. "Do I have to wait all day, Magician?"

*Jesus Christ.* She had no idea why she'd been worried about being comfortable with this dynamic that was growing between them. At this moment Finn would have crawled over to the car and kissed Bridge's shoes. There was nothing contrived about this energy between them. It was natural and it appeared that they both fed off it. Finn only prayed she would be allowed to touch Bridge.

"Did you hear me?" Bridge said.

Finn jumped into action, locked her cottage door, and walked down to the car. She tried to play it as cool as she could. "When you said you were borrowing one of your friend's cars, I didn't think you'd roll up in an Aston Martin."

Bridge smiled. "You wanted me to show you the other side of me, what my life used to be like. This is it, champagne and sports cars. Put your bag in and we can get going."

Finn put her bag in the back seat and got in the front. The interior was so gorgeous it was making her horny. She turned to watch Bridge slip into the driver's seat and throw her heels into the back seat, and felt even more aroused. She needed to touch Bridge at least once.

"Bridge?" Finn leaned over to kiss her, and Bridge grasped her chin.

"Oh dear, oh dear, oh dear. We are starting off on the wrong foot, boy. What did I tell you about taking? You don't want to be bad, do you?"

Finn smiled. "Maybe I want to do bad things with you."

Bridge laughed and switched on the engine. "I bet you do. Let's go."

❖

Bridge had booked them into a small hotel around the corner from the private members' club she was taking Finn to. The club was run by some old friends of hers from her Red's days, and she was sure they would be discreet. She couldn't face going to Red's again and facing her painful memories, so this was the next best thing.

She had gotten two rooms to assure discretion but there was an interconnecting door between the two. Bridge sat at her dressing table applying her make-up after showering, and she was already getting that tingle of excitement she used to get when she went out regularly. It amazed her how easily Mistress Black came out from under her armour. It never had been difficult to keep that side of her under wraps, but since Finn came to the village and slammed the cottage door in her face, Mistress Black had wanted Finn, and on her knees.

Bridge finished with her eye pencil and blotted her lipstick one last time. This was it, the moment she had been most excited about, donning her black leather corset and leather miniskirt. It crossed her mind how much she would love to have Finn dress her, but if she invited that now, they might not make it out of the hotel room.

A little voice at the back of her mind told her to stop this before it went too far, but her need to explore her feelings for Finn were too loud.

As she dressed, Bridge felt a rush of confidence and power. The leather, the way her corset held her, the feel of her sheer stockings and suspenders that hung below the hem of her skirt, and her high, high heels magnified that part of her personality, the part that loved to control, to coerce her play partner to their ultimate pleasure. She loved giving someone that, and to think of holding Finn on the edge of pleasure before giving her release made Bridge shiver.

She checked her corset in the full-length mirror on the wardrobe, and considered the similarity to dressing in her vestments. Each costume amplified another part of her personality. Both were part of Bridge, and she'd always believed that the two couldn't coexist, but that need that Finn was bringing out in her made her wonder if she was wrong.

There was a knock at the connecting door. "Wait," Bridge said firmly.

She went over to the bed and picked up the last piece of her outfit, the part that made her persona of Mistress Black complete—her riding crop.

Bridge stood by the four-poster bed and said, "Come in."

Finn opened the door and walked in. She stopped suddenly when she saw Bridge and said, "Jesus fucking Christ."

❖

Finn could hardly breathe at the sight before her. Bridget looked sexy, exquisite, terrifying…all of the above. She wore a tight black leather corset and a tiny black leather skirt that was so short Finn could see her lace underwear and the tops of her stockings.

Finn longed to touch and kiss those legs that had tormented her. Bridget's bright red lipstick matched the nails that she longed to feel dig into her back.

Bridge stood nonchalantly by the bed, tapping a riding crop on her thigh. "That mouth of yours is filthy, boy."

"Sorry."

Bridge cupped her ear, "What was that? Speak up."

"I'm sorry," Finn said again.

Bridge laughed and strolled over to her. "So much for the arrogant little brat who turned up in my village. I soon brought you into line, didn't I?"

"Yes," Finn said. Her heart was hammering out of her chest. She felt a swat on the side of her leg from the riding crop.

"Yes, what?"

"Yes, Mistress," Finn said quickly. Every time she used that title, it made her even more turned on, but she had a feeling she would be driven to distraction all night, and who knew if Bridge would allow her any relief.

Bridge walked around her, assessing her outfit. Finn had gone up to London the week before to buy something appropriate to wear. She wasn't quite sure what the correct thing would be, so she'd opted for something simple, black jeans and black sleeveless T-shirt, and she made sure her hair was just how Bridge liked it.

Bridge stopped in front of her and was silent for a few seconds, then placed the end of her riding crop on her forehead. "This will do, I suppose," Bridge said as she drew the crop down Finn's face and chest and, finally, down her belt buckle, and rested it on her crotch.

Finn noticed recognition and excitement in Bridge's eyes as she quickly moved closer to Finn. Bridge took the crop away and out of the blue grasped Finn's crotch lightly.

"My, my, what do we have here? You like wearing a cock?"

"Yes, Mistress," Finn croaked.

Bridge got even closer and whispered in her ear, "A bit presumptuous, isn't it, boy? Do you really think I'll allow you to use this with me?"

*Jesus!* Finn screamed inside. She had never been as turned on as this. She was so wet and needed Bridge so badly. "I didn't presume. I just thought I'd like to wear it for you, Mistress."

Bridge softly massaged the bulge in her jeans. "Well, we'll just need to see how much of a good boy you can be. Get my jacket."

Finn was breathing heavily, and they hadn't even done anything yet. "We don't have to go out to the club if you don't want to, Mistress. We could just stay here—" Her sentence was ended by a strong thwack to her backside by Bridge's riding crop. "God," she groaned in surprise.

"Did I ask for your opinion, boy?"

It was exciting when Bridge called her *boy*. It was another way of stripping down her ego and making her feel she belonged to her mistress. She wanted more than anything to be Mistress Black's boy on a permanent basis.

"No, you didn't. Sorry, Mistress."

"Go and get my jacket." Bridge pointed to a black raincoat hanging on the back of the door. She hurried to get it, and held it while Bridge slipped into it. It was long enough to cover Bridge's outfit, so that she could walk to the club without too many strange looks.

"We'll go for a few dances and then I'll see how I feel. Oh, one more thing." Bridge went to her bag on the bed and took out a leather wrist strap with a chain and a leather handle at the other end. Bridge wrapped the strap around Finn's wrist and yanked the handle, showing Finn was now under her control.

Finn felt crazy and they weren't even at the club yet. She said desperately, "Mistress, please? Let's stay here. I can't—"

Instead of being reprimanded this time, Bridge leaned in and gave her the softest of kisses, then whispered, "Trust me to take care of you. A few dances are all I want."

Finn immediately calmed. "Yes, Mistress."

❖

Bridge sat back and sipped her drink. She had loved the look of excitement and nervousness on Finn's face as they came down into the club. It felt so good to share this with her.

When they arrived, Bridge got them drinks from the bar and nodded to a few old acquaintances. She loved the look of envy from the other women as they admired Finn, and then saw the wrist strap and chain binding Finn to her. It was such a rush.

Even as she'd planned this night out, Bridge never thought they would actually sleep together. She simply thought it would be fun, and exciting. But as soon as Finn came into her hotel room, and looked at her the way she did, Bridge was sure she wanted her.

It was a risk to her career, her way of life, but she couldn't not have Finn touch her. All she could think of was slipping Finn's cock inside herself, and driving them both wild.

Bridge stood and pulled Finn's wrist strap. "Let's dance, boy."

The music had a deep heavy beat, and the atmosphere in the club was heady with sex. Finn slipped her arms around Bridge's waist, and Bridge held her riding crop across Finn's backside, keeping her as close and under control as possible.

They started to sway to the music, and Finn rubbed her face in the crook of Bridge's neck. "I love the way you smell, Mistress."

"Do you?"

Finn nodded. "Can I kiss you?"

"Yes." Bridge groaned as she felt small kisses all over her neck, and then finally Finn kissed her on the lips. Their kiss was slow and deep. Tasting, needing, showing how much they wanted each other. Finn's hips started to grind into hers, as if Finn wasn't even aware any more that they were on a dance floor surround by strangers.

Finn sucked her tongue, and Bridge responded by scratching her nails down Finn's head and neck. When they broke apart, Bridge looked at Finn's heavy-lidded eyes, and thought, *I'm falling in love with her. I need her.*

Bridge didn't care that they'd only had one drink and one dance. She needed Finn and she needed her now.

"Let's go back to the hotel."

Finn nodded enthusiastically.

❖

The walk back to the hotel was the longest of Finn's life. Her body was on fire for Bridge, and touching her just couldn't come quick enough.

When they walked through the bedroom door, Finn broke. She pushed Bridge back against the door and began to kiss her roughly.

Bridge grasped her hair and yanked her head back. "I think you're forgetting yourself, boy. You think you can just take from me?"

"I'm sorry, I just need you so much, Bridge."

Bridge pulled her harder. "Excuse me? Is that how you address your mistress?"

Finn realized her mistake and quickly said, "I'm sorry. I need you, Mistress Black."

Bridge pushed her away, let the wrist strap drop, and walked over to the bed. "I think you need to learn some restraint, boy."

Bridge laid down her riding crop and took off her coat. "Drop your jeans, and stand against the door."

Finn experienced a feeling of excitement mixed with fear. She hesitated, and Bridge said again, more forcefully this time, "Drop those jeans and turn around, palms against the door."

Finn's fingers tremored as she unbuttoned her jeans, and let them fall to her ankles, leaving her in a pair of tight jockey shorts.

"Take everything off up top too," Bridge added.

Finn quickly pulled off her T-shirt and sports bra, then placed her palms against the wooden door. The cold was a sharp contrast to the heat all over her body.

Finn heard a zip and some shuffling behind her. She imagined Bridge was taking off her leather skirt. Her sex throbbed uncontrollably, and she wondered if she'd be able to survive whatever her mistress had in mind.

*My mistress.*

Finn's ears pricked up when she heard Bridge's heels clatter against the wooden floor.

*Please, don't let me disappoint her.*

She heard Bridge stop behind her. "I would have liked to have your cock inside me by now, but you had to take when I made it clear that wasn't allowed."

"I'm sorry, Mistress."

Finn shivered when she felt the tip of Bridge's riding crop trace its way from her neck, down her back, coming to rest on her backside.

"Maybe I need to make things clearer for you."

Finn jumped in shock when Bridge gave her a thwack. Not hard enough to be too painful, but enough to make her gasp, and her sex throb even more.

She got another two swats to her behind, and Bridge stepped close to her. "How did that feel?"

"Good, I'd like more," Finn said.

Bridge laughed softly. "I thought you'd turn out to be a bad boy. Only four more then."

She stood back and gave her two swats, and paused to listen to Finn's groans of pleasure. Bridge had never experienced this kind of arousal while playing with someone. She cared for Finn so much, it made everything more intense. She gave Finn another two quick hits, and told her to turn around.

She grasped Finn's hair tightly, and pulled her into a deep passionate kiss, before pulling back. "That's my good boy. Kick off those jeans and follow me."

Finn looked ready to explode, and Bridge wasn't much better. She needed Finn to touch her. Bridge scratched her nails down Finn's chest and stomach, and then began to massage the bulge in her jockey shorts.

"If you're a good boy, I'll let you use your cock. *If* you're good."

"I'll be good, Mistress," Finn said quickly.

"Let's see. You like magic, Finn? I think I know your magic words."

Finn looked confused for a second, and then Bridge leaned forward and whispered, "Kneel, boy."

Finn dropped in a second. "Yes, please. I've been waiting to worship at your feet since I met you, Mistress."

Bridge gazed lovingly at Finn down on her knees, and stroked her face gently. "Worship your mistress then."

Finn prostrated herself so that she could kiss her shoes, and Bridge said, "Put your head on the floor."

Finn did as asked and was breathing heavily, no doubt wondering what was coming next. Bridge carefully put her stiletto on top of Finn's head, allowing the heel to dig into Finn's cheek.

It gave Bridge such a rush to watch the formerly arrogant celebrity on her knees, delighting in being under Bridge's heel and control.

"What do you want, Finn?"

Finn groaned, and gasped. "I want to be allowed to lick and kiss your feet and legs, Mistress."

Bridge was so wet, and all she could think about was Finn's tongue on her sex. She lifted her foot and said, "You may."

Finn complied, gave lots of licks and kisses to her heels, and then kissed her way up Bridge's ankles and shins. Bridge knew how much Finn loved her legs, so she let her linger a while longer before pulling her head back by the hair. "I need you to lick a lot higher. Do you want to make Mistress feel good?"

Finn threw her arms around Bridge's legs, and buried her face in Bridge's sex, trying to lick and bite through the lacy material of her underwear.

"Wait." Bridge stepped back and quickly took off her underwear before sitting on the edge of the bed. "Come and taste me, boy."

Finn was over like a shot and kissed her way up Bridge's thighs. It had been so long since Bridge had been touched like this, the feeling was almost overwhelming. When Finn's tongue finally licked the whole length of her sex, Bridge called, "Yes, Finn! Just like that. Good boy," as she ran her fingers through that wonderful hair of Finn's that attracted her so much.

It was clear that Finn loved her heels, so Bridge leaned back and slipped her legs over Finn's shoulders, and dug her heels into her back. She heard Finn moan into her sex, and then suck her clit between her lips.

Bridge's head fell back and she moaned as her orgasm grew fast. All her fears about what this relationship meant for her life were forgotten. All Bridge cared about were Finn's mouth, lips, and tongue, and how good Finn made her feel.

Her hips bucked and her heels dug further into Finn's back as she approached the pinnacle of her release. "Faster, faster." Bridge moaned. "Good boy, good boy—"

Then Bridge's orgasm hit her hard, and took her breath away. "Finn," she shouted as the waves of pleasure spread all throughout her body.

In this moment, she felt whole again. The two sides of herself which she had so carefully kept apart, Finn had made whole in one delicious moment.

When she regained her breath, she looked down at Finn, who was breathing hard and looking like she was going to shake apart.

"Take off your jockey shorts and get up on the bed. You've been very good."

Finn nearly tripped trying to get out of her underwear and up onto the bed. Bridge straddled her and began slowly to take off her corset. She threw it to the side and grabbed Finn's hand and placed it on her breast.

"Do you like that?"

"Yes, please kiss me, Bridge."

She let that slip go, since Finn was feeling so emotional, and leaned over to kiss her. Bridge slipped her hand between them and grasped Finn's strap-on. Finn groaned. "Do you like that?"

Finn nodded, and Bridge said, "Do you want to come inside me?"

"Jesus, yes, Mistress. I need you so much."

She leaned over and kissed Finn's lips softly. "How could I refuse my beautiful boy?"

"Yes, I'm yours," Finn replied.

Bridge positioned herself over Finn's hips, grasped her cock, and lowered herself onto it. She was so wet, Finn's cock slipped in easily, and they both groaned when it filled her up.

"Fuck, Bridge, please can I touch you?" Finn pleaded.

Bridge took off Finn's wrist strap and threw it away, and placed Finn's hands on her hips.

"I'm going to take care of you, darling. Just relax and let go, okay?"

"Yes," Finn gasped.

Bridge started to roll her hips and Finn thrust inside her. Normally she would withhold her partner's orgasm till the very last moment, but this was different. This wasn't just sex—it was so much more. Even though Bridge wouldn't admit it out loud, there was love growing between them, and she couldn't ignore Finn's emotional and physical need any longer.

Finn's hips started to pump faster, and Bridge met them just as fast as she lifted and impaled herself on Finn's strap-on.

"Fuck, Mistress. I'm going to come soon. You feel so good." Finn reached up and pulled her down into a passionate kiss.

Bridge broke away, and said, "Are you going to come inside me, boy?"

"Yeah," Finn gasped, "soon."

Bridge was so close to her second orgasm, but she wanted to come with Finn. She whispered something that she thought might tip Finn over. "I would have you keep your cock on all the time, wherever we are, so that I knew my beautiful boy was ready to serve me and pleasure me when I needed it. Would you like that?"

Finn leaned back and closed her eyes tightly. "Coming, coming now."

"Yes, yes, come for me." Bridge watched the orgasm crash over Finn, and heard her cry out, "Fuck!"

That was all Bridge needed. She ground her hips onto Finn and let go of all her restraint.

❖

Early the next morning, Bridge lay awake watching Finn sleep. Bridge didn't think she had seen anything more beautiful. Finn had her arm slung across Bridge's waist and her head tucked just below her breast, her hair flopping across her face.

Bridge stroked the hair away from her eyes, and loved the feel of her silky blond locks so much she continued running her fingers through it. Finn let out a little sigh of contentment. There was something very innocent about Finn. As accomplished a woman as she was and as controversial a figure as she might be, Bridge could see that so much of Finn was the little girl who had been let down, disappointed, and deceived by her father and, as she thought, God. She'd gotten through it by looking after her sister, Carrie. Being the tough one, the strong one, fighting against the world to give them both a life. Now Carrie was gone, and there was no one to fight for, to keep busy and successful for every day.

She gently caressed Finn's cheek with her fingers. "You're beautiful like an angelic boy, and you need someone to love you and look after you, don't you?"

Bridge would give anything to be mistress of Finn's heart and her body, enabling her to walk out to her audience of hundreds of thousands, to perform with freedom, knowing that Bridget was there waiting for her, taking care of her, but above all loving her.

But that could never be, could it? Bridget knew she could never be with Finn and be celibate. Finn brought out such passion in her that she had to express herself physically.

Would it come down to a choice? Could she choose to give up the Church, the village, and her life for Finn? But could she really survive losing Finn and her heart breaking again?

Bridge needed to think. She got up and got dressed, then left a note on the pillow for Finn that she would be back shortly.

She sighed and stroked Finn's face one last time. *I'm not falling in love. I am in love.*

❖

As soon as Finn read the note on her pillow, she knew where Bridge would be, and she had to get to her quickly before the past made her run away from what they had.

She pulled on her clothes and hurried out of the hotel. She ran the half mile down to where Red's was and saw Bridge standing on the pavement outside, staring at the club.

When she got close enough, Finn said, "Bridge? Are you all right?"

"How did you know where I'd be?" Bridge asked.

"I guessed you'd want to come to Red's to relive your memories."

Bridge sighed. "Why do you think I'd want to do that?"

Finn walked closer and took her hand. "Because when you woke up with me this morning, you admitted to yourself that we were falling in love with each other. You got frightened and came here to remind yourself why falling in love is a bad idea."

Bridge turned to look at Finn, and she had tears in her eyes. "You're very sure of yourself, Finnian Kane."

"I'm a mentalist, I know how the human mind works, but I also know you, Bridge. We shared something so special last night. You trusted me. You showed me that part of yourself you've kept hidden for so long. That's why I know you care about me, and that we have something special."

Bridge focused her gaze forward again and said nothing for a few minutes. "You know I can't be this person when we go back to Axedale."

Finn's heart sank. "This is who you are, Bridge. You must face the fact you are a woman of God, who enjoys a normal, healthy sex life. The Church are the ones who are wrong, and you've told me that you have colleagues who have managed to live a normal life. Please, Bridge, I—"

"Don't, Finn. I need time, time to think. Let's go home."

Finn was terrified that when they returned to Axedale, and Bridge was surrounded by the church and everything she thought she might lose, Bridge would retreat from her. Perhaps for good.

## CHAPTER NINETEEN

For the next few days, Bridge spent her time praying and trying to come to terms with her feelings for Finn. She felt in her heart that God did not want her to turn her back on a loving and fulfilling relationship, but the Church was way behind where she was sure God wanted them to be. After evening services, Bridge walked up to the stables at Axedale. Her mind was going at a million miles an hour, and she thought feeding the horses might help her clear her thoughts. She had seen much less of Finn since their excursion, and yet she thought about her even more. Deep inside she knew that when she went to London with Finn, she had opened a Pandora's box. Not only were there the concerns about her vocation and her job, there was also a deep-seated fear that she would have to choose between her love of the Church, and her growing love for Finn. And even if she could take a chance and pursue this, Finn would leave sometime. Finn had demands and commitments that would force her to leave, and she would be heartbroken.

Bridge took out her phone and dialled Harry's number, but it just went to her voicemail. "Hi, Harry, um…it's nothing important. I just wanted a chat. Bye."

She felt tears start to fall from her eyes, but heard the slamming of a car door outside, so she quickly wiped them away.

Quade came walking into the stable. "Bridge, you are a hard woman to get hold of. I called you a few times, but it just went to voicemail."

Bridge forced a small smile on her face. "Sorry, Quade. I've needed some time to myself."

Quade leaned against the stall and sighed. "Is this to do with our magician friend?"

She thought about saying no, but she couldn't lie to Quade. "Yes, mostly. How did you know?"

"Finn's been working with me today. Said she needed to take her mind off things with some hard work. Hasn't seemed to help much—she's had face like a a wet weekend all day."

She knew Finn was hurting too, but Finn just didn't see the risks she was taking. Bridge stroked the horse's soft nose. "Yes, it's about Finn. I'm falling in love with her."

"Jesus Christ," Quade said.

Bridge's head snapped around. "Everyone has such bad language around me. I think you all forget I'm a vicar."

"I'm sorry. What are you going to do? It's clear Finn feels the same. She's like a lovesick puppy."

"I have no idea."

Bridge heard another car door slam shut. "Who's that?"

"Finn, she was following me in another truck," Quade said.

"Oh, hell's bells," Bridge said in a panic. "I can't face her right now."

But it was too late. Finn walked in before she had the chance to leave. "Hi, sorry to interrupt," Finn said.

"Don't worry." Quade clapped her on the back. "You helped me out a lot today, Finn. Could you do me one last favour and drive Bridge home?"

Bridget tensed immediately. She was being set up and she didn't like it. "It's okay, I'll walk home."

"No, I can take you," Finn said. "I'm going that way anyway."

"Great," Quade said. "Thanks again, Finn, and I'll see you later, Bridge."

Then they were alone and there was an awkwardness in the air.

Finn finally broke the silence. "Do you come up here a lot, Bridge?"

Bridge gave Willow one last carrot and brushed down her skirt from the stray bits of straw and dust. "I try to come up every night. I promised Riley I'd feed her horse its nightly treat of carrots and make sure she isn't lonely."

Finn stepped beside her and put her hands on the stall door, so their fingers were inches apart. Bridge couldn't take her eyes off them, and ached to touch her.

"Riley? That's your Harry and Annie's daughter, yes?"

Bridge nodded. "Yes, that's right."

Finn shook her head angrily. "Why are you being so cold, Bridge? You can't keep hiding from me."

"I'm not hiding from you. I'm trying to sort out things in my mind."

"Things?" Finn was getting so frustrated. "You want to sort out things? What, like how much we feel for each other?"

Bridge moved to walk to the door, but Finn caught her waist and pushed her back against the side of the stables and said, "How we can't keep our hands off each other?"

When Finn moved in for a kiss, Bridge pulled her head back by her fringe, and said firmly, "We don't take without asking. I thought I had made that perfectly clear."

*Oh God.* Finn groaned internally. That voice, the way Bridge talked to her, made Finn's sex throb instantly. She would do anything for this woman if she commanded it, but she had to want her too.

"I'm sorry. I—the past few days have been so hard. I just wanted to see you. I can't stop thinking about you."

Bridge cupped Finn's cheeks and whispered, "I know. I just need time to talk to God and make sure I'm doing the right thing. Please, darling. Just give me a little more time."

Finn nodded, and sighed audibly. "If that's what you want."

"I do. Drive me back to the vicarage, would you?"

"My pleasure," Finn said.

Finn helped Bridge up into the Land Rover and started to drive her home. Although she had pledged to give Bridge time, her frustration was still there, and it was eating away at her. They should be cherishing every moment of their relationship, not worrying about what God thought, what the bishop thought. This was *their* life. Yet again God was dictating Finn's happiness, and she didn't like it.

She pulled into the vicarage driveway and saw a car she didn't recognize.

"Bloody hell," Bridge exclaimed. "It's Bishop Sprat."

"Your bishop?" Finn said.

Bridge nodded, and was clearly panicking. "Why is he here? We don't have an appointment. He's going to think something is going on."

"There is something going on," Finn noted.

"Please, Finn. This is my life."

"Fine, I'll help you out, then leave." Finn slammed out of her door and walked around to the other side of the truck, just as Bishop Sprat's chauffeur was opening his door and he got out.

Finn helped Bridge out and saw Bishop Sprat staring at them accusingly.

"I'll see you later, Finn," Bridge whispered.

"Claremont?" Bishop Sprat said sharply. "Is that *her*? Is that the atheist, Finnian Kane?"

Finn was furious at his question and his tone. "Yeah, I'm Finnian Kane, the ungodly atheist who's been sent to spiritually corrupt your vicar."

There was silence after that comment, and when she turned to look at Bridge, she looked shocked and hurt.

The reality of what Finn had said came crashing down on her. *Oh, shit.*

Bridge walked away from her towards the front door and didn't look back once.

*What have I done?*

❖

Bridge stood in front of her own desk in her study, while Bishop Sprat sat behind her desk in her chair. She felt like she had been called to the headmistress's office at boarding school, only this was much more serious.

"I came to see you this evening because I've had complaints about your behaviour from your parishioners," Bishop Sprat said.

"Parishioners or parishioner? Winchester, by any chance?" Bridge said.

Bishop Sprat sat back in the chair, and said smugly, "I'm not at liberty to discuss that, but after what I saw out there, thank goodness I came to see you."

"She was only joking. Finn gave me a lift home, that's all."

"I told you the last time we spoke that your family connections can't protect you forever, and it's getting close to that time. Have you any idea what the press would do with this story? Besides the fact that you're breaking every covenant you've made with God, and the Church."

Bridge started to feel the panic of her church and her life slipping away from her. "I have not broken any covenant, with God or the Church."

Bishop Sprat was silent for a moment. "Have you remained celibate, Miss Claremont?"

The question that she'd dreaded him asking, and he just came out with it.

"I think that the unwritten rule is that you don't ask that question, My Lord. Do you ask your straight clergy that question?"

"I don't have to. They are not engaging in immoral acts that the Bible condemns. I ask again, have you remained celibate, and are you engaged in an illicit affair with Finnian Kane?"

Bridget's whole future flashed before her eyes. What could she say? God knew the secrets that she kept hidden in her heart.

"Well?" Sprat repeated.

❖

Finn downed a bottle of lager, and immediately took another from the fridge. She just couldn't believe she had said what she had to Bridge's bishop. If she hoped to get Bridge onside she'd probably blown it now.

"Fucking idiot."

Finn heard loud thumps on her front door, and she just knew it was Bridge. She put down her bottle and went to the door. As soon as she opened it, Bridge pushed through the door full of anger.

"Bloody Sprat. He wanted to discipline me. If I didn't have friends in high places, I would have been called to a disciplinary meeting in London."

Finn followed Bridge into the living room. "Bridge, I'm sorry if I made things worse—"

Bridge balled her fists and let out an angry sigh. "It's not your fault—it's that pompous bastard Winchester's fault. He's been sneaking behind my back, making phone calls to Sprat. Says he has seen evidence of my impropriety with his own eyes. Bloody fool. It would be bad enough if I was getting into a relationship with another woman, but not Finnian Kane the world-renowned atheist."

Bridge was so angry she looked near tears, and then they started to fall.

"Bridge, don't cry, please."

Finn tried to take Bridge's hand but she pushed it away. "No, don't touch me, don't touch me right now."

Bridge turned away from her and stood in front of the fire. Her hands were shaking with emotion. The anger she had stormed over here with started to morph to something else as soon as she saw Finn's contrite and emotional face. She was angry at the bishop for making her think what she had with Finn was wrong, immoral, and angry at the Church for dragging their feet into the twenty-first century.

She turned around and her heart ached when she looked at Finn. How could anything be bad about falling for this woman?

"I'm so sorry, Bridge. You've been so good to me and helped me through my grief. I'm sorry what we have between us is bringing you unhappiness."

Bridge stepped closer and reached out to caress Finn's cheek. "You know I had to stand there and deny that I had any kind of sexual relationship with you?"

"I'm so sorry."

Bridge couldn't stop herself from touching Finn some more, and she ran her fingers through her hair. She searched Finn's eyes and only saw mirrored the want she felt inside. Her breathing became shallow and she couldn't take her eyes off Finn's lips. "I had to deny what I felt for my beautiful boy."

Finn turned her head and kissed her palm. "Then don't, Mistress."

Bridge broke and kissed Finn hard. When they broke apart, Finn breathed, "Please may I touch you, Mistress?"

"Yes, you may." Bridget gasped when Finn took her hand and placed it on the fly of Finn's jeans.

"I remembered what you told me," Finn whispered. "That you would like me to be always ready for you. I wanted to please you."

Their lips came crashing together with pure and utter passion. Bridget shrugged off her jacket and pulled Finn's T-shirt off. It was such a turn on to have Finn ready for her, ready to give her pleasure.

She scratched her nails down Finn's bare chest, knowing how much she'd enjoyed it the last time.

"I'm sorry," Finn said.

"I'm not," Bridge replied.

"Bridge, please…"

"Please what, beautiful boy?" Bridge loved to hear Finn ask for what she wanted.

Finn kissed her neck while she grasped Bridge's thighs. "I want to be inside you, please."

Bridge rubbed Finn's strap-on through her jeans. "You want to be inside me with your cock? Would that make you feel good?"

Finn put her arms around Bridge's waist and held her in a tight embrace while she nodded in the crook of Bridge's neck.

Bridge's sex clenched, and she shivered at the sweet request. Bridge realized in this one embrace that this was real. They were so sexually in tune with each other. Each gave the other something she needed. Finn needed a place in her arms where she could be vulnerable and let go, and Bridge needed to take care of Finn and give her what she needed.

"You ask so sweetly, how could I refuse? Go and sit on the couch."

Bridge took off her black blouse and dog collar and threw them to the side. She resented them at this moment. She resented that they'd made her lie, made her deny someone she was falling in love with.

Bridge needed to feel what she had with Finn, after denying it. She needed to revel in everything that made their blossoming relationship. Finn sat on the couch, muscles visibly taut, waiting for Bridge to give her what she needed.

Bridge stood in front of the couch and slowly took off her skirt and panties, leaving just her stockings, suspenders, and bra. She watched Finn's eyes glued to every move her fingers made.

"Undo your belt, and pop open your jeans."

She pointed to her stockings. "I think I'll leave these and my stilettos on. You like them, don't you, boy?"

"Yes." Finn groaned.

Bridge raised an eyebrow. "Yes, what?"

Finn's eyes went wide. "Yes, Mistress. I'm sorry."

Bridget walked closer and said, "You're lucky I don't have my riding crop with me."

Again, Finn groaned, and clenched her fists tight. She was clearly finding it difficult to remain still and not touch herself or Bridge.

Bridge decided to help her just a little bit. She eyed Finn's crotch and said, "Take it out. Take out your cock and let me see what you've got for me."

Finn fumbled opening her fly, so eager was she to follow Bridge's instructions. She got her strap-on out and squeezed it in her hand.

"Good boy," Bridge said.

She walked right up to the couch and straddled Finn's lap. Finn's hands were on her buttocks and thighs in a second. Bridge caught her hands and held them above her head.

"Tut, tut. Did I say you could touch me?"

"No, Mistress."

"Keep them there and don't move. I see you're going to need some help remembering the rules."

Bridge took off her bra and trailed it over Finn's face before using it to tie Finn's wrists above her head on the back of her couch. Finn shuddered when she pulled it tight. Bridge said, "Now my hands are free to keep you under control."

Bridge grasped her hair and pulled her head back. When she looked into Finn's eyes they looked totally lost in passion. She placed kisses all over Finn's face and lips, and ended by biting her lip hard enough to make her jump.

"Just checking to see if I had your attention. What would you like to do, boy?"

"I'd like to kiss your breasts and suck your nipples, Mistress."

She leaned forward so Finn could pleasure her breasts with her mouth. Bridge groaned as Finn's mouth sucked, and her tongue licked her nipples. She felt the electrical tug from her nipples right down to her sex, which was throbbing with anticipation of accepting Finn's cock inside her.

Bridge needed this so badly, needed to revel in everything that she'd had to deny she wanted to her bishop. Without any more preamble, Bridge grasped Finn's strap-on and positioned it so she could lower herself onto it. The feeling of it inching its way inside her, filling her up, was exquisite, and even more so that she was controlling it at all times.

When she let it fill her completely they both moaned out loud, and Bridge whispered in Finn's ear, "Oh, you are my good boy. Don't you dare thrust until I tell you to."

"Yes, Mistress." Finn struggled against her bonds, knowing she could get out at any time, but also knowing that she didn't want to. Being under Bridge's control was like nothing she could have ever imagined. Her heart hammered like a drum in her chest, her skin was covered in goosebumps, and everything—all her feelings of fear that she had messed everything up, frustration that they couldn't just be together, and all her sexual energy—was centred in her groin, under her strap-on.

There was nothing she wanted more in the world than to thrust inside Bridge, but her mistress had said no.

Bridge grasped onto her hair as she raised herself up and down, riding Finn's cock. Finn was starting to sweat, just with the effort of not moving her hips.

"Please, Mistress. Please can I thrust inside you?"

Bridge grasped her chin with thumb and forefinger, and said, "How much do you need to thrust?"

"More than anything, Mistress. Please, I'm going to explode. I need it."

Bridge laughed softly and scratched her nails down Finn's shoulders. "Did any of the little groupies you fucked make you feel like this? Hmm?"

Finn screwed up her eyes and began to gasp. Her urge to thrust was so bad. "No, never. I never felt anything till you touched me, Mistress."

Bridge leaned forward and breathed in her ear, "Then you may. Fuck me like the good boy I know you are."

As soon as Finn was let off the leash she realized she wouldn't be thrusting for long. Bridge had wound her up so much. Bridge met every thrust, and they moved faster and faster towards the orgasm that ended Finn's torment.

"Fuck, fuck, going to come," Finn shouted.

"Not till I tell you to, boy." Bridge groaned. "Don't you dare come till I'm ready."

Finn felt like her whole body was on fire. She didn't think there was any way she could stop the inferno that was burning inside her. "Can't, Mistress. Can't."

Bridge's movements got faster and faster until she dug her nails into Finn's shoulder. "Come, come *now*."

At Bridge's command, Finn's body exploded. "Jesus, fuck."

Bridge flung her head back, ground her hips on Finn's cock, and groaned. "Good boy, I knew you could be good."

Finn broke free from her restraints, and they clung together long after their orgasms had subsided. Holding each other like it could be their last time. Finn looked up into Bridge's eyes. "I'm so sorry I made things more difficult. I promise I'll follow any lead you set."

"I told you, it's not your fault. I just need some time, to pray, to talk to God, and to make peace with what I feel. I know you don't understand that—"

Finn cupped Bridge's cheek tenderly, and said, "I do. You've helped me understand. I talk to Carrie all the time. The first time we met you told me you would work on the atheist bit, and you have. I think you can safely assume I'm now agnostic."

Bridget laughed softly and kissed her brow. "Good boy. I'm training you well then."

"I think, considering our positions, I'd say yes," Finn joked. "Seriously, take all the time you need. When you talk to God, remember one thing, Bridget Claremont, Mistress Black, I'm in love with you.

I'll keep my distance and let you have your space, but you are all I never knew I needed." Bridget tensed up when she said that and tried to move. Finn caught her and kept her from moving. "What's wrong with saying I love you?"

"You know why. I don't know if I can risk my whole life, my vocation—I'm frightened of hurting you."

Finn took Bridge's palm and kissed it softly. "When I knew I had to get away from London, I had no idea where to go. So I decided to do something so against what I believed in, but something Carrie believed in. I got a map and Carrie's dousing crystal and held it over the map. It led me to Axedale. It led me to you."

"You did?"

Finn nodded. "Yes, and for an atheist-slash-agnostic to think there is some purpose in that, then I'm sure a woman of God should see that as a sign, don't you think?"

Bridget gasped. "A sign?"

"A sign," Finn repeated.

## CHAPTER TWENTY

Finn was true to her word. She did keep her distance from Bridge, all week in fact. Finn didn't see their separation as a good sign, but she'd promised she would give Bridge space, so she did. It was still very hard. To fill the time she tried to help Quade and took Martha out in her wheelchair.

This morning Finn accompanied Quade and the Axedale gamekeeper to check up on the deer herd that lived on estate land. It was different and interesting work. From there she and Quade headed to the pub for lunch. She waited at the table while Quade ordered the food.

Finn took out her cards, the cards that Bridge gave her, and started to shuffle. Everything reminded Finn of Bridge. She'd never experienced the feeling of aching for someone physically before, but that's what she felt for Bridge. She ached to touch her, to be allowed to touch her and hold her. How could she ever handle it if Bridge thought they shouldn't pursue this?

Quade came over with two pints of lager. "Here, get that down your neck."

"Cheers." Finn lifted her glass to Quade and then took a drink. "Tastes good after working from six o'clock in the morning."

"You did well, Finn. Especially for someone who hasn't done that type of work before."

Finn smiled and held up her hands and showed the blisters starting to form on her palms. "I know. I'll be a rugged butch, as Bridge puts it, before I know it."

Quade smiled and took a drink. "Have you talked to her yet?"

Finn sighed and shook her head. "No, I said I would give her time, and I have. I haven't gone to the church to paint or anything. After everything with her bishop, I'm not taking the chance of pushing her any more."

"Good idea." Quade looked at her cards and said, "They look different from your other ones."

"Yeah." Finn quite naturally started an elaborate shuffle and fanned them out in front of Quade. "Pick one, and look at it carefully. They belonged to Bridge's grandpa. He got them from Houdini. She thought I would appreciate them."

Quade picked a card and held it close.

Finn continued, "I couldn't believe she would give me something so personal. It's like she really understands me."

"She is one of the kindest women I know," Quade said.

Finn reshuffled the pack and said, "Pick another, and decide which card is going to be your first choice, then give me back the card that you don't want, but remember what it was."

Finn took the card and put it back in the pack. "Okay, now give me your first choice, and remember it."

Quade gave her the card.

Finn shuffled and fanned out the deck on the table. "Remember your card?"

"Three of hearts," Quade said.

"Okay. Three of hearts, count to three when I say so, and your card will jump from the pack over to you, okay?"

She nodded, and Finn held her hand over the cards, and said, "Go for it."

Quade counted, "One, two, three—"

Finn smacked her hands together and Quade's card, the three of hearts, fell by her pint glass.

Quade laughed and clapped her hands together. Soon other people in the bar, who had gathered around without them noticing, started to clap.

Finn wasn't finished yet, and said, "What was your second choice?"

"Five of clubs."

Finn pulled her palms apart and there was the card.

Quade was astonished. "What? No way. How did you do that?"

Finn tapped her nose. "Trade secret."

The other villagers gathered closer and patted her on the back. Mr. Peters said, "Show us one more before I have to get back to the post office."

Finn looked around at the expectant faces and didn't feel panic or fear at performing. She felt excited, just as when she had shown the children. Maybe she didn't have to feel guilty any more. Magic was part of her, and while she might have been wrong about rubbishing other people's belief in God, that didn't change the fundamental purpose of her act, which was to entertain and bring joy and wonder to people's faces.

After showing the bar patrons a few more tricks and eating lunch, Finn walked Quade to her Land Rover. "So, do you think I should go and talk to Bridge?" Finn asked.

Quade thought for a few seconds and said, "Maybe you need to work on yourself first."

Finn nodded.

Quade added, "Well, maybe you need to show her that you're not going anywhere, that you'll be here for the foreseeable future. Axedale is everything to Bridge, but she maybe thinks you'll eventually be tempted back to the bright lights of London. That maybe it's not worth gambling her career on someone who might leave. Can you make a life in our little village?"

"You're right," Finn said. "I need to think and face my future. I'll work on that."

Quade unlocked the truck and said, "I enjoyed that, Finn. I always wanted to see some of your magic, but Bridge said you didn't like to perform any more."

Finn leaned against the side of the truck. "I didn't mean to—it just happened. Magic was a part of myself I didn't want to know any more."

Quade smacked her on the shoulder. "It's hard to hide such an important part of your life, Finn. Sometimes you have to face what's inside of you."

That struck a chord with Finn. She was trying to get Bridge to face and accept another side of herself, and she wasn't doing the same. *I need to show her we can have a future, and live being true to ourselves.*

"Quade? Do you know where Mr. Butterstone lives?"

❖

The next day Bridge was out walking her usual evening route, trying to sort out her thoughts and come up with some sermon ideas for this week's sermon. It was very difficult to put her all into writing a sermon for a church organization that was making her feel guilty about who she was falling in love with, but it had to be done.

She stopped and sat on the bench overlooking the estate where she and Finn had their first skirmish. Bridge chuckled to herself thinking of how angry, arrogant, and dismissive Finn was then, but mostly she recalled how damaged she was. That wasn't Finn any more, but if Bridge let go of what they had together, would she return to that state of mind?

No. Bridge was overestimating her importance in Finn's life. She could navigate life without Bridge. But could Bridge navigate life without Finn? She had missed her so much this week that it was hard not to give in and visit her. She missed talking to her, missed laughing with her, and missed soothing and taking care of her. It felt so natural to be with Finn, so natural and easy to love her, and yet the Church she loved, or some parts of the Church she loved, were telling her it was unnatural.

After staring at her blank notepad for ten minutes, all she had managed to write down for her sermon notes was the word *love*. Love should be a wonderful, happy, hopeful word, but at the moment her two loves, Finn and the Church, were pulling her in opposite directions.

"I give up." Bridge put her notebook back in her handbag.

"Giving up? That doesn't sound like a Claremont, Bridge."

Bridge turned her head and was full of joy to see Harry standing there. She jumped up and hugged her tightly. "Harry! How…when?"

"The dig was a wash, so we did all the tourist things and Annie and Riley were anxious to get back home. Plus, I was concerned about you, after your voicemail, so we caught a flight this morning."

Bridge clung to her like a limpet. She could already feel the relief of having her oldest friend by her side spreading through her heart and soul, and the joy showed itself in the tears that sprang from her eyes.

Harry pulled back and said to Bridge, "What's wrong?"

Bridget took a tissue from her pocket and dried her eyes. "Ignore me. I've become an overemotional fool since you left Axedale. How did you find me?"

They sat down on the bench together. "Your housekeeper thought you might be up here."

"Where's Annie and Riley?"

"Annie is getting unpacked and I was apparently getting in the way. Riley went to visit Willow. She missed that pony a great deal."

Bridge smiled. "Quade and I took good care of her."

"I'm quite sure. I bumped into Quade up at Axedale," Harry said.

Bridge sighed. "I suppose she told you about my troubles then."

"Not much. You know she's not one for gossip and chit-chat, but she did say you could use someone to talk to."

"And here you are."

"And here I am. Tell me what's been happening. I understand your atheist magician friend has made quite the impression on Martha. I popped in to see her on my way."

"Yes. Martha is quite taken with her," Bridge said.

Harry sat back and crossed her legs. "And you, Vicar?"

Bridge nodded. "I think I'm in love with her."

Harry did a double take. "Love? Bloody hell. I understood you liked her but...in love? I didn't think she'd be your type."

Bridget laughed ironically. "Oh yes, I've tried to tell myself she's not my type since the first time I looked into her beautiful, sad, and confused eyes, but alas, she is exactly my type. She fits with me, every part of me, not just the vicar but also—"

Harry smiled. "Mistress Black."

"Yes, I've been trying to hide that side of me for so long, but Finn just brings her out of me, whether I like it or not."

"So what's the problem? If you both like each other, then what is to stop you being with her?"

Bridget said, "I could write you a list, but it would take too long. The long and short of it is that if I pursue this I may lose my church, my job, and my home here in Axedale. You know what a hardliner Bishop Sprat is. He's had some phone calls from concerned parishioners about the propriety of my relationship with Finn."

"Let me guess, Archie Winchester, by any chance?" Harry said.

"Probably."

"Bloody fool. I don't see the problem. You can be in a relationship with the same sex—"

"But I'd have to remain celibate. I can't, in good conscience, lie to my bishop, and to be in a celibate relationship...I just couldn't ask that of Finn or myself. I just couldn't. We're too"—Bridge searched for a term to describe them—"compatible."

Harry laughed. "More like you can't keep your hands, or your whip, off her."

"Maybe. I've prayed and tried to understand what God wants me to do. All I feel is this is right, God is love and wants me to love, but maybe that's my wants that I'm listening to."

Harry got up from the bench and started to pace in front of her. "You should have prayed to Bacchus—he'd have given you a much clearer answer, and probably sent you a new whip."

"Oh, shush about your bloody Roman gods."

Harry shook her head. "I don't know why you're in turmoil about this. Bridget Claremont doesn't run from a fight. You've been campaigning for gay rights in the Church for years, and this is the chance for you to lead and show the Church the way. Your Christian group is full of couples—in fact I've met Kate and her partner at one of your fundraisers, and there's no way in hell they are celibate."

Why did this seem such an easy choice to everyone else? Why couldn't they see how difficult it was?

"What does your aunt Gertie say?" Harry added.

"Follow my heart and my conscience."

Harry knelt in front of her and took Bridge's hand. "Then do it. Remember what you said to me when I was falling in love with Annie? The only Bible verse that I will remember till the day I die. 1 Corinthians 13, *Love bears all things, believes all things, hopes all things, endures all things.* Faith, hope, and love are all that matters. You taught me that."

"I never thought I'd have you quote scripture at me, Harry," Bridge said with emotion in her voice.

"Well, I'd like you to be happy, like you helped me to be."

"Harry, the Church is the only thing that has kept me afloat. It saved me from myself. If I were to lose it—"

"You won't lose it. You have too many important friends for even Sprat to get rid of you. Besides, this is my village, my church, and I choose you as my vicar," Harry said angrily.

"You can't control the Church of England, Harry, and do you really think a celebrity magician is going to stay in a little village like this forever?"

Harry stood and crossed her arms. "Maybe you need to talk to her about this. I don't even know the woman, although she will be getting a visit from me in the future."

"Oh, Harry, protecting my honour? I don't think I have any left to protect," Bridge joked.

"I do know one thing. Annie and Riley are going down to the church hall tonight to sign up for the big winter show. Riley's friend, Sophie, texted her the exciting news as soon as we got back."

"What exciting news?" Bridge asked.

"The famous Finnian Kane is directing the show. She told Mr. Butterstone yesterday. Doesn't sound like your magician is in a hurry to leave."

❖

Finn stood in the middle of the church hall with her clipboard, surrounded with what looked and sounded like the whole village. This was more chaotic than rehearsals for her arena tour. She was astonished when she arrived at the church to find the villagers lined up out of the door to sign up for the show.

After she'd spoken to a delighted Mr. Butterstone yesterday, he put posters up in the pub and on the church noticeboard. She had no idea the response would be this big. By making her presence so public, it also made her realize it wouldn't be long before the press found her here. She was surprised she had been given this time as it was. If they found her now, what was the worst that could happen? She was happy here in Axedale and had begun to make her peace with her sister's death, and had met someone who gave her the strength to move on with her life.

*If they come, they come.*

"Finn?" Mrs. Peters interrupted her from her thoughts.

"Sorry, I was miles away. We better get started."

Finn tried to catch everyone's attention with her voice, and when that didn't work she brought her fingers to her lips and whistled loudly.

Everyone in the hall stopped and turned to look. "Listen up, everyone. Thank you all for coming tonight. We'll try and get through this first night as quickly and as painlessly as possible. The theme for this year's show is Winter Wonderland."

Everyone clapped and chattered excitedly. Finn was glad they were so impressed. That was all she had so far—she still had to write the show.

"There are tables set up and manned by Mrs. Peters and the church committee in each corner of the room. So everyone who wants to be considered for dancing, follow Mrs. Peters, all the singers, head over to Mrs. McCrae, if you'd like to be involved with some magic, then sign up with Mr. Butterstone, and if you're interested in costumes, props, and backstage work, then Beverly will take your names."

Finn leaned over and whispered to Mrs. Peters, "Good luck, you'll need it."

She sighed in relief as all the people started to drift over to the respective desks. Finn grabbed a bottle of water and took a seat on the edge of the stage. She took out her iPad and started scrolling through the brief notes she had made for the show so far.

*I wish Bridge was here.* She controlled these sorts of things with military precision.

Once some of the children were signed up for the various parts of the show, they started to gravitate over to Finn. She was fast becoming a Pied Piper with the children. It was a good reminder for Finn of what magic was all about—childlike wonder. That was the feeling she wanted to capture, wonder and joy. It occurred to her that was something she could get the kids to help her with.

She asked Mrs. Peters if there were any art supplies, and luckily, they had what she needed in the Sunday School room.

Finn handed out the pens and paper and said, "Okay, kids, I want you to draw and write everything that you think is magical about winter, and we'll incorporate it into the show."

The assembled kids were very excited about this and set to work.

A short time later the church hall door opened and a blond-haired woman came in with a child, four plastic boxes piled high in their arms. Some of the kids got up and ran over to them. Finn heard some of the adults exclaim, "It's Lady Annie."

Mrs. Peters and quite a few others went to greet them warmly. *Lady Annie?* Must be the famous Lady Harry's wife. Bridge didn't mention they were due to come back home. Annie was everything she'd imagined her to be—beautiful, warm and friendly.

She and the girl who must have been her daughter Riley started giving out cookies. Mrs. Peters guided Annie over to her, and Finn suddenly got very nervous.

"Finn?" Mrs. Peters said. "This is Lady Annie, Lady Harry's wife."

Annie was warm and smiling. "Please, it's Annie. I'm happy to meet you, Finn. We've heard so much about you."

She shook Annie's hand and felt her cheeks heat up. It was easy to see why Lady Harry loved her. "Hi, nice to meet you."

"This is my daughter, Riley," Annie said.

"Hi, Finn, I've got every one of your DVDs. Your show is so cool," Riley said excitedly.

"Thanks. Are you going to sign up for the show, Riley?" Finn said.

"Yeah, I'd love that. I'm going to put my name down for magic.

Mum, take this?" Riley placed her box of cookies on top of Annie's and rushed off.

Annie laughed. "You'll have to excuse Riley—she's very excitable today. We just got back from Rome, and she's been high as a kite since we landed. She's going to crash any time now and sleep for three days, I think."

"She seems like a great kid. Bridge talks about her a lot," Finn said.

"Is Bridge around? I was hoping we'd see her here." Annie looked around the hall. "She's usually at the centre of these village events."

Finn didn't know what to say. This was Bridge's friend, and she didn't want to lie to her. "Uh...this was kind of a last-minute thing. Mr. Butterstone just put up the posters for it yesterday. I'm not sure she knows yet."

Annie gazed at her carefully, as if trying to work out what exactly was going on here. Annie put down her boxes on the stage and brought out a large cookie. "Why don't we sit and have a cup of tea and a chat? You can fill me in on everything that's happening, and about your friendship with Bridge. I have super-duper cookies or Harry's favourite, fudgie-wudgies. All freshly baked this afternoon."

"Okay," Finn said slowly. For some reason, she had the impression Lady Annie was about to psych her out.

Finn went to the refreshment table and returned with two cups of tea. They sat on the stage, and Annie gave her a choice of treat.

"I'll take a fudgie-wudgie." When Finn bit into it, she moaned in pleasure, it tasted so good. "This tastes amazing."

Annie took a sip of tea and smiled. "I have been told fudgie-wudgies can mend a broken heart. So tell me...you've gotten close to Bridge?"

Finn stopped mid-chew. *Is this woman clairvoyant?* She had been right. She was getting manipulated in the nicest way. Lady Annie used her cakes and sweet treats as a form of distraction, exactly the kind of thing she did when doing sleight of hand.

❖

Finn was given the most delightful form of interrogation from Annie, but their conversation was cut short when Mrs. Peters gave her a message that the vicar would like to see her in the back office.

She made her way to Bridge's office, and as she got near the door, her heart started to beat faster. It was so long since she'd seen Bridge, and she was aching to see her, to touch her. But what if Bridge wanted to tell her it was over?

She took a breath and knocked.

Bridge's voice came from behind the door. "Come in."

Finn opened the door and found Bridge standing against the front of her desk, arms crossed, and looking like the epitome of female sexual power. She fought the urge to drop to her knees right now and crawl across the floor to her.

"Hi," Finn said.

"Come here." Bridge beckoned her over with a finger.

It was like this woman had some magical power over Finn. A look or a few words could set her on fire. Her skin, her heart all burned, and her sex throbbed with unquenchable want.

Finn walked over, her focus on Bridge's legs the whole way. When she arrived in front of Bridge, she felt Bridge's finger under her chin pushing her head up.

"Eyes up, Magician," Bridge said.

"Sorry. I've tried to give you your space like you asked, but I missed you," Finn said.

Bridge reached out and caressed her cheek. "I know, and I missed you too."

Finn couldn't stop herself taking a step closer, but Bridge put a palm on her chest to keep her at arm's length.

"Why are you doing this, Finn. The show? I need to understand."

"To show you that I want to make a future here, get involved with the community," Finn said.

"What about your career?"

Finn shrugged. "I haven't decided if I ever want to perform again, but if I did I would just do a select number of shows, but base myself here if—"

"If what?" Bridge said.

"If you wanted me to. If you gave us a chance."

Finn saw Bridge's emotional side rise to the surface, the part of her that was still scared her heart could be broken.

She took Finn's hands and rested her forehead against hers. "I want to."

"I'll do whatever you need me to, Bridge, I just want to be with you. You've given my life meaning again. Every day I wake up, and I don't think of the bad times with Carrie, I think of the good times. I'm not angry at God and the world any more. All I think about is being with you and the happiness it brings. Please give us a chance."

Bridge sighed and said, "I've spoken to Aunt Gertie, and she tells me to follow my heart and my conscience. So I prayed long and hard, and I know in my heart that God wants me to love you, but we have to be discreet."

Finn's heart soared with happiness. "I'll follow your lead. As long as I can be with you."

"I won't deny our love ever again, if pushed, but I would rather avoid questions altogether," Bridge said.

"Whatever you say," Finn said. "You're the mistress of my heart and my body."

"And what about your soul, boy?" Bridge smiled, half joking.

"Because of you I think I believe in the soul again, so you are most certainly mistress of it. Thank you for giving us a chance. I—" Finn hesitated. She knew she loved Bridge, but she was frightened of scaring her off, so she said, "Just like your favourite song, 'Can't Help Falling In Love.'"

Bridge smiled. "Neither can I, my beautiful boy. Kiss me."

The kiss turned from loving to passionate in seconds since they hadn't touched each other for so long. Finn's hands went straight to the hem of Bridge's skirt and she slid her hand up to her thigh, massaging and grasping the flesh she found there.

Bridge pushed her back and said, "Uh-uh. Calm your little trickster hands, not in the house of God."

"Then let's go to mine after we're finished here. I need you so much, Bridge."

Bridge pushed one finger into the centre of Finn's chest, and moved it down her stomach slowly. "I think you are getting a bit presumptuous and above yourself," Bridge said.

She then traced her finger over Finn's belt buckle, lingering there and enjoying Finn's breath hitching, before grasping her crotch through her jeans.

"Oh dear, oh dear. You aren't ready for me. That is a punishable offence." Bridge chuckled internally at the look on Finn's face.

"But...but we weren't together for a whole week. You weren't even talking to me."

Bridge leaned forward and whispered in her ear. "If we are going to be together, you must understand the most important thing is to follow my rules, no matter what is going on around us. I need to know you're ready for me, and you need to know that wherever we are or whatever we are doing, you belong to me, boy."

Finn groaned. Bridge knew Finn loved it when she talked to her like that. Bridge took Finn's hand and placed it on her own thigh. "That is, if you want this."

"God, yes, I want it. Say my magic words, Mistress."

Bridge laughed and pushed her hand away. "Oh no, that is a reward. The second thing you're going to learn is about punishment. I don't have my riding crop to whip that muscled little backside of yours into shape, so instead you can learn about abstinence." Bridge walked to the office door. "Let's go and finish up your show's sign-up."

"I'm going to explode, Bridge." Finn sighed and stuffed her hands in her pockets.

As she walked past her through the door, Bridge gave her a swat on the backside. "That's the point. Now go and be a good little magician."

## CHAPTER TWENTY-ONE

The next few days were torture for Finn. Bridge was consuming her every thought, and yet they'd done nothing more than kiss since the night in her office. What made things harder was that the press had finally found her. Finn woke up on Sunday morning with a few paparazzi sitting across the road from her cottage. But she wasn't going to panic. It didn't matter, as long as they couldn't connect her with Bridge and embarrass her.

Finn called her publicist Allegra and walked to her living room window.

"Finn? Are you all right? I'm sorry about the press. How are you coping?"

"It's fine. It was going to happen sooner or later," Finn said.

There was a silence on the other end of the phone and then Allegra said, "You sound awfully calm. You were dreading them finding you."

Finn looked out at the photographers sitting across the street, and did feel calm, because she knew Bridge loved her, and she had found a place of safety here in Axedale.

"Yeah, well, maybe it's the country air, but I am not concerned. Let them post pictures of me walking to the post office and back. What's the worst they can do?"

She knew they would do worse if they found out about her relationship with Bridge, but that was not going to happen.

Finn heard Allegra sigh. "If you're sure. You do sound so much better. Country life must suit you. Let me know when you want to get back to work."

That was one thing she didn't want to contemplate at the moment. In Axedale and Bridge she had found safety, and she didn't want to change that now.

"I'll call you. Thanks, Ally. Bye."

As soon as that was done, Finn called Bridge. She was supposed to be going to church this morning then up to Axedale Hall with Bridge and Martha for Sunday lunch. Although Annie was delightful and welcoming, she sensed Lady Harry was more cynical and wanted to give her best friend's new girlfriend a proper talking to.

Finn sneaked another look outside. There were now four people with cameras standing around and drinking coffee. *You'll soon get bored.*

She phoned Bridge, who greeted her with, "Hello, darling, I hope you're not phoning to weasel out of going to church."

"Morning, I'm sorry but I am, but it's not my doing. The paparazzi have finally found me. I've got four across the street just now. I think me going to your church on a Sunday would give them a story and cause you unnecessary problems."

Bridge sighed. "You're right, I suppose. I wrote a sermon for you. I wanted you to hear it."

"Tell me what verse it was based on and I'll read it here," Finn said.

"You have a Bible?" Bridge said sceptically.

"Of course. Atheists or former atheists always have a Bible. It's part of knowing thine enemy better than you know yourself, or checking for inconsistencies to throw like hand grenades at sexy vicars."

Bridge laughed. "Very true, Magician. It was taken from 1 John 4:18. *There is no fear in love; but perfect love casteth out fear: because fear hath torment. He that feareth is not made perfect in love.*"

"That is perfect. Do you know how much I want to kiss you right now, Bridge?"

"Probably as much as I want to kiss you, but it is a Sunday."

"You have some reason to stop me touching you every day. I got more kisses before we were together than I do now."

"Don't pout, boy. We can spend some time together tonight," Bridge promised.

"But what about the cameras? They'll follow me whether we're at the vicarage or here. They can't see me with you like that."

"Let me work something out. Just make sure you bring an overnight bag to lunch at Axedale. I'll get Quade to pick me and Martha up, and we'll see you there. They can't follow you past the Axedale estate's gates. It's private property."

Finn felt excitement start to gather in her stomach already. "You are clever, Mistress."

Bridge laughed and then said, "I know. I better run, I have a sermon to deliver, but I'll see you at Axedale later. Oh, and do something interesting with your hair. You know how much your mistress loves it."

Finn shivered and looked over at her strap-on waiting for her beside her clothes. "Oh, I know. See you later."

❖

Finn couldn't wait to see Bridge. She could feel her in every cell in her body, even when they were apart. She needed to connect with her soon—abstinence really did work as a punishment, but a good punishment. When Bridge did allow Finn to touch her, their separation would make it so good.

She put her overnight bag over her shoulder and checked her hair in the mirror. *She's going to love it.*

Finn didn't take her bike so she wouldn't ruin her hair with her helmet, so she had to walk past the photographers waiting for her to appear. She had dealt with the paparazzi many times over the years, so she was no stranger to ignoring them. She would have found them difficult to deal with when she first came to Axedale, when she was torn up inside about Carrie, but now knowing that Bridge cared for her, wanted her, and she had a place to call home, she felt strong.

The village roads were busy, because Axedale was a favourite Sunday outing for tourists. The paparazzi snapped their pictures as she walked down the road to the post office, and when the tourists turned to watch and realized who she was, then the smartphones came out to video her.

She tried to keep calm and keep walking. A few of the photographers said a few things to try to get a reaction from her stoic mask. Instead of reacting, she said, "You're all going to get really bored following me around the village."

One taller man said, "I wouldn't count on it."

Finn ignored that comment and noticed Mrs. Peters standing outside the post office. "Good morning, Finn, in you come."

As soon as she walked in, Mrs. Peters shut the door on the photographer's face, and turned the shop sign to Closed.

"Thank you, Mrs. Peters. You're a lifesaver."

"Don't you worry—you're one of us now. They won't get past me," Mrs. Peters said.

"That means a lot. Thank you. I wondered if I could get something to take to Axedale. I'm having lunch there, and I think I should take Lady Annie something."

Mrs. Peters smiled and clapped her hands together. "You've come to the right place. I happen to have Lady Annie's favourite chocolates. She does have a sweet tooth."

"Perfect."

The postmistress went over to a shelf and held up two boxes of chocolates. "The smaller or the larger one, Finn?"

"Large, please—oh, could you make it three large? Mrs. Castle and the vicar will be there."

"Of course." When she brought them over, Finn remembered Riley.

"You wouldn't happen to know Riley's favourite sweets, do you?"

"I know just the thing." When she was done packing up the sweets, Mrs. Peters leaned over the counter and said in a low voice, "Why don't you go out my back door, and then you can leave these buffoons behind."

"You are a treasure, Mrs. Peters."

❖

Archie Winchester watched from a distance with a grin on his face as the photographers waited for Finn to come out of the village shop and post office. *It's all going to fall around your ears, Vicar, once your immoral love affair is exposed.*

Thee he noticed one of the photographers packing up by his car and preparing to leave. He walked over to him and said, "You're not leaving, are you? There's much more to this story. I'm the one that called your newspaper."

The photographer patted him on the shoulder. "Don't you worry, mate. I've got more than enough. These idiots"—he pointed over to the other photographers—"they're too late. I have everything we need."

Archie rubbed his hands together with glee. "I can't wait to see her deviant face all over the newspapers."

❖

Harry, Bridge, and Finn sat in front of the fire in the blue drawing room. They had spent a wonderful afternoon together with Martha, Quade, and Riley, enjoying Annie's food and warm hospitality.

Quade had taken Martha home and Annie was just putting Riley to bed. Harry was over at the drinks table and Finn was mentally undressing Bridge with her eyes. She just couldn't wait to touch her.

Harry brought over a brandy for each of them, and Finn sniffed it suspiciously. "Everything all right, Finn?" Harry asked.

"Oh yes. I've just never had brandy before."

Bridge chuckled and looked at her adoringly. "Isn't she so sweetly innocent, Harry?"

Finn cleared her throat and felt her cheeks go red.

Harry stood by the fireplace and raised a quizzical eyebrow at her old friend. "I'll leave that judgement to you, Bridge."

Just then, Annie came back in the room. "Oh my goodness, Riley was high with excitement at meeting you, Finn, I doubt she'll sleep for hours." Annie stepped into Harry's arms and hugged her. "I left her watching magic videos on YouTube."

She saw Harry roll her eyes. Finn wasn't quite sure she had Harry's approval yet. She got on great with Annie, and had spent most of the day teaching Riley some simple magic tricks, and she was a quick learner.

"Would you like a drink, my darling?" Harry said to Annie.

Annie thought for a moment and looked to Bridge and smiled. "No thanks, sweetheart. I think I've had enough. Besides, remember, we were going to have an early night."

Finn caught on to Annie immediately, and could have kissed her, but Harry seemed confused. Finn smiled at Bridge and winked.

"We did?" Harry said.

"Yes, remember, we want to be up early to start cataloguing the attics." Annie finished her sentence with a dig in Harry's ribs.

Bridge chuckled and said, "Harry, your wonderful wife is trying to tell you it would be nice to leave Finn and me alone, since we're staying over."

"Oh, I see," Harry said at last.

Finn thought it was funny to watch Annie gently coerce her partner. They had a completely different dynamic to her and Bridge. Harry was a total butch top. She couldn't imagine for a second Harry giving up her control in the bedroom. And yet, were they so different?

Annie led Harry, just as Bridge led Finn, they just had different ways of going about it. Certainly, in Axedale Hall, Finn was sure that the real power behind the throne was wielded by a very sweet, very femme Lady Annie.

"It was lovely to spend the day with you, Finn, and get to know you. We're so happy for you both," Annie said.

Bridge said, "Thank you for allowing us to stay over at Axedale. We have to be so careful."

"It's our pleasure, isn't it, Harry?"

Another soft dig in the ribs got the reply, "Yes, yes, of course." Harry finished her brandy quickly, and said, "Well, we'll turn in and leave you...to it, as it were."

Finn stood when Harry offered her hand to shake. "Finn, Bridge is my best friend in the world. I hope you will be good to her, and treat her with respect."

"Oh, shush, Harry," Bridget said. "Don't be so protective."

Finn returned her firm handshake and said, "I promise to always put Bridge first."

Harry nodded and went over to Bridge. As Annie gave Finn a kiss on the cheek goodnight, she heard Harry say to Bridge, "Thank God Axedale has thick walls. Try not to strip the plaster off them, okay?"

When Harry and Annie left, Bridge sauntered over to Finn, and said, "Come to bed, boy." By the time they got up to the guest bedroom, Finn was nearly jumping out of her skin, but Bridge wanted to take things slowly, and enjoy loving Finn, not just having sex. She knew she would have to calm her down considerably.

Bridge kissed her, and when Finn tried to deepen the kiss, she pushed her back and placed a finger on her lips. "Patience, boy."

Finn groaned. "Say my magic words, Mistress. You know how much they turn me on."

Bridge cupped Finn's cheek with her hand, and kissed her way up the other side of her jawline, and ended with whispering in her ear, "Kneel, boy."

Finn moaned and fell to her knees. "It makes me want to come when you say that."

Bridge smiled, and stroked her head. "I know. I want you to undress me, starting with my shoes."

"Yes, Mistress." Finn kissed all over Bridge's shoes before easing them off her feet and placing them carefully on the side. She kissed all the way up Bridge's legs, and unzipped her skirt, letting it fall. As soon as it was gone, Finn pressed her face into Bridge's sex, while her hands massaged her buttocks.

"Please, may I taste you?" Finn asked.

"No. Finish undressing me, take your clothes off, and get into bed."

Finn looked at her with surprise. "But—"

"No buts. On your feet, and finish undressing me." Finn got up and helped Bridge off with the rest of her clothes, dispensed with her own, then went into bed.

Bridge stalked towards it and slipped in beside her. She pushed off the sheets, and leaned on her side next to Finn.

Bridge caressed Finn's body with her fingertips. She loved the look of confusion on Finn's face. Finn had given over control to Bridge in the bedroom, and she probably thought she knew what pattern their lovemaking would follow, but Bridge promised herself that she would always keep Finn on her toes by not letting her anticipate what was coming next.

"Bridge—" Finn got a quick slap on the thigh for that. "Sorry, Mistress. What are you going to do to me?"

Bridge chuckled. "What am I going to do to you? You really want to know?"

Finn nodded.

"I want to show my boy how much I love her, and I want you to fuck me long, but oh so slow."

"I don't want to disappoint you, Mistress," Finn said with a hint of desperation in her voice. She closed her eyes for a second and whimpered. She had waited so long to be alone with Bridge again, that she thought one touch would set off her orgasm.

Bridge leaned over and kissed her lips softly. "Mistress knows how you feel, and I'm going to make you feel better, so you can please me."

Again, Finn had no idea what was going to happen, which thrilled her. Bridge casually traced her fingernails across Finn's breasts, making her nipples go rock hard.

"Tell me, did you think about your mistress when we were apart?" Bridge asked.

The question might have sounded casual, but it kick-started a huge ball of excitement low in Finn's stomach.

"Yes, Mistress."

Bridge smiled. "What did you do when you thought about me?"

Finn hesitated. Was she really asking her to do that?

Bridge seemed to sense her hesitation and grasped Finn's hand, and put it down on her sex.

"Show me, boy. I'll make you feel better," Bridge said huskily.

Finn didn't hesitate this time. She would do anything for Bridge, anything. She slipped her finger under the base of her strap-on and into her wet sex. She groaned when her finger first touched her clit.

"That's my good boy."

While Finn stroked her clit, Bridge grasped her strap-on and started giving it a soft massage.

"Jesus Christ." Finn's eyes went wide and her orgasm very nearly came too soon, as she watched Bridge's fingers with their red-painted nail polish stroking and squeezing her cock.

"Now, now. Don't blaspheme, bad boy. Do you like your mistress massaging your cock for you?"

"Fuck, yes. Don't stop please, Mistress." Finn couldn't take her eyes off Bridge's hand. She had never seen such an erotic sight, and her own fingers on her clit matched the pace of Bridge's massage, convincing Finn all her pleasure was coming from her cock in Bridge's hand. "Faster, Mistress. I'm going to come."

Bridge rubbed faster and squeezed harder, while placing soft loving kisses on her jaw. "Come for me, beautiful boy. Come in my hand."

Finn couldn't take any more. An orgasm exploded throughout Finn's body. "Yes, yes, Mistress, fuck!"

Her orgasm was so intense, it took away that desperate, desperate need that was causing fires beneath her skin.

Finn lay gasping, trying to make her breathing normalize.

"Did Mistress make you feel better, boy?"

Finn smiled, and quickly rolled over so she was on top of Bridge. "I'm ready for anything you need from me, Mistress."

Bridge pulled her down into a deep kiss. "I want you, boy. I want you to fuck your mistress, and make me come long and slow. Can you do that?"

Finn grinned. "I can do anything for you. I want to make you scream, Mistress."

## CHAPTER TWENTY-TWO

Finn had never been happier. She had Bridge and they were together as much as possible. They had to be discreet, but the paparazzi appeared to be bored with camping outside her house, and their number dwindled with each passing day. She was also getting to know Harry and Annie, although Harry still wasn't totally sure about her intentions towards her friend. Everything was going perfectly and Finn was ready to tell Bridge she loved her, again.

Finn was awakened by the incessant ring of her phone. She barely woke up, but answered. It was her publicist. "Ally, do you know what time it is?"

"I'm sorry, but you need to know this. I take it you've gotten involved with someone in Axedale."

Now Finn was fully awake. "Ally, I don't think that's really any of your business."

"It is when I've had a tip off from the journalist at the newspaper. They will make your relationship with Bridget Claremont as scandalous as possible, considering the right-wing agenda of the newspaper."

Finn held her head in her hands. "Jesus Christ."

This was what she had always been afraid of. This could be how she lost Bridge, if she was forced to choose.

"What do you want us to do, Finn? I could contact your lawyers, get them to try and delay publication, try and get an injunction of some sort, although I don't know if that would do any good."

Finn heard a knock at her cottage door. She looked out of her bedroom window, and Bridge looked up.

"I need time to think, Ally. I'll get back to you in a few hours, okay?" Finn hung up the phone quickly, pulled on a T-shirt to go with the boxers she had on, and ran downstairs.

She opened the door and Bridge fell straight into her arms. "I needed you to hold me," Bridge said.

"Always." Finn squeezed her tighter and said, "I take it you've heard then?"

Bridge nodded. "Yes, the *Daily Tribune* called the bishop for a reaction, and he called me."

Finn led Bridge through to the living room. Bridge sat on the couch while Finn lit the log-burning fire.

Bridge watched the flames dance and crackle, and it brought some comfort to her confused mind. When Finn found out the whole truth, she was worried what her reaction would be.

Finn sat beside her and said, "What did Sprat the prat say? I bet he was delighted at the chance to stick the knife in."

Bridge snorted. "You could say that. He contacted the archbishop and I am to come to London in three weeks' time to attend a disciplinary committee."

Finn took her hand. "God, I'm sorry. I never wanted this to happen."

"I know, but it has, and we have to face it."

"What will happen at this meeting?" Finn asked.

"They'll question me on the nature of my relationship, and if I admit or deny the accusation of immoral conduct."

"Then you could get away with it, if you deny the accusations? You could keep your job, your life?"

Bridget looked at Finn with surprise. "What are you talking about? I'm not going to deny you, deny my lo—what we feel for each other."

Bridge saw Finn gulp down a lump in her throat as the emotion threatened to overwhelm her.

Finn dropped to her knees in front of Bridge and pleaded, "Bridge, you have to deny us. You have so much good work to do. The people of this village rely on you, they need you. You need to fight for your job, fight to stay in your church."

"How can you say that, Finn?" Bridge caressed Finn's cheek with her hand. "I can't deny my beautiful boy and I can't deny what I feel for you. I am your mistress." Bridge pulled Finn to her and gripped her tight. "I will never let you go as long as you stand beside me."

Finn sighed sadly. "I know."

❖

Finn had never seen Bridge so emotional, so much so that it threatened to overwhelm her.

She held her tightly and tried to give her comfort, but inside she knew there could be no comfort. Finn couldn't let Bridge lose her job, her life. She felt Bridge's kisses on her neck and jaw.

"I need you, Finn," Bridge said desperately.

"I'm here," Finn said.

Bridge's kisses became more frantic, which wasn't like her. She was always so controlled, knew what she wanted, and demanded it.

Finn pulled back and saw tears running down her cheeks. "Hey, hey, it's okay."

"It's not okay. I'm scared what we have will be taken away from me, but I'm going to fight with every ounce of my being to hold on to you. I—I love you, Finn."

Finn's heart ached with joy and hurt. This was the first time Bridge had said *I love you*, and yet it could be goodbye. She closed her eyes for a second and knew what she had to do. Bridge had given her everything since she'd arrived in Axedale, heartbroken and angry. She had shaken her up, helped her heal, and shepherded her back into the fold. It was time Finn took care of Bridge for once. That meant loving her, and doing the right thing for Bridge, whether she liked it or not.

"I love you with all my heart." Finn took Bridge's hand to her lips and kissed it softly.

"Finn, I need you. I need to feel you," Bridge said breathlessly.

Finn leaned her forehead against Bridge's and said, "Mistress, you've taken care of me, made me feel again. Will you let me take care of you? Just this once?"

"Yes, but promise it's not goodbye," Bridge said.

Finn answered as honestly as she could. "I will never say goodbye to you, Bridge." She held her lips inches from Bridge's. "Let me worship you, Mistress. May I?"

"Yes, I need my beautiful boy to touch me."

"I will. I'm going to love you, everywhere, Mistress."

Finn gave her the gentlest, most loving kiss she could, and simply enjoyed the softness and feel of Bridge's lips. When she kissed Bridge it felt like currents of electricity ran all over her body and straight to her heart.

She shrugged off Bridge's biker jacket, and went to take off her dog collar and blouse, but stopped. The collar was a symbol of all that stood against them. Finn wanted to rip it off, but at the same time couldn't take all that it represented away from her lover.

Bridge must have understood her reluctance, because she took it off herself and threw it onto the couch. Finn stared at it lying there, the thing that was going to break her heart.

Bridge put her hand on Finn's cheek and turned her head back towards her. "I don't want anything between us now. Just tell me you love me—"

"And worship you?" Finn finished for her.

Bridge nodded. "Tell me what's in your heart."

"I love you," Finn said, and then pulled off her T-shirt, leaving her just in her boxers.

Bridge ran a red fingernail down Finn's shoulder, then chest, and down her stomach. "Then that just leaves worshipping me."

Finn's body was covered with goosebumps—it always was when Bridge touched her. She pulled Bridge into her arms and kissed her deeply, tasting her slowly with her lips and tongue.

Bridge's hands were touching, and her nails tracing, all over her neck and back.

In between kisses Bridge said, "I love the way your body feels, Finn."

It was hard not to get lost in her own feelings of pleasure. Finn didn't want to lose control and take this too fast. She wanted to savour her worship. "I want to feel your skin on mine," Finn said, and then took off Bridge's bra, and quickly unzipped her black skirt.

When it pooled at Bridge's feet, she kicked it away. Finn lifted her and laid her carefully on the rug in front of the fire. She kicked off her boxers and knelt by her feet.

Finn lifted Bridge's foot and kissed her shoe before slipping it off, and then she did the same with the other, and placed tender kisses on her ankle and up her gorgeous legs.

She wanted to remember every inch of the legs that had tormented her since she first laid eyes on them. As she got up to her thighs, Bridge's hand was in her hair, roughly grasping it just the way she liked.

Bridge moaned and said, "Good boy."

One of Finn's favourite parts of Bridge's sexy legs were the suspenders on her thighs. There was something about suspenders, something so utterly female about them that made her crazy and willing to do anything to touch them.

Bridge had once told her that her suspenders, her biker jacket, and her heels were the three little ways she could keep Mistress Black in her life as a vicar.

Finn was apparently spending too much time kissing Bridge's thighs, because she felt her head pushed to her lover's sex.

Bridge was wearing a black G-string, and was so wet it made Finn groan. Before she allowed herself to touch Bridge there, she looked up to her lover and said, "May I, Mistress?"

"God, yes." The look of adoration and want in Finn's eyes made Bridge moan. She felt feather-like soft kisses at first and then Finn sucking her clit. Bridge clenched her thighs together around Finn's head, the feeling intense. Every kiss and lick from her lover was making her forget what problems lay outside these cottage walls.

Bridge's hips started to buck when Finn simply pushed her G-string to the side and teased the entrance to her sex. She grasped her own breasts and squeezed. "Good boy. Just like that." She was aching for her lover's fingers, but instead Finn stopped abruptly and started kissing her breasts. Bridge wrapped her arms around Finn's head and her legs around Finn's waist. Finn kissed every inch of her breast, and sucked and teased her nipple.

Bridge was so ready to come it was unreal. "Finn, I need you inside, now."

Finn stopped her attentions on her breasts, and came up to look in her eyes. She stroked Bridge's cheek softly. "You're so beautiful, Mistress. I love you. I want you to really believe that."

"Of course I believe that, darling. I can see it in your gorgeous eyes, Finn."

"May I make you come?" Finn asked.

Bridge grasped Finn's hand and placed it on her sex. "Make me come while you kiss me."

Finn's lips were on her instantly, while her fingers pushed past her underwear and inside her.

Bridge groaned into the kiss and grasped Finn's hair. Nothing had ever felt like Finn and nothing ever would. She couldn't give this up, this love that was pouring from her heart into Finn's.

She gripped Finn's hair harder as her orgasm was fast approaching. Their kiss deepened ever more, and Finn's thrust hastened to match

Bridge's hips. Bridge's orgasm hit her, and then washed all over her body. It felt like all the residual hurt and pain that she had been keeping locked up inside her soul was released by Finn in this one exquisite moment. Her moans of pleasure were swallowed by their kiss, until her body went limp.

Finn pulled back and placed tiny kisses on Bridge's chin, nose, and cheeks. Bridge gasped, trying to calm her heart. She felt truly worshipped, just as Finn promised.

"I love you, Finn. I love you."

Finn gave her a small smile, stroked her hair, and looked deeply into her eyes. "You're the mistress of my heart, and no matter what, I'll love you forever."

Bridget sat in the vicarage dining room, with a plate of uneaten food in front of her. The news of her relationship with Finn was due to hit the *Daily Tribune* as an exclusive at midnight. How could she eat? She hadn't told Harry yet. She knew if she did, Harry and Annie would gather around her and try to comfort her, but she didn't want comfort. She wanted to be alone and contemplate what came next.

She gazed around the vicarage and thought about how she would miss the old place. It was draughty, falling apart in places, but had been her home at the happiest time of her life. But with Finn she hoped she would have more happiness in the future.

Bridge got up and walked to the dining room window. She wondered if she and Finn would stay in the village. She would hate to leave Harry, Annie, and Riley, and Mrs. Castle, but Bridge also doubted whether she could watch another vicar take over her church and her parishioners. It might be too painful.

She clasped her hands together and prayed for God's guidance. The sound of tyres on the gravel driveway made Bridge's eyes spring open. It was Finn's motorbike. She ran to the front door, but by the time she got there, Finn was driving out of the vicarage driveway.

"Finn, wait!" she shouted after her, but Finn never slowed down or looked back.

Bridge looked down and discovered what looked like a canvas wrapped in brown paper. Sitting next to it was an envelope.

Bridge's heart started to crack. She instinctively knew this was not good. She pulled the paper from the canvas and found the finished painting of the church that Finn had been doing. Then, with shaking hands, she picked up and opened the letter.

*Dear Bridge,*

*I know you won't deny us while I'm here, so I'm going to do the right thing and leave. I won't take your life away from you and you away from the people of Axedale. Your work is too important. I want you to keep fighting for the rights of gay people in the Church. You must be the trailblazer like your ancestors were, so that the Church changes, and no other woman or man of God has to choose between their love of their faith and the love of their partner. You are just the Claremont to do it. I believe in you.*

*I'm going back to work. My manager got me some shows at the London Arena after Adele cut short her tour. You gave me back my hope that there might be a greater power out there, and that Carrie is safely with them. I'll always be thankful, and I'll always love you.*

*For now I want you to be able to deny us with a clear conscience, but I'll always wait for you, Mistress. If and when it becomes safe for us, we can be together. Until then you don't need me complicating your life. Remember, I love you.*

*Your boy xx*

Bridge clasped her hand to her mouth, and tears ran down her face. "No, no, Finn."

She screwed up the letter in anger and threw it on the ground. "Why do you need to be so bloody noble, Finn? I love you."

She closed her eyes and she was back on the side of the road watching Ellen leaving her, and it was happening again, as she'd always feared. Except this time her lover was riding away into the sunset to protect her. She wiped away her tears.

"You can't get away from me that easily, boy. I'm going to fight for us, even if you can't."

## CHAPTER TWENTY-THREE

The three weeks that followed were the most heart-wrenching and stressful of Bridget's life and career. Each day that counted down to her disciplinary meeting was a day without Finn, and only emphasized how much she loved her, how much she needed her, but she was gone now. Gone back to her life before Bridge, the life of celebrity, fawning audiences, and probably fawning dancers. The thought of anyone touching her beautiful boy made her feel sick, but she could do nothing about it, for the moment. Finn had left her here alone to deal with the fight, even though Finn thought she was doing the noble thing.

Bridge had stayed with her aunt Gertie the night before and she was accompanying her to the meeting. Harry was by her side, as she had always been.

The radio in the taxi started to play a new cover version of "Can't Help Falling In Love." She thought of dancing with Finn to that song at the barn dance, and felt the tears threatening to come.

"Are you all right, Bridge?" Harry said across from her.

She quickly pulled herself together and put a forced smile on her face. "I'm fine."

Aunt Gertie squeezed her hand. "Not long now."

Harry checked her phone and said, "There's a lot of people and protest groups there, according to social media, Bridge. You really have caught the public imagination with this fight."

It had happened quite naturally over the three weeks since she had been notified about this meeting. Her own protest group had spread the word about this issue, and other gay Christian groups had joined them, and then non-religious gay groups, and it had gotten bigger and bigger. Suddenly the conversation on TV and the internet was whether two people in love should have to choose between the Church and their love, and it had captured the public imagination, with Bridget as its figurehead. Of course, anti-gay protestors joined the debate and were making themselves heard loudly, but it seemed as if everyone else prayed that love would win.

Bridget never thought she'd be one of those Claremonts who blazed a trail, but here she was about to give a speech on equal rights before going into her meeting.

"We're here," Harry said.

Aunt Gertie kissed her on the cheek, and whispered, "Remember, you're a Claremont, and we don't run from a fight. Blaze that trail."

Bridget smiled and nodded. She didn't know where she'd get the strength, and could only hope for God's guidance.

Harry helped her out of the taxi, and she was hit with a wall of noise and shouts from journalists. She walked up to the microphone, and the crowds of protestors and gathered media quietened down, and all she could hear were the clicks and pops and cameras going off around her. She had written this speech from her heart, and practised it last night with her aunt's help, and it was a shortened version of what she would present to the disciplinary council.

She was a confident speaker, but something so personal as this was a different matter. Bridge tried to think of all the wonderful support she had been given by those liberal elements within the Christian community, and the world at large, and she gained strength from that, but the cameras and eyes upon her made her waver.

It was then that she noticed a big red double-decker bus drive by with a huge advert for Finn's show. Seeing Finn's face reminded her what she was fighting for. She was fighting for their love and her heart.

Finn thought she was being noble letting Bridge go. She thought she was protecting Bridge's career and way of life, and she didn't believe that it was possible for their two lives to coexist. Bridge realized that it was her job to lead the way, her job to show Finn that their love was worth fighting for, because that's what a mistress did. She took control and led the way, and helped her submissive push their limits and realize just what was possible if they tried hard enough.

A new surge of strength and confidence came over Bridge, and it was Mistress Black who was giving her the strength to fight for Finn. Bridge realized in that moment that she could only move forward to a new, happier, truthful life when she accepted Mistress Black was part of her, a big part of her that couldn't and should never be hidden.

Bridge stood taller, and smiled at the assembled press pack.

❖

"Not now, Christian," Finn shouted at her assistant.

Finn was sitting in her dressing room backstage at her arena show, waiting to see Bridge on the rolling news.

"I'm sorry, Finn, it's just the director wants—"

"He'll have to wait. I'm not to be disturbed, okay?"

Christian nodded. "Is it today?"

"Yes, I need to see her," Finn said sadly.

Christian put a comforting arm on her shoulder. "Okay, I'll keep the director off your back for a bit."

When he left, Finn looked up to the TV on the wall, and saw Bridge exit her taxi and walk to the assembled press pack. *I love you, Bridge.*

*Ladies and Gentlemen, I joined the Church because I wanted to spread the word of God. I wanted to spread his word because his love for us is infinite. God loves us no matter if we are straight, gay, black, white, rich, poor, spiritual, or atheist. It doesn't matter how far we run from him—he will always take us back into the warmth of his love.*

*I joined the Church as a gay woman, and I have always been sure of God's love for me, and my place in the Church. I have never had a relationship until recently, when I fell in love with someone who means everything to me.*

*The Church has moved forward leaps and bounds in terms of gay rights, but it still lags way behind society's norms. I say to the Church that I love, it's time to move forward again. If we hope to stay relevant to the population we serve as clergy, we must reflect those people and their families. If we do not, the Church will wither and die.*

*God made us to love one another, not to hate. So today and every day in the Church, love must win!*

A huge cheer went up from all Bridget's supporters, and Finn couldn't have been prouder of her.

Finn knew then that Bridge truly loved her, and she was fighting for them.

❖

Finn took the applause of the audience for the last time doing this version of her show. Her next tour show would be all about close-up magic, and bringing wonder and belief back to people's faces.

She took off her top hat and bowed, but didn't get the rush she used to. Her heart wasn't in it any more, because her heart was aching for another life, a simpler life in Axedale with Bridge and her friends.

Christian met her at the side of the stage with a towel and a bottle of water. "Great show, Finn. The audience loved it."

"Thanks," Finn said with no conviction. She had the feeling the clamour for tickets after her return to the stage was more about the scandal surrounding her, rather than the magic.

She walked towards her dressing room and one of the crew said, "Layla is looking for you, Finn."

Finn sighed and nodded. "I bet." Since she had returned, she had barely escaped the attentions of her overeager dancer. The thought of being with another woman was just beyond the pale, and after being with Bridge, her mistress, she didn't think she'd find joy in sex ever again. She hesitated before turning the corner to her dressing room, worried that Layla might be there. Finn just couldn't deal with her, not today.

Finn took a moment and walked around the corner. She stopped breathing. Instead of the dreaded Layla standing by her dressing room door, Bridge stood there nonchalantly, hands in her biker jacket pockets, and her gorgeous legs crossed at the ankles.

"Bridge? What?" Finn stumbled.

Bridge smiled, walked over, and took Finn's hands. "I was at your show. It was wonderful, although I had to hiss at one of your dancers who was hanging around waiting for you back here. She soon ran away when I told her you were taken."

"You did?" Finn couldn't quite understand what this meant. "What happened at your disciplinary meeting? I just saw you going in—"

Bridge caressed her cheek with the back of her hand. "Come with me."

They went into Finn's dressing room, and Bridge immediately pulled Finn into an embrace.

Finn held her with desperation. "I missed you so much, Bridge. I feel like my heart is being ripped out every day I'm apart from you."

Bridge scratched her nails soothingly down the shaved short hairs at the back of her head. "Shh, I know. You've been so noble in trying to protect me, but I had to fight for us, Finn. Claremonts never run from a fight. I won't be forced to choose between God and the woman I love, when I know in my heart that God wants me to love you. Your sister Carrie sent you to me. We were meant to love each other."

"But I can't live with knowing that our relationship has driven you from the Church you love, from the people of Axedale—"

Bridge silenced her with a finger on her the lips. "We won."

"What?"

"I'm to return to my parish and continue as vicar there, and my private life is my business, if I am discreet."

"You're kidding."

Bridge smiled and shook her head. "Not kidding."

Finn couldn't quite believe this was happening. They were being given another chance.

Bridge gave her a serious look, and said, "There's just one thing."

She knew there must be some catch. "What?"

"I have to live my life in Axedale. Can you give up your life in London to be with me?"

"Are you kidding? I have no life in London. My life is with you, Bridge, in Axedale."

Bridge smiled broadly. "Then you're mine, Magician."

Finn had never felt such joy in her life. She picked up Bridge and twirled her around. "I can't believe it."

Bridge slid down Finn's body and lightly grasped her chin. "That's what I've been trying to teach you ever since I met you, Magician. You have to believe." She kissed Finn's lips and felt the thrill that she knew she would never tire of.

When they separated, Finn asked, "What happened after your speech?"

"Apparently while I was in the meeting, the clip of my speech went viral. I suppose having a well-known, well-connected family has its benefits."

"So?"

"Aunt Gertie says that they were frightened of making a martyr of me, because of the public opinion, and some senior closeted figures in the Church hierarchy, including my old bishop, threatened to come out, which would cause havoc and a split in the Church. The council felt it best to send me back to work, and to make their don't ask, don't tell policy stronger. Plus, marriage for clergy is back on the policy agenda."

"So we can be together," Finn said with a huge smile.

Bridge nodded. "Forever."

"And one day I might be able to marry my mistress."

"Yes, my beautiful boy."

Finn picked her up and spun her around. "I can't believe it."

Bridge caressed her cheek. "Believe it."

Finn was bursting with happiness, elation, and energy from just finishing the show. She kissed Bridge passionately and grasped her thigh.

Bridge pulled away and said, "Uh-uh. Have you forgotten the rules already?"

Finn felt dazed. She just needed to touch her lover. "I'm sorry. I'm hungry for you."

"I know you are." Bridge rested her forehead against Finn's, and whispered, "So am I, but things don't change just because we're in your world. We don't touch without asking."

Finn groaned. Her mistress was back.

Bridge pulled back and took from her pocket the leather wrist strap and chain they had used on their night out together. She opened the cuff and said, "As much as I love your sweet little costume, Magician, take off the jacket."

Finn had that indescribable excitement of not knowing what was coming next, which was one of the biggest reasons she loved Bridge. She threw her jacket to the side, and was left in sleeveless T-shirt and trousers.

"Lift your arm, Finn," Bridge said.

Once she did, Bridge held the cuff around her arm, but didn't close the buckles. "I've come to take back possession of my boy. Do you wish to have me as your mistress?"

Finn smiled, knowing there was much more significance to this than met the eye. They would be tethered emotionally as well as physically.

"There's only one mistress who'll ever have my heart," Finn said sincerely.

Bridge smiled and fastened up the cuff. "I love you, Judith Maxwell and Finnian Kane. I love all of you."

Finn was taken aback but touched by the use of her former name. Bridge loved all of her, and that couldn't be clearer.

"I love you, Mistress Black and Bridget Claremont."

Bridge pulled Finn closer by the chain and whispered close to her lips, "I bet you've had lots of little groupies in this dressing room."

Finn gulped and nodded. She had to be honest, but Bridge just smiled.

"I bet they couldn't do this." Bridge gave her a tender kiss and whispered, "Kneel, boy."

Finn dropped like a shot. Only coming from Bridge's mouth could those words make her do this, and make her feel so turned on.

Bridge chuckled. "You are so good when you want to be. Now go and get dressed. I'm going to take you home and do unspeakable things to you."

Finn grinned. "You promise?"

Bridge winked at her. "If you're a good little magician."

# EPILOGUE

Axedale church hall had never been so full. There wasn't even any standing room left around the sides of the hall for the winter show. In the front row sat Harry, Annie, Quade, and Bridge.

So much work had gone into the show, with Annie working on costumes and props, and Quade making sets, and of course their resident celebrity as director, Finnian Kane.

The lights went down and the large video screens Finn had installed on the back wall of the stage started to project wintery, snowy scenes. Suddenly Finn appeared in the middle of the stage, apparently out of thin air. She was wearing her trademark ringmaster costume and top hat, and leaning on a cane.

Bridget smiled, and her heart fluttered when Finn winked at her. Bridge was so proud of Finn. She alone knew how much Finn had put into this village show, putting on hold her own new show, financing everything, just to help the village charities.

But Finn did it gladly, because she had a home now in Axedale, and a home in Bridge's arms, somewhere she could be safe and let go.

Finn tipped her hat to the audience and said, "The show you are about to see is the magic of winter, through a child's eyes, and for that you need a child—"

She clicked her fingers, there was a puff of smoke, and there where she had been standing was Riley, dressed in an outfit the same as Finn's, like a mini-me.

Bridge glanced at Harry and Annie. Harry held Annie's hand tightly, and Annie was crying with pride. She was such a sweet woman.

Riley said, "You will now experience the magic of winter through a child's eyes…"

Riley ran around the stage, seemingly producing kid dancers out of thin air all over the stage. Then the music came on and they all went into the first dance number.

Bridge felt Quade nudge her and whisper, "You looked so proud watching her there. You really must be in love, Vicar."

"I truly am. I never thought I'd have this," Bridge replied with a smile.

"I don't have to marry you and your whip when we're forty-five then?" Quade joked.

"You're safe, Quade. My whip is more than delighted with Finn. It's your turn next."

Quade raised her eyebrows and shook her head. "I won't hold my breath. What woman wants to be a farmer's wife these days?"

Bridge patted her hand. "If it can happen to a celibate vicar, it can happen to you, Quade. Excuse me."

Bridge got up quietly and sneaked into the kitchen next door to the church hall. When she walked through she found Finn watching the show on monitors she had set up there.

She slinked up behind Finn and whispered, "Hello, Magician."

Finn turned around with want in her eyes. "I love that voice."

"What voice?" Bridge teased.

Finn kissed her palm. "My mistress's voice."

Bridge laughed. "I know you do. Everyone is loving the show in there. You've done so well."

"The kids have done well. Riley Knight has taken to magic like a duck to water."

"She does to most things. Riley is very intelligent." Bridge ran her fingers through the blond fringe that she found so fascinating. "If you play your cards right, Magician, I might say your magic words later, at home."

Finn lifted Bridge and placed her on the table.

"I always play my cards right, Vicar. I'm the best." Finn grinned, knowing how much Bridge loved it when she got a bit cocky.

Bridge pulled Finn close and whispered, "I'll enjoy wiping that cocky smirk off your face tonight, boy."

"So will I, Mistress. I love you," Finn said softly.

"I love you too." Their lips came together in a kiss just as applause erupted from the hall next door.

"We must be good," Finn joked.

# About the Author

Jenny Frame is from the small town of Motherwell in Scotland, where she lives with her partner, Lou, and their well-loved and very spoiled dog.

She has a diverse range of qualifications, including a BA in public management and a diploma in acting and performance. Nowadays she likes to put her creative energies into writing rather than treading the boards.

When not writing or reading, Jenny loves cheering on her local football team, cooking, and spending time with her family.

Jenny can be contacted at http://www.jennyframe.com/

# Books Available From Bold Strokes Books

**Between Sand and Stardust** by Tina Michele. Are the lifelong bonds of love strong enough to conquer time, distance, and heartache when Haven Thorne and Willa Bennette are given another chance at forever? (978-1-62639-940-2)

**Charming the Vicar** by Jenny Frame. When magician and atheist Finn Kane seeks refuge in an English village after a spiritual crisis, can local vicar Bridget Claremont restore her faith in life and love? (978-1-63555-029-0)

**Data Capture** by Jesse J. Thoma. Lola Walker is undercover on the hunt for cybercriminals while trying not to notice the woman who might be perfectly wrong for her for all the right reasons. (978-1-62639-985-3)

**Epicurean Delights** by Renee Roman. Ariana Marks had no idea a leisure swim would lead to being rescued, in more ways than one, by the charismatic Hudson Frost. (978-1-63555-100-6)

**Heart of the Devil** by Ali Vali. We know most of Cain and Emma Casey's story, but Heart of the Devil will take you back to where it began one fateful night with a tray loaded with beer. (978-1-63555-045-0)

**Known Threat** by Kara A. McLeod. When Special Agent Ryan O'Connor reluctantly questions who protects the Secret Service, she learns courage truly is found in unlikely places. Agent O'Connor Series #3 (978-1-63555-132-7)

**Seer and the Shield** by D. Jackson Leigh. Time is running out for the Dragon Horse Army while two unlikely heroines struggle to put aside their attraction and find a way to stop a deadly cult. Dragon Horse War, Book 3 (978-1-63555-170-9)

**The Universe Between Us** by Jane C. Esther. Ana Mitchell must make the hardest choice of her life: the promise of new love Jolie Dann on Earth, or a humanity-saving mission to colonize Mars. (978-1-63555-106-8)

**Touch** by Kris Bryant. Can one touch heal a heart? (978-1-63555-084-9)

**A More Perfect Union** by Carsen Taite. Major Zoey Granger and DC fixer Rook Daniels risk their reputations for a chance at true love while dealing with a scandal that threatens to rock the military. (978-1-62639-754-5)

**Arrival** by Gun Brooke. The spaceship *Pathfinder* reaches its passengers' new homeworld where danger lurks in the shadows while Pamas Seclan disembarks and finds unexpected love in young science genius Darmiya Do Voy. (978-1-62639-859-7)

**Captain's Choice** by VK Powell. Architect Kerstin Anthony's life is going to plan until Bennett Carlyle, the first girl she ever kissed, is assigned to her latest and most important project, a police district substation. (978-1-62639-997-6)

**Falling Into Her** by Erin Zak. Pam Phillips, widow at the age of forty, meets Kathryn Hawthorne, local Chicago celebrity, and it changes her life forever—in ways she hadn't even considered possible. (978-1-63555-092-4)

**Hookin' Up** by MJ Williamz. Will Leah get what she needs from casual hookups or will she see the love she desires right in front of her? (978-1-63555-051-1)

**King of Thieves** by Shea Godfrey. When art thief Casey Marinos meets bounty hunter Finnegan Starkweather, the crimes of the past just might set the stage for a payoff worth more than she ever dreamed possible. (978-1-63555-007-8)

**Lucy's Chance** by Jackie D. As a serial killer haunts the streets, Lucy tries to stitch up old wounds with her first love in the wake of a small town's rapid descent into chaos. (978-1-63555-027-6)

**Right Here, Right Now** by Georgia Beers. When Alicia Wright moves into the office next door to Lacey Chamberlain's accounting firm, Lacey is about to find out that sometimes the last person you want is exactly the person you need. (978-1-63555-154-9)

**Strictly Need to Know** by MB Austin. Covert operator Maji Rios will do whatever she must to complete her mission, but saving a gorgeous stranger from Russian mobsters was not in her plans. (978-1-63555-114-3)

**Tailor-Made** by Yolanda Wallace. Tailor Grace Henderson doesn't date clients, but when she meets gender-bending model Dakota Lane, she's tempted to throw all the rules out the window. (978-1-63555-081-8)

**Time Will Tell** by M. Ullrich. With the ability to time travel, Eva Caldwell will have to decide between having it all and erasing it all. (978-1-63555-088-7)

**Change in Time** by Robyn Nyx. Working in the past is hell on your future. The Extractor series: Book Two. (978-1-62639-880-1)

**Love After Hours** by Radclyffe. When Gina Antonelli agrees to renovate Carrie Longmire's new house, she doesn't welcome Carrie's overtures at friendship or her own unexpected attraction. A Rivers Community Novel. (978-1-63555-090-0)

**Nantucket Rose** by CF Frizzell. Maggie Jordan can't wait to convert a historic Nantucket home into a B&B, but doesn't expect to fall for mariner Ellis Chilton, who has more claim to the house than Maggie realizes. (978-1-63555-056-6)

**Picture Perfect** by Lisa Moreau. Falling in love wasn't supposed to be part of the stakes for Olive and Gabby, rival photographers in the competition of a lifetime. (978-1-62639-975-4)

**Set the Stage** by Karis Walsh. Actress Emilie Danvers takes the stage again in Ashland, Oregon, little realizing that landscaper Arden Philips is about to offer her a very personal romantic lead role. (978-1-63555-087-0)

**Strike a Match** by Fiona Riley. When their attempts at matchmaking fizzle out, firefighter Sasha and reluctant millionairess Abby find themselves turning to each other to strike a perfect match. (978-1-62639-999-0)

**The Price of Cash** by Ashley Bartlett. Cash Braddock is doing her best to keep her business afloat, stay out of jail, and avoid Detective Kallen. It's not working. (978-1-62639-708-8)

**Captured Soul** by Laydin Michaels. Can Kadence Munroe save the woman she loves from a twisted killer, or will she lose her to a collector of souls? (978-1-62639-915-0)

**Under Her Wing** by Ronica Black. At Angel's Wings Rescue, dogs are usually the ones saved, but when quiet Kassandra Haden meets outspoken owner Jayden Beaumont, the two stubborn women just might end up saving each other. (978-1-63555-077-1)

**Underwater Vibes** by Mickey Brent. When Hélène, a translator in Brussels, Belgium, meets Sylvie, a young Greek photographer and swim coach, unsettling feelings hijack Hélène's mind and body—even her poems. (978-1-63555-002-3)

**A Date to Die** by Anne Laughlin. Someone is killing people close to Detective Kay Adler, who must look to her own troubled past for a suspect. There she finds more than one person seeking revenge against her. (978-1-63555-023-8)

**Dawn's New Day** by TJ Thomas. Can Dawn Oliver and Cam Cooper, two women who have loved and lost, open their hearts to love again? (978-1-63555-072-6)

**Definite Possibility** by Maggie Cummings. Sam Miller is just out for good times, but Lucy Weston makes her realize happily ever after is a definite possibility. (978-1-62639-909-9)

**Eyes Like Those** by Melissa Brayden. Isabel Chase and Taylor Andrews struggle between love and ambition from the writers' room on one of Hollywood's hottest TV shows. (978-1-63555-012-2)

**Heart's Orders** by Jaycie Morrison. Helen Tucker and Tee Owens escape hardscrabble lives to careers in the Women's Army Corps, but more than their hearts are at risk as friendship blossoms into love. (978-1-63555-073-3)

**Hiding Out** by Kay Bigelow. Treat Dandridge is unaware that her life is in danger from the murderer who is hunting the woman she's falling in love with, Mickey Heiden. (978-1-62639-983-9)

**Omnipotence Enough** by Sophia Kell Hagin. Can the tiny tool that abducted war veteran Jamie Gwynmorgan accidentally acquires help her escape an unknown enemy to reclaim her stolen life and the woman she deeply loves? (978-1-63555-037-5)